HAMMER DOWN

OTHER TEAM REAPER THRILLERS

Retribution

Deadly Intent

Termination Order

Blood Rush

Kill Count

Relentless

Lethal Tender

Empty Quiver

Barracuda!

African White

Kill Theory

Danger Close

Collateral Damage

The Death Bringers

Hunting Ghosts

London's Burning

The Cold Hand of Death

Global War

Companions of Death

HAMMER DOWN

A TEAM REAPER THRILLER
BOOK 20

BRENT TOWNS

ROUGH
EDGES
PRESS

Hammer Down
Paperback Edition
Copyright © 2025 Brent Towns

Rough Edges Press
An Imprint of Wolfpack Publishing
1707 E. Diana Street
Tampa, FL 33610

roughedgespress.com

Paperback ISBN 978-1-68549-469-8
Ebook ISBN 978-1-68549-468-1
LCCN 2025951558

HAMMER DOWN

HAMMER DOWN

TEAM REAPER

Command:
Mary Thurston
Cara Billings
Luis Ferrero

Team Reaper:
John "Reaper" Kane
Raymond "Knocker" Jensen
Les "Lofty" Travers
Richard "Brick" Peters
Kagiso

Bravo:
Rani Perera
Pete Teller
Sam "Slick" Swift
Doctor Rosana Morales

PROLOGUE

IRAN

What would you do if you knew you were about to die?
The hapless sentry had no chance to contemplate an
answer before a 7.62 round streaked out of the darkness
and touched him between the eyes, blowing brains and
bone fragments out the back of his head.

"Tango down."

The call was repeated four additional times before a
big man in a black skull-faced ski mask said, "Move in."

Five figures materialized like wraiths from the darkness and moved into the small Iranian village. The
buildings were of mud brick construction, some crumbling, others destroyed. Many were occupied by
followers of the most wanted man in the Middle East.
He was known as The Persian. Responsible for
multiple bombings and mass slaughter across the globe.
Everyone wanted him but the Brits had asked Global to
assemble the team who were about to get him.

Chosen to execute the extraction was Team Reaper,

led by their adept leader John 'Reaper' Kane: Reaper because of the Grim Reaper tattoo on his back.

"Reaper One, we're approaching the well from the east," said a familiar voice over the comms.

Raymond 'Knocker' Jensen was a longtime compatriot and one of Kane's closest friends. A Brit with a short beard, Knocker was former SAS, and reliable as he was tough. He was also one of the best operators Kane had ever worked with.

"Copy," Kane replied.

Edging stealthily around the corner of a crumbling building, the man they called Reaper saw one of the terrorist's men approaching along the street. The suppressed Heckler and Koch HK433 came up and fired twice. When the man dropped to the ground, Kane said, "Kagiso, get him."

Originating from Africa, Kagiso's skin was as dark as the night and her skills as a shooter were as good as anyone in the team. She stepped from behind Kane onto the dirt street and dragged the dead terrorist into the shadows.

With the body out of sight, the operators pressed forward silently toward their target building.

———

HAVING BEEN DROPPED into Iran three hours earlier, the team had proceeded on foot to the target area. Intel provided by MI6 had specified this area as being the location of The Persian. Hence the request for a Deep Black team for an off-the-books mission into Iran. The terrorist was being sheltered by special guards supplied by the Iranian government.

During an interdiction of ivory shipments coming out of Africa, the team had gathered intelligence which MI6 then utilized to track The Persian. There were big terrorist dollars in the ivory trade.

Kane had been on leave in Greece when two MI6 officers had tracked him down, one of whom he'd once considered a friend. Rachel Locke. Upon catching a glimpse of her on the street outside the taverna he was in, Kane knew something was up. Based on their history, that something was bound to be far from good.

"I need you and that ratbag friend of yours," she had told him. "For a mission into Iran."

"Are you going to fuck us over like last time?" Kane had asked her.

"Only if I have to," came the succinct reply.

"What is the mission?" He looked around the quiet bar to make sure nobody was paying them any attention.

"Ever heard of The Persian?"

"Who hasn't?" he replied.

"We have intel he's hiding in a village about a hundred kilometers from the Iraq border."

"Stupid thing to do," allowed Kane, taking a mouthful of beer.

"Pick your team, go in, get him, and we'll get you out," Locke had said.

"I don't need to pick a team. I have one. I'll run it up the flagpole."

Locke nodded. "Are you in?"

Kane looked at the beer in front of him as though seeking some brewski guidance. "Sure, why not?"

———

Raymond 'Knocker' Jensen used his knife to dispatch a guard walking past the dark alley. The unsuspecting terrorist died with three puncture wounds in his chest and a savage slash across his throat.

Dragging the dead man into the shadows, the burly Brit said to the man with him, "Let's go, Lofty."

Former SAS Corporal Les "Lofty" Travers. The dark-haired man stood around six foot one and had known Knocker back in the day.

Leading out across the intersection, Lofty swept it with his 433. He was almost across when another gunman appeared. The weapon in his hands spat a semi-quiet burst of fire and the new arrival dropped in the ground.

Lofty slung his rifle and bent to drag the body into the shadows on the far side, drawing his suppressed P30 handgun and shooting the downed man in the head just to make sure.

Knocker covered him and once Lofty was done, they continued along the street.

"Everyone, hold." The voice was low, calm, female. Cara Billings, Bravo.

"What's up?" Knocker heard Kane ask over the comms.

"I have a sniper on the rooftop to the south of the well."

"Copy, holding."

The callsign allocated by Cara for this op was Ares, after the Greek god of war. She was hiding in a rock formation on a hill outside of town with a Remington MSR (Modular Sniper Rifle), suppressed, and chambered for .338 Lapua Magnum rounds.

Normally excluded from missions in the field, being

the team's new overall commander, her ideology was that command gave her the prerogative to do what she wanted.

She had found the sniper by accident. The fool had blended perfectly with his background until he'd lit a cigarette. Even then all Cara had to go by was the glowing ember on the tip. But that was all she needed and sighted on the miniature target. Saw it brighten. Squeezed the trigger.

The Remington slammed back into her shoulder as the bullet left the barrel at 3,200 feet per second. "Target down."

"Roger that, Ares," Kane replied, and the mission continued.

———

"TEAM ONE IN POSITION. I have the target building in sight," Kane whispered. "Preparing to breach."

"Team Two in position," Knocker replied.

"Bravo One, sitrep?"

A Brit by birth to Sri Lankan parents, Rani Perera had flown Apache helicopters then crossed over to UAVs before coming to work for Global. Now she was in command of Bravo Element. "Nothing out of the ordinary, Reaper One. There is no evidence to suggest they know you're there."

"Roger that."

Outside the target building stood two terrorists. Both were armed with Masaf 1 assault rifles supplied by the Iranian Army.

Kane said to Kagiso, "You take the one on the left."

"Roger that."

They each sighted on their target and paused momentarily.

"In three...two...one...execute!"

Triggers depressed and both terrorists died like many of their comrades did that night during the incursion. Kane and Kagiso hurried across the street and took up a position either side of the doorway. From their right, Knocker and Lofty appeared, closing in to back up the two breachers. Bringing up the rear was Richard "Brick" Peters, the team's combat medic who was bald, sported a beard and tattoos. Brick would pull security outside the building while the others cleared it.

Kane took out a stun grenade and pulled the pin. He squeezed Kagiso's shoulder, and she cracked the door far enough for Kane to throw the flashbang inside.

Moments later it detonated, and Kane pulled the door wide and entered. Then all hell broke loose.

Gunfire erupted, forcing Kane to throw himself sideways. Bullets barely missed their target and peppered the wall behind him. Kagiso opened fire and took out the shooter.

Kane came to his feet and checked the fallen man. "No joy."

In the meantime, Knocker and Lofty had slipped through the door behind them and were methodically clearing the other rooms, which so far were empty.

However, reaching the last one, when Knocker breached, he found a man standing in the center of the room, hands in the air.

"Get on the fucking floor," Knocker snapped.

Following the order, the man got onto his knees before lowering himself onto the floor and laid face down, his arms away from his body.

"Lofty, secure him."

The former SAS operator moved in quickly, securing the man's hands behind his back before dragging the prisoner to his feet. Knocker shone a flashlight on his face to confirm the identity and nodded with satisfaction. "Reaper, we got our man."

"On my way."

Kane joined them about a minute later. He said to Lofty and Kagiso, "Sweep the room. Get everything you can."

While they began searching the space, Kane looked at the prisoner. His face was white, almost pale. Even after months in the desert. Kane removed his mask. "Hello, Roman."

"Reaper, it's been a while." The accent was unmistakably German.

"Not long enough. Knocker, get that helicopter in here, we've got what we came for. It's time to go home."

Roman smiled. It was cold, mirthless. "You may have me, Reaper, but can they keep me?"

"I guess we'll find out."

One hour later, word had leaked of the capture of The Persian. Someone wanted him dead. Signals went out across the globe and the wolves started sharpening their teeth. They all wanted a piece of the most wanted man on the planet. There were $50,000,000 US reasons for it. And they meant to have it.

CHAPTER 1

IN THE AIR, 20,000 FT

An hour after the modified C-17 took off from the airbase in Iraq, a signal came through from Mary Thurston. Cara changed position and sat beside Kane. "Something is happening. We've been diverted to Kuwait. Once we reach there, we'll get follow-up orders."

Kane nodded. "Any idea what?"

Cara shook her head. "No. I was hoping to get back to Africa after we were done, to have a crack at those Chinese poachers."

"Looks like that will be on hold."

"Yes."

"Did they say what was happening with Roman?" Kane asked.

"No, I guess we babysit him until we're told not to."

Kane felt the plane begin its turn. Walking over to them, Knocker asked, "What's happening?"

"We're headed to Kuwait."

"Really? Shit. I was hoping to get back to Africa."

Cara nodded. "Yes. That's what I said."

The Brit shook his head. "Bollocks. They'd better have beer."

An hour later they were on the ground once more. This time at Ali Al Salem Air Base just outside Kuwait City. Cara came over to Kane and Knocker who were putting their tac gear on. Kane slapped home a magazine into his 433 and asked, "Have they got something secure for us?"

"From what I can gather, yes. Is everyone wearing their suit?"

The suits to which she was referring were the Synoprathetic form-hugging bodysuits. Made from bullet proof material, they would stop a lot of calibers, but the impacts still hurt like hell when you got hit. "As far as I know."

The whine of the hydraulics could be heard and daylight from outside could be seen as the ramp commenced its descent. Kane noticed a well-dressed man standing on the tarmac at the bottom of the ramp. He tapped Knocker. "I bet this prick is melting."

"Dumb fuck ought to know better. I bet he's fucking head shed."

———

ALI AL SALEM AIR BASE, KUWAIT

Making his way up the ramp, the man was approached by Cara and Luis Ferrero. In his late forties, Ferrero was solidly built, his hair seemingly a little grayer with each passing day. An experienced commander, Ferrero was just below Cara in the pecking order in charge of the teams overall. Mary Thurston had stepped into the role vacated by an ill Hank Jones.

"What can we do for you?" Cara asked.

The man wiped his face with a small rag. "Are you Cara Billings?"

"That's right," replied Cara with a sharp nod. "This is Luis Ferrero."

"I'm Jorgensen, from Six," he said, shortening the name of the intelligence service. "Sorry to have you diverted but there seems to be a problem."

"What is it?"

"It seems no one wants our terrorist in London."

"What do you mean?" Ferrero asked.

"It seems someone has put a fifty-million US bounty on his head. Whitehall fears that if he is in London, or anywhere else in England, all hell could break loose. The MPs in the Parliament are climbing the walls."

"What about Interpol or The Hague?"

"That takes time, I'm afraid. The higher-ups are trying to work out a deal with either one."

"In the meantime, we're in limbo," Cara said. "Shit."

"I'm afraid so."

Kane and Knocker walked over to them. By now they had their 433s strapped, their tac gear on, and were wearing sunglasses against the Kuwaiti sun. "What's happening?"

"Once more, we're being screwed," Cara said, shaking her head. "Do one of you want to bend over?"

"Depends on who is doing the screwing," Knocker replied dryly.

"It's not like that," Jorgensen said. "Just look upon it as a couple of days layover."

"You got beer?" asked Knocker.

"Why—ah—yes, yes we have beer."

"Good, I'm in."

"You would be," Kane said.

A line of Humvees pulled up outside the loading ramp of the C-17. "Are they our rides?" Cara asked.

"Yes."

She turned to Kane. "Load them up."

"Yes, ma'am."

———

KNOCKER LICKED HIS LIPS. "It's not British beer but it'll do. At least it's cold."

Kane took a pull of his own. "Yankee beer not good enough for you?"

"That wasn't what I said." Knocker grinned. "I like most beer. Hey, I bet Lofty wishes he was us right now."

Lofty and Kagiso were standing guard on Roman until the MPs could get a team to take over from them. Kane said, "Should only be an hour longer."

"An hour longer what?" Lofty asked as he and Kagiso walked into the recreation room.

"Shit," said Knocker. "He must have heard you crack that beer."

Both newcomers unstrapped their weapons and removed their body armor. All present had their gear with them. You just never knew when shit was about to rain down. And from experience, Team Reaper attracted flies like shit on a bedsheet.

Lofty grabbed a beer and passed one to Kagiso. She

sat on a sofa near Knocker who was holding a book. "What are you reading?"

"A western by some guy named Robert Vaughan."

"Any good?"

"Not bad, actually," Knocker replied.

"Can I have it when you're done?" she asked.

His eyebrows shot up. "You read?"

"Of course I do," Kagiso replied. "We're not all neanderthals like you."

"Sorry, not how I meant it to sound."

"Where is Brick?" Lofty asked.

"Going through his medical supplies," Kane replied.

Cara walked into the large room, carrying her kit and weapon which she had changed to a 433. On her head was a baseball cap covering her collar-length hair. She asked, "Who's drinking my beer?"

Kane held his up and she took it from his hand. "You know there is more in the refrigerator, right?"

"Yours is better."

They spent the next hour talking and doing other things. When the sun went down, chaos ruled the night.

———

OVER KUWAIT

"Sir, we're coming up to the jump point. Two minutes," the voice said in Sergei Andropov's headset. "Radar jamming is still working."

"Understood," he replied. Then, "Ilya, get them up.

We're two minutes out. Make sure they have their oxygen masks on."

"Sir."

Andropov checked his equipment, ensuring his AK-12 had a fresh magazine in it ready to go when he hit the ground. They were cruising in the Ilyushin Il-76 at 40,000 feet. Every man fitted their oxygen mask and waited for the rear ramp to drop.

Andropov looked at his men with pride. Many were veterans of the Syrian campaign, of Ukraine, and Mali. All were former soldiers of the Russian army and special forces. Now they were working for him as mercenaries. These were but a select few of the force he had on offer. Andropov, the former Russian general, had his own private army.

"Sir," said Ilya. "The men are ready."

Andropov nodded. He toggled the transmit button on his comms. "Strike One, this is Scorpion, over."

"Read you, Scorpion," came the reply.

"Execute Plan Ivan."

"Copy, Scorpion. Executing Plan Ivan."

In the time it had taken to finish the brief conversation with the strike fighter commander, the ramp on the Ilyushin Il-76 had fully descended. Now the light was green. Time to go.

———

THEY WERE A FLIGHT OF SIX. Sukhoi Su-57s with stealth capabilities. They came out of the desert hugging the deck doing Mach 1. Their hardpoints were filled with Kh-38 Air to Surface missiles. The commander of the flight was Genady Kuzlov.

Ahead of him, Kuzlov could see Ali Al Salem Air Base seemingly growing out of the desert darkness before him. "Strike Flight, get ready to pull up and engage."

The jets hammered toward the target, their turbo fan engines screaming. The men and women of the air base unaware of the imminent threat. Then when they reached two kilometers, Kuzlov gave the order. "Strike team pull up. Acquire targets and fire at will."

Pushing the aircraft's throttle all the way forward, Kuzlov pulled back on the joystick. He began seeking a target and found what he wanted. The control tower. The plane's targeting system acquired it and then Kuzlov fired. Under the direct impact, the tower exploded violently.

By the time the flight had passed over, six targets were burning.

Kuzlov said calmly, "Come back around, Strike Flight. Good hunting."

———

THE ROAR of low aircraft followed by shattering explosions rocked Team Reaper to their cores. As the base alarm began to wail, they knew what was happening. "Fuck, we're under attack," Kane shouted. "Gear up."

By the time they reached the door, everyone was in their kit and was ready to fight. Up ahead in the gloaming, Kane saw the orange glow of fires and burning objects. An Air Force member was running past and Cara called out, "What the fuck is going on?"

"We're under air attack, ma'am!"

No shit. Cara turned and pointed at Lofty and Kagiso. "Go and sit on The Persian."

"Boss," Lofty replied and the pair ran off.

"What about us—" Kane started.

Suddenly more deafening roars were punctuated by missiles exploding. A fuel truck disappeared along with some stationary aircraft. Multiple buildings and other infrastructure were shattered.

"What the fuck is going on?" Cara wondered out loud.

Knocker said, "They're Russian Sukhoi Su-57s, boss."

"How do you know, Ray, it's damn dark."

"I can tell," Knocker replied.

"They're not military," Kane said.

"How the fuck do you know that?" Knocker asked.

Kane pointed at the sky. Parachutes were floating down in the spotlights, with men hanging beneath them. Knocker's face screwed up. "Ah, bollocks. Fucking mercenaries."

Brick suddenly appeared with Rosana Morales in tow, her shoulder-length black hair tucked under a ball cap. Her face was laced with concern. "I need to help with casualties," she shouted.

"In case you hadn't noticed," Knocker said. "It's raining fucking mercenaries."

"What are they doing?" Brick asked.

"What the fuck do you think?" Cara replied. "You go with Rosana. The rest of you, with me. We'll join Lofty and Kagiso with The Persian."

"What about the others?" Brick asked.

"They'll have to look after themselves. Everyone, move."

ANOTHER PASS from the Sukhoi Su-57s and the base was fast becoming a burning wreck. By now the mercenaries were touching down. They separated into teams and started pushing toward the secure facility where The Persian was sequestered. Others set up a security perimeter. The plan for the operation was to hit hard and fast and get out.

Andropov gathered a team of twenty men around him. "Sergeant Volkov, take five men and move toward the target building."

"Yes, Comrade."

"The rest of you, follow me."

Small arms fire was breaking out everywhere. Almost all of Andropov's men had landed and the planes were still making runs. The Russian attack force moved quickly past burning vehicles and bodies on the ground. Off to the left, a group of defenders opened fire. A couple of the Russian's men fell with a cry of pain.

Two others broke away and took cover behind an intact Humvee, laying down suppressive fire. A third, with a grenade launcher underslung on his weapon, joined them. Once in position he fired, and the defenders took a direct hit.

All the personnel were killed instantly and the incoming fire ceased. With that, the force moved forward.

As they pressed on, the mercenaries were joined by an additional twenty men while another part of the attacking force attempted to secure the flanks long enough for Andropov and those with him to kill The

Persian. For proof of death, they needed his head. The reward would be paid for nothing less.

It was an objective the Russian intended to accomplish.

———

"Set up a perimeter here," Kane barked at the MPs. "Knocker, you're in command of this section."

"Roger that."

"Now wait a damn minute," the MP sergeant snapped. "My men, my command."

Kane didn't have time to argue. However, he needed the sergeant on side. "Listen, with the amount of combat experience he's had, you want him in charge. He will keep at least some of you alive."

The sergeant nodded. Knocker said, "All right you bloody pillocks, get whatever you can and set up a line of cover. Right fucking here."

Kane tapped four more. "You, with me."

"I'll stay here with Knocker," Cara said.

Nodding stoically, he said, "Keep your head down."

Relocating with his four MPs, Kane found Kagiso and Lofty still standing their post with two other MPs. "What's happening, Reaper?"

"No idea. But I have a feeling—"

The roar of jet engines along with explosions cut him off. "Take up defensive positions."

"Roger that."

"No one gets the package."

Lofty nodded. "Understood."

Kane turned to an MP. "Come with me."

"Where are you going, Reaper?" Lofty asked, watching him walk away.

"To the plane. We need more firepower."

Running toward a Humvee with the MP behind him, Kane called to him, "You drive."

The young man jumped behind the wheel while Kane climbed onto the passenger side. "Let's go."

Kane gave him directions, and the MP kept his foot down. The sound of bullets ricocheting off the armored skin of the vehicle sounded like it was being pounded by a ballpeen hammer. Kane pointed ahead of them. "Over there."

An explosion in front of them caused the MP to swerve. A few moments later the Humvee skidded to a stop. "What's your name, kid?"

"Gomer, sir."

"Who didn't like you, son?"

"My father. He was a Gomer Pyle fan," the MP replied with a reluctant smirk.

Climbing from the vehicle Kane entered the plane through the side hatch. He ran forward and stopped in front of the armory. Once it was unlocked, he started removing weapons. He grabbed two M320s and a SAW (Squad Automatic Weapon) that was belt fed.

With Gomer's help, they loaded them into the Humvee followed by ammunition. Kane then took the SAW and climbed up into the turret. "All right, Gomer, take us back."

———

KNOCKER GLANCED down at the MP who had been standing beside him, now lying on the tarmac. In the orange glow of multiple fires, he could see the blood pooling from the ghastly throat wound.

"Fuck." He slapped another nearby MP on the shoulder and said, "See to him."

Reloading his 433 Knocker opened fire once more, his target thrown back with arms in the air as he fell. The MP leaning over his comrade spoke gruffly, "He's fucked."

"Drag him back and then start shooting—" a grenade exploded in front of their position. "Fuck! Boss, are you okay?"

Cara stopped firing as her weapon ran dry. She dropped down and began reloading. Seeing blood on her cheek, Knocker asked, concern in his tone, "Are you hit?"

"Scratch," she replied.

"Don't get shot. Reaper will have my bollocks."

"*RPG!*"

The shouted warning was like a bomb going off. Everyone on the firing line fell flat and covered themselves. The rocket propelled grenade detonated in front of Knocker's position, bringing a shower of debris down on him. "Why the fuck do they pick me?" he coughed.

Cara dragged him up. "Come on, Raymond."

"Don't fucking call me Raymond," he growled and opened fire.

———

KAGISO WAS DOING the same thing for one of the MPs who'd been knocked down by a blast. "Get up and fight like the lion," she hissed. "Tonight, we die with honor."

"I'd prefer not to die tonight, ma'am," the MP replied.

"But if you do, make your people proud."

The young MP grunted and returned to firing. As did Kagiso. She picked out a target and stroked the trigger twice. The Russian mercenary fell and then tried to rise. She fired once more and hit him in the head. Blood spurted from the man who would never rise again.

More gunfire hammered out through the night illuminated by flaming buildings. Sirens wailed across the base as the fighter bombers made another pass setting off calamitous explosions.

Emerging from the chaos, Jorgensen had a HK416 tucked under his arm and wore body armor. He came over to Kagiso and said, "Where the bloody hell do you want me?"

"Right here will do," Kagiso replied.

The battle continued unabated for a few more minutes when the roar of a Humvee sounded close by. Then through a pall of smoke, Kagiso saw the vehicle with Kane firing a SAW from the turret.

The vehicle pulled up inside their perimeter and Kane climbed down. Unloading their booty, Gomer began passing out the grenade launchers to the others. Kane came over to Kagiso. "How is it?"

Kagiso looked around her. "We are dying well."

"If it's all the same to you, I think I prefer to live."

Lofty joined them. "Can I make a suggestion, Reaper?"

"Suggest away."

"We need to take the package and get the fuck out

of here. If we can get airborne, then that'll be a good start because of our stealth capabilities."

"And go where?"

"Antarctica," Jorgensen said.

"What?" Kane looked at the Six man.

"If we can get airborne then I'll explain. I don't think we can because I think we're fucked. But if we can, then you might have a chance."

Kane stared at Jorgensen and then glanced at the carnage all around. If they were going to make a decision, now was the time. Kane turned to Gomer. "Feel like another drive?"

"Point and shoot, sir, point and shoot."

Kane toggled his comms. "Ares from Reaper One."

"Copy, Reaper One."

"I've come up with a plan."

"Send."

"Everyone back to the plane and we get the hell out of here."

Cara thought for a moment. Then, "From one death trap to another. I like it. Let's go."

"Reaper One to all callsigns, rally on the plane. Say again, rally on the plane. Out."

"Kagiso, Lofty, pick some people and bring out our package."

"Copy, Reaper."

Moments later they had Roman restrained and in the Humvee. Gomer was already in the driver's seat and Kagiso and Lofty climbed in the rear with the package. Out of the smoke ran three more MPs. The leader was a short female sergeant with a dirty, blood-smeared face. "Permission to come with you, sir?"

"We have no idea where we're going, Sergeant."

"Anywhere is better than fucking here, sir."

"Climb aboard."

The three MPs climbed onto the running boards along with Jorgensen, and Gomer floored the gas pedal. As the vehicle accelerated away, the MPs lay down heavy fire in addition to that coming from Lofty in the turret. Another Humvee fell in behind them and Cara's voice came over the radio. "I see you have some passengers, Reaper."

"We have ourselves a regular party happening." Kane paused and then said, "Reaper One to Hammer."

"This is Hammer."

"Hammer, we need immediate exfil."

"Roger, Reaper One. Engines are already warming up. Some passengers already aboard."

"We'll be there directly."

––––––––

ANDROPOV SAW the Humvees speed away and knew they were too late. While the battle had raged his men had been held up long enough that had given their targets the opportunity to escape with the terrorist. "Where are those Humvees going?"

"Sir, they have a plane on the runway they are communicating with. That would be my guess."

"Shit. Strike One this is Scorpion."

"Read you, Scorpion," came the reply.

"There is a plane on the runway. I need it destroyed."

"Sorry, Scorpion, we just expended the last of our missiles on that run, over."

"Then use your fucking guns."

"We have enough for one run—fuck."

Suddenly there was an explosion in the sky as Kuzlov's plane disintegrated in a massive explosion.

Somebody had managed to get one of the Patriot missile systems working.

"I thought those systems were knocked out. Fucking fix it."

Two more Sukhoi Su-57s fell from the sky hit by missiles. Andropov's anger raged at the commander's ineptitude of carrying out a simple task. He got back on the radio and contacted the Ilyushin Il-76. "Get that fucking plane on the ground and block the runway."

"But it is unsafe, sir," the pilot radioed back.

"No shit. Just fucking do it."

———

THEY FORCED Roman onto the modified C-17 and locked him in a small one-person cell. Kane set up a perimeter at the bottom of the ramp with the MPs, the small sergeant beside him.

As a handful of incoming mercenaries emerged from the smoky darkness they opened fire. Kane and the defenders returned fire and soon put their pursuers down. Beside him, he heard the sergeant say, "Get the fuck up, you're not hurt."

He saw her dragging another MP to his feet. Kane asked, "What's your name, soldier?"

"They call me Burner, sir. Short for Hell Burner," she replied, reloading.

"Well, Burner, get your ass on the plane. Your friends too."

"We should stay, sir."

"I have a feeling we'll need you, Sergeant. My boss will square it with yours."

"Yes, sir. Right. You lot, get on the fucking plane."

Running up the ramp, Kane began checking on the rest of his team. All were battered and bruised in some way. Knocker looked no different than normal. "Been in the thick of it, Knocker, I see."

"I'm a fucking armaments magnet, Reaper, I swear. Now, where are we going?"

"No idea."

The plane was already moving. It had sustained bullet strikes on its armored skin but anything short of a missile wouldn't penetrate it. However, as the plane rumbled along the runway, the pilots were dealing with their own dilemma.

———

Former Wing Commander Regina Smythe concentrated on the end of the runway and everything she could control from her pilot's seat. Beside her sat former Squadron Leader Harvey Keller. It was Keller that picked up the alarm.

"Ma'am, we have a collision alarm."

"Where?" Reggie snapped back.

"Twelve o'clock. There is another plane trying to land on our runway."

"Bollocks," Reggie growled. "Push the throttles to the wall and ready the Hellfires."

Keller flicked the switch that opened a compartment in each wing of the modified C-17. From these, two hard points lowered with attached Hellfire missiles.

While this was happening, he pushed the throttles all the way forward.

The plane's engines rose to a high-pitched scream. From her seat Reggie could now make out the incoming plane. "Is that a fucking Ilyushin?"

"Would appear so, ma'am."

"Get ready," Reggie told Keller.

"We already have lock."

Reggie switched over to the intercom. "Hang on back there. Things are about to get rough."

Easing the joystick back, the nose of the plane started to rise as she said, "Let the bastard have it, Harvey."

The missiles fired and streaked out in front of the C-17. The twin dots of their engines glowed orange in the dark. Two pairs of eyes followed them right up until the point of impact.

The Ilyushin exploded and dropped to the runway. The C-17 continued its climb, barely missing the wreckage, but flying through the orange ball of flame produced by the explosion. The plane bucked and lurched. Alarms went off but were quickly switched off

"Are we all good?" Reggie asked.

"We're still flying," Keller replied with a relieved smirk.

"Great, now let's find out where we're going."

CHAPTER 2

IN THE AIR, 30,000 FT

"We're going where?" Cara blurted out when Jorgensen told her of their destination.

"Antarctica," he repeated.

"Why the hell would we want to go there?"

"Because no one wants us—him," the Six man replied, meaning Roman. "The UK has a secret facility there which they use to house certain people."

"Like who?" Kane asked.

It was Knocker who answered. "People like terrorists, serial killers beyond help, all the ones the British government wants to disappear."

Kane was surprised. "You know about it?"

"Delivered there before with an SAS team," Knocker said. "They use private contractors to guard it."

"What are we meant to do when we get there?" Cara asked.

"Wait and see what needs to be done," Jorgensen replied.

"Shit. They wanted us to get him but now no one fucking wants him."

"That's about it."

Cara looked at Kane. "What do you think?"

"We get Roman on the deck and locked away. Team Reaper stays behind but we get the plane and Bravo out of there. They can operate remotely."

"Bravo can go, but I'm staying."

"No—"

"Command, remember, Reaper. Me boss."

He wasn't happy. "Fine."

"What about the MPs?" Knocker asked. "A few extra weapons might come in handy."

"Get them sorted. New kit. We've got cold-weather gear to go around. Watch out for their sergeant. She bites."

"Most small terriers do," Knocker replied.

Cara sighed. "I'll let the boss know. Reaper, fill the others in."

"Roger that."

"Knocker, before you do anything else, get Rosanna to patch you up instead of bleeding all over my plane."

The Brit looked at his arm. "Just a scratch."

"Get it tended to."

"Yes, boss."

———

TEN MINUTES LATER, Rosanna was stitching the wound together when Burner approached Knocker.

"You wanted to see me, sir?"

"Name's not sir, it's Knocker as in those things you have on your chest," the Brit replied. "Some people call me Raymond. If you do that, I'll kick your Geordie ass all the fucking way back home."

"You think you can, mate?" Burner asked defiantly.

"I'll give it a red-hot go."

Without her helmet, Burner's red hair was revealed and her freckles were more pronounced. "All right then. My name is Burner. Also known as Rosie. Call me that and I'll burn your fucking house down."

Knocker smiled. "I like you already. Who are your friends?"

"Guy with the blond hair is Ralph. Tall guy is Shorty. The other guy is Gomer. He already met your Reaper mate."

"Fine. Once I'm done here with Doc Morales here, I'll get you lot some new kit."

"Where are we going?" Burner asked.

"Antarctica."

"Fuck me."

———

HEREFORD, ENGLAND

Mary Thurston was at her desk watching a real-time feed of the incident still occurring at Ali Al Salem Air Base. She had seen the C-17 take off and felt a wave of relief wash over her. Where they were headed, she had no idea, but knowing her people, they would have a plan.

Mary was the spitting image of actress Rhona Mitra, and had they been of similar age they could have been mistaken as twins. A former general in the United States Rangers, she had taken over command of Team Reaper at the team's inception, and then ultimately became overall charge of Global, a private contract and research facility when General Hank Jones had become sick.

The encrypted cell on her desk rang. Only one guess was needed as to who it would be. "I was wondering when I would hear from you."

"Things have been a little hectic, General," Cara told her.

"Do you have the package?"

"Yes, ma'am."

"All your people in one piece?"

"Yes, ma'am," Cara replied. "We have a few more as well. A man from Six and four MPs."

"What's the plan?" Thurston asked.

"Antarctica," Cara said, waiting for the explosion.

"Tell me quick before my head blows off."

"The Brits have a facility there they keep highly undesirables in. Seeing as no one wants Roman, we're up the proverbial creek without a paddle. And we need somewhere to stash him."

Thurston nodded slowly. "After what happened at the airbase, I can't see anyone wanting him. Not with that bounty on his head."

"What's happening at Ali Al Salem?"

"The mercenaries are scattering. However, the place is a mess. Casualties are high. What is the plan once you reach the South Pole?"

"I'll send Bravo back to Hereford and I'll stay here with Reaper and the others."

"Why?" Thurston asked.

"Because I have a feeling this isn't over. And other than putting a bullet in Roman's head, wherever we go, it's going to be a war zone."

"The bullet thing sounds tempting," Thurston said, contemplating the idea. Then she said, "All right, Cara, keep me informed. I'll see if I can find you a refueling tanker."

"Thank you, Mary."

"Take care."

Thurston disconnected the call and shook her head. "What a damn fuck-up."

IN THE AIR, 30,000 FT

Kane opened the cubicle door and took the bag off Roman's head. He was chained securely, so presented no threat.

"I see you made it." The German sneered.

"If there was ever any doubt, I would have put a bullet in your head, Roman," Kane replied.

"Just the same John Kane I see," Roman opined.

"The fuck I am. I've grown harder."

"Harder than the Congo?"

"Yeah."

During Kane's previous encounter with Roman, the German had been a captain in the Kommando Spezialkräfte, or KSK. These were frontline German special forces. They were working with the Recon Marines evacuating missionaries in the path of rebel soldiers. Catching Roman shooting some of the prisoners they had picked up, Kane had flattened Roman in front of his men, the emasculation creating instant enmity. The two had been enemies ever since. Now this.

"You think you can hold me? After what happened at the air base?"

"Someone has offered a lot of money to rescue you?"

"They don't want me alive, Reaper. They want me dead."

Kane nodded. "You have pissed off a lot of people."

Roman shook his head. "I did work for a syndicate. Don't ask me who they were. But not all the targets were of my choosing."

"What are you talking about, Roman?" Kane asked.

"The bombing on Wall Street, the Russian pipeline, the coup in Sierra Leone, I could go on but it was all for the benefit of a syndicate. Everything I did was to manipulate something so they could make money."

"Who is the syndicate?"

"That I can't tell you. All I had was a name. Chrysalis."

"Never heard of it," Kane said doubtfully. "For all I know, you could be lying to me."

Roman smiled. "Yes, I could."

Kane placed the hood back over the German's head. "Get some sleep."

"You haven't told me where we're going?"

"And I'm not going to."

Five minutes later, Kane had gathered Cara, Knocker, and Sam Swift, A.K.A., Slick, their red-headed computer tech. "This could be something, or it could be nothing. I was just talking to Roman. Have any of you heard the name Chrysalis?"

"Yeah, it's the thing butterflies come from," Knocker replied. Everyone in the group looked at him. "What? I read books."

"It is tied with some kind of syndicate. Roman eluded that they were the ones that put the bounty on his head to keep him quiet."

"What about?"

"He did a lot of work for them."

"Are you sure he's not feeding you a line of shit?" Knocker asked.

"He could be," Kane allowed. "I was just running things past you guys."

Slick nodded. "Leave it with me, Reaper. I'll see what I can dig up."

"Thanks, Slick."

Cara said, "Everybody else, get some rest."

———

Two hours later, their flight was redirected to Australia for refueling, and Slick found a lead.

He sat with Kane and Cara and explained. "Chrysalis popped in Hong Kong. Chrysalis Holdings. They are a consortium made up of companies from Saudi Arabia, South Korea, Russia, Singapore, and Switzerland."

"What kind of companies?" Cara asked.

"Very rich ones," Slick replied. "And they all keep a healthy stock of gold in Switzerland."

"Names?"

"Saudi Arabia: Khalid Al-Mansour, oil. South Korea: Ji-Hyun Park, electronics. Russia: Viktor Ivanovich Petrov, arms. Singapore: Adrian Tan Wei, global logistics. Switzerland: Sofia Meier, she is their banker."

"Okay," Kane said. "Now impress me."

Slick did just that. "Oil? Roman blew up the Russia pipeline and forced the price in Saudi Arabia to climb. Electronics? Roman infected all the new Chinese military software with a virus which rendered it useless. They went to Park to fix it. Arms? Roman took out the biggest arms dealer the globe had seen last year."

"Hiram Kleist?"

"That's it. That leaves us with global logistics. Roman kidnapped the wife of one of the world's biggest shipping magnates and forced him to sign everything over to an LLC which was—is owned by Wei. After that he killed the woman and the husband at the handover."

"You have evidence of this?" Cara asked.

"Not exactly but it all adds up."

"Now they want him dead before he can tell all," Kane said.

"And they've got the money to succeed," Slick said.

"Which one is the overall commander of The Syndicate?" Cara asked.

"From what I can gather, they are all equal."

"So we can't just take one of them out?"

Slick shook his head. "No, it doesn't work that way. Take out one, they are still operational."

"Then they all have to go," Kane said. "Why haven't we heard of these people before?"

"Because, like all clever criminals, they live in the shadows. I just turned the light on."

"Good work."

"They will know I found them," Slick said. "There was no way to avoid it."

Cara nodded. "Thanks, Slick."

After he had gone, Kane turned to Cara. "Are you thinking what I am?"

"We take five heads off the hydra?"

Kane nodded. "That's what I was thinking. But unlike a hydra, these ones shouldn't grow back."

"Who do you propose do it, Reaper?" Cara asked.

"Normally I'd say Knocker, but I need him with me. Which leaves one other."

"Borden Hunt?"

"Yes. Borden Hunt."

"I'll get Slick to do up an intel package just in case he accepts. Do you know where he is?"

"Bangkok, riding herd on some rich kid," Kane said.

Cara grinned. "Oh, how the mighty have fallen."

"That's what happens when you go it solo."

"Call him, see if he's interested."

CHAPTER 3

BANGKOK, THAILAND

The last thing former SEAL chief Borden Hunt wanted to be doing was babysitting three rich American brats as they went out nightclubbing.

Amelia Strait was the daughter of Magnus Strait, one of the biggest real estate tycoons in Thailand. Having sold everything in his portfolio in LA, he'd headed overseas with his family. After twelve months in Thailand, this was Amelia's first opportunity to host her friends. At twenty, each member of the group scraped in over the legal drinking age.

Worse luck.

Attired in a black suit, Hunt had a SIG P226 tucked away inside the jacket. While the streets of Bangkok were relatively safe, after dark, the creatures came out. It wouldn't be the first time a young woman was snatched from a nightclub.

But that was why he got paid the big bucks. Make

sure that nothing happened to the group. The girls' job was to have fun and not make trouble for Hunt.

What could possibly go wrong?

He pulled the SUV they were in over into the gutter and parked two doors down from the nightclub. Nodding toward a neon sign that said: **PINK PUSSYCAT**, he asked, "Is that it?"

"That's it," Amelia replied.

"Sounds more like a damn strip club than a nightclub."

"Cheer up, Senior Chief," she retorted.

"I will if you lot stay out of trouble," Hunt growled. "Do you have your panic buttons?"

"Yes," all three replied in a bored drone.

"Right, have fun."

"You're not coming in, Borden?" Amy asked. She was the redhead of the group, and it looked like she had a crush on the former SEAL.

"No, Amy, I'm sure you don't want me raining on your parade."

"You can rain on me anytime," she replied.

Hunt shook his head. The girl was brazen; he'd give her that.

"You should relax, Borden," Kellie said, putting a long strand of her black hair behind her ear.

"I'm not paid to relax," Hunt told her. "Now get out of here and keep an eye on each other."

They climbed out of the SUV and started along the sidewalk, playfully giggling and arm in arm. Hunt watched as they reached the line to go in. He looked at the sign again. "Pink fucking Pussycat."

His cell rang. Not his work one, his personal

encrypted one. He looked at the screen and automatically thought about rejecting it. "Ah, shit."

Somehow his thumb came down on the accept button. "Hey, Reaper."

"Hey, Bord, what's up?"

"I'm sitting here looking at a sign that screams strip club watching three layers of trouble about to go inside."

"Ouch. I bet you wish you were downrange."

"What do you want, John?"

"I need Scimitar."

"Tell me more," Hunt said.

"It'll be dangerous."

"As dangerous as riding herd on three females in party mode?" Hunt asked.

"Yeah...no. But it could get you killed."

He thought about his current assignment. "Good, I'm in."

"You don't know what it is," Kane said.

"I don't give a fuck. I'm in. I just need to finish tonight, and I'll be good to go."

"Do you want to know what you have to do?" Kane asked.

"I suppose."

"We need five people dropped. Different countries, possibly different danger levels."

"What did they do?"

As they talked, Hunt saw a black BMW stop outside the nightclub and three men climbed out before it drove off. Kane said, "They're part of a conglomerate called The Syndicate. We picked up a little terrorist called The Persian and now they have a big bounty on his head which we need removed."

"Hunting whales, Reaper," Hunt said.

"He's one I wish I could throw back," Kane replied. "Instead, we'll settle for killing the five-headed snake."

Hunt looked up. The girls had gone inside. "I gather I'm on the books?"

"All the help you need from Global including weapons, transport, and spending money."

"Backup?"

"Lone wolf."

"I can deal with that. Now, you mentioned money," Hunt said.

"Big job, big risk, five million."

Hunt nearly fell out of the SUV. "Shit, Reaper, I could retire on that."

"I don't want you to retire, Bord. I just want you alive when all this is over."

"Roger that."

"There will be a car waiting for you tomorrow when you wake up. Text me your details. There'll also be a plane at the airport with everything you need. Including a file on each target that Slick will put together."

"What did everyone's favorite general have to say?"

"I haven't told her yet," Kane replied.

Hunt grinned. "Keep your head down, Reaper."

"You too, Bord."

The call disconnected and Hunt suddenly felt calm again. He always did when he was running into fire. A white van drove past on the same side as he was parked. He didn't think much of it at first. The third time it went by, his attention piqued. "What are you up to?"

With a sense of foreboding, Hunt turned to look in

the rear seat. His eyes widened when he saw the three panic buttons. "Ah, fuck me."

Climbing out of the SUV Hunt hurried toward the nightclub. When he reached the line, he circumvented it and walked to the front. Reaching inside his jacket for his close security credentials which gave him permission to work in Thailand, he flipped it so that the doorman got a look and nodded, allowing him to pass.

Inside the music was loud and the dance floor packed with jumping and writing bodies. The females outnumbered the males by at least two to one. Back in his youthful years, he would have called this heaven. Now, he called it a smorgasbord for kidnappers.

Spying the girls on the dance floor, Hunt walked over to the bar where a Swedish girl was working wearing cutoff jeans and a bikini top. "What can I get you?" she shouted at him.

"Beer," he shouted back.

Bending to open a fridge door, she pulled out a bottle of Heineken and cracked the top, placing it on the bar in front of him. Hunt paid her and took a pull. The bargirl stared at him. The former SEAL was in his late thirties and cut a fine figure in his suit. "American?" she asked.

"Yeah."

The bargirl nodded and grabbed a bit of paper and scribbled on it then passed it to him. On it was the name Ingrid and number. She smiled. Hunt stared at her. He figured she was in her mid-twenties. She had a tattoo of a bear on her side, extending from her jeans to the area covered by her bikini wrap. Hunt held the paper up to be polite. "Thanks."

"Don't forget to call it." Then she walked away.

Hunt turned his attention back to the girls who were now jumping up and down to the beat of a different song. He slowly drank his beer and only had about a third left when he noticed a man watching the girls from a distant corner.

Hunt's eyes narrowed. He wasn't quite sure if the man was one of those from the BMW or not. He scanned the room and picked out another watcher. Now his internal alarm was jingling hard. He turned back to the first man and saw he was gone. Hunt looked at the girls.

The two girls.

Amy, the redhead, was gone.

"Shit!"

The former SEAL placed his beer on the bar and walked out onto the dance floor. Revelers jostled him as they tried to keep up with the beat of the music. He finally reached Amelia and Kellie who seemed surprised to see him. "Bord, what are you—"

"Where is Amy?"

Kellie said, "She wasn't feeling well. She went to the bathroom."

Hunt looked around and saw that the second man was gone now. "Go over to the bar and don't move."

"What?" Amelia protested. "Why on earth—"

"Just damn well do it," Hunt hissed.

"Okay, okay."

He made firm eye contact with her to show he wasn't messing around. "Stay there until I come for you."

"You're scaring us," Kellie said.

"Just go."

Hunt turned and looked around for a sign to indicate the direction of the bathrooms. He saw it above the open doorway to his left. Pushing his way through the crowd, he finally reached the doorway. It led to a narrow hallway with a tiled floor. Halfway along, a guy and girl were wrapped in each other's arms, their tongues intertwined like serpents. Hunt's first stop was the male bathroom to make sure the two suspicious men weren't in there just pissing. Instead, he found another couple having sex. The young woman seated on the bathroom bench, her legs wrapped around her lover, her head against the wall below a sign promoting condoms.

Hunt pushed the door into each cubicle and found them empty. Leaving the bathroom he went back out into the hallway. Suddenly the ladies' bathroom door crashed open and three men emerged. Two carried a struggling Amy.

All three were Asian in appearance. The first man through the door turned and saw Hunt. "What the fuck are you looking at?" he asked with a thick accent.

"Let the girl go," Hunt ordered.

The two men carrying Amy continued along the hallway to where it turned a corner. The third bad guy moved swiftly toward Hunt, taking his suit as a sign of weakness. He found out different.

As soon as he was within reach, Hunt's right fist streaked out and caught the man in the throat. He gagged, unable to breathe. Clutching at his throat with his left hand, his right went under his coat. Hunt saw the flash of a handgun.

The former SEAL went for his P226. It appeared just as the kidnappers did. Hunt's left hand grabbed the wrist of the gun hand and pushed it wide. The man squeezed the trigger twice and the bullets hammered into the wall.

Hunt rammed his SIG into the kidnapper's middle and fired two shots of his own. The sound of all four shots was deafening in the hallway. Letting the man fall to the floor, Hunt stepped over him, firing once more, the bullet punching into the fallen kidnapper's head.

Now Hunt was moving fast. He turned the corner in the hallway and saw the door at the far end closing. He picked up his pace even further and was running now. His shoulder hit the door and it flew wide open.

Hunt stumbled into the alley and looked left then right. He spotted a van; the one he'd seen earlier while waiting in the SUV. The two remaining kidnappers were climbing in. The first disappeared and the second had just put his foot inside when Hunt fired the SIG once more.

Although the first shot missed, the second didn't, and the kidnapper cried out in pain and fell backward. He staggered and Hunt shot him again.

This time he went down and never moved.

The van's engine roared as the driver stood hard on the gas pedal. The van shot forward directly toward the former SEAL.

Hunt opened fire and put the rest of the magazine through the windshield on the driver's side. Pulling to the right, the white van ran into the wall of the building.

Dropping out the magazine from his SIG the former SEAL replaced it with a fresh one. He walked toward the van with his gun raised. As he reached the driver's door and looked through the smashed window he saw the dead driver.

Hunt was about to take another step when the side door slid open and the final man appeared. The kidnapper snapped off a shot at Hunt who fired two in return. Both rounds hit the man in the chest, and he fell to the pavement.

Taking cautious steps, Hunt looked inside and saw Amy lying, bound with a bag over her head. "Amy, it's Bord."

Her struggling stopped immediately, and she let him remove the bag. Her eyes were filled with tears; her cheeks streaked with makeup. Hunt helped her out of the vehicle and cut the zippy ties binding her wrists. She twisted violently and threw her arms around his neck, starting to sob uncontrollably. Hunt eased her back and said, "We have to get the others and leave. Understand? Before anything else happens."

Amy nodded jerkily. "I understand."

With his arm around her, they started walking back the way they had come.

CHAPTER 4

ROGER RAAF BASE, AUSTRALIA

The loading ramp came down and Kane and Knocker emerged from the plane to stand at the bottom on the warm tarmac. Rogers RAAF base was a secret site in central Australia utilized by the Air Force for UAVs and their Next Gen program. It was small but adequate for what the Global people needed.

Overhead a wedge-tailed eagle did lazy circles as it looked for something to eat. Knocker and Kane were wearing jeans and T-shirts with reversed baseball caps on. They wore body armor and carried their 433s.

"Something is wrong," Knocker said, charging his weapon.

Kane followed suit. "What tells you that?"

"Maybe the fact that no one is here."

"Cara was talking to them an hour ago," Kane replied. "Has to be someone here."

Knocker toggled his transmit button on his radio. "Boss, you're needed outside."

"Now?" Cara asked.

"Preferably yesterday."

"On my way."

Kane raised his weapon and started using his sights to sweep the area. "I can't see anything."

"That's the problem, Reaper. There is nothing to fucking see."

"What's up?" Cara asked as she came down the ramp.

"Tell me what you see," Knocker said.

She looked around. Then said, "Nothing."

"Exactly. A base like this should be bustling. Our fuel tanker should be on its way here to refuel."

"Hammer, copy?" Cara said into her comms.

"Copy, ma'am."

"How many pounds of fuel do you have left?"

"Twenty thousand, ma'am."

Cara nodded. "Get us in the air."

"Ma'am?"

"Now, Hammer."

"Roger that."

Kane said, "Brick, Kagiso, Lofty, on the ramp now. Bring your weapons."

"Roger."

The engines which had been winding down suddenly began increasing in pitch. Kane was about to speak to Knocker when he saw him frowning, looking to the sky. Kane followed his gaze and saw what the Brit was looking at. Five dots, hovering in the air about one hundred meters out. "Are they..."

"Drones," Knocker said. "And I bet my left bollock that they are the fucking exploding kind."

"Lofty, get the AMX-6 up," Kane said.

The AMX-6, was based on Global's AMX-4, code-named Rhino. It was a quadcopter platform which mounted a small four-barreled rotary machine gun that fired a 5.56 bullet. It also carried a hundred round magazine like the M249. They had deployed it before in Africa with some success. But the AMX-6 had been upgraded with automatic targeting. They called it the Taipan.

"Roger," came the reply.

"What are they waiting for?" Cara growled.

They were soon joined by the others. The plane started rolling and on cue, the drones began to close the distance.

Knocker brought his 433 up and sighted on the first killer. He opened fire but missed. Firing again, he was joined by the others who began firing at the drones too. Two of them exploded and fell to pieces on the apron. The other three kept on flying.

The Global team changed their aim. More rounds ripped through the air. Meanwhile, Lofty was clipping the Taipan together.

The three remaining drones exploded like the others and fell to the ground. Knocker turned to Lofty. "Lofty, you got that bird ready to go yet?"

"Almost."

"Well hurry the fuck up, we've got more incoming."

Kane glanced at his friend and then in the direction he was looking. He saw ten more shapes in the air and then the SUVs appeared. "What the hell is going on here?" Kane snarled, bringing his weapon up.

Cara said, "I get the feeling that a lot of people want our package."

"Don't get off the ramp," Kane said into his comms. By now the turbines were screaming.

"Taipan away," Lofty said and the aerial killer took off.

CAPTAIN RICHARD CARMICHAEL, SASR, sat in the front passenger seat of the first SUV. Also in the vehicle were the driver and two other shooters. Behind them, in the five other SUVs came the rest of his two patrols of SAS vehicle-mounted troop.

He was under orders from someone inside the government to seize or destroy the plane and the terrorist inside. His mission was not to ask why, just to carry it out. Upon his arrival at the site, he ordered everyone off the base so they could have a free rein.

From the back of the SUV, a voice said, "Skipper, the advance drones are all down."

"Get the rest into the attack, Trigger. That plane doesn't leave here."

"Roger that."

Carmichael said into his comms, "This is Blue Lead. Keep that plane on the ground. Fan out and open fire."

Each of the following vehicles acknowledged and fanned out as ordered. Soon they were bristling with guns and ready to fire.

"WE'VE GOT MORE INCOMING," Slick said. "Listen to this."

He opened a line to Rani. *"This is Blue Lead. Keep that plane on the ground. Fan out and open fire."*

"This is bad," Rani Perera said as she watched everything unfold on her screen. "Very, very, bad."

Luis Ferrero stepped in beside her. "What do we have?"

"Incoming SUVs. Slick intercepted their transmissions. They're Australians."

Ferrero's face grew grim. "I see. Launch the Stingers."

She toggled a switch on her headset and said, "Launch the Stingers."

The Stingers were four-wheeled drones. Built low to the ground and loaded with explosives. All their operator had to do was drive them to the target. Vehicles were ideal.

Two of the onboard crew chiefs hurried to a couple large boxes. Opening the lids they reached inside and withdrew a pair of Stingers. About the size of a remote-controlled car, they were almost as light. Running toward the ramp where the operators of Team Reaper were starting to engage, one of the crew chiefs called out:

"Make a hole!"

Looking over his shoulder, Kane saw what was about to happen and stepped aside. The crew chief put the Stingers on the ramp. "One and two ready."

Rani acknowledged the call. She took hold of her control stick and glanced at Pete Teller, the former Master Sergeant in the US Air Force, now the right-hand man in the UAV team, with eyes on his screen. She said, "Launch One, Pete."

"Boss," he acknowledged with a nod of his head.

Out on the ramp, the first Stinger came to life and streaked forward off the ramp. Close behind, Stinger Two, controlled by Rani, came to life and followed its sister.

Back inside the onboard ops room, the two operators watched their screens. Rani said, "You take the first on the right, I'll take the one on the left."

"Roger that," Teller replied.

His eyebrows knitted with concentration as the Stinger bounced over the runway. It raced toward the target, jumping left and right. Then it slipped beneath the vehicle and Teller hit the detonate button.

In an orange ball of flame, the armored SUV disappeared. The explosion flicked it over into a roll. Then moments later, Rani's target did the same thing.

She said in her comms, "Get two more out and put the ramp up."

"The Taipan is still out," Lofty said.

"Leave it, we have more."

"Roger that."

The crew chief grabbed two more Stingers and released them as the rest of the team pulled back and the ramp came up.

At her console, Rani guided her Stinger toward the remaining SUVs. Through the camera, the SUVs grew larger until the Stingers reached them and once more the picture disappeared.

"Is that all of them?" Cara asked as she stepped in behind Rani.

"I think there's two left."

"What the fuck was that?" Burner asked Kane.

"Welcoming committee."

"You guys must be popular."

"As popular as a goat at a lion's banquet," Kagiso said.

"Everyone, strap in," Kane said. "We're getting out of here."

"Reggie, how are we looking?" Cara asked the pilot.

"Runway is clear, ma'am. I just need a destination."

"Standby, we're working on it." Cara said to Rani, "We need a gas station."

"Yes, ma'am." Then, "Slick, I need to know if the Australians have any gas stations in the air."

"On it." His fingers moved across the keyboard like he was a tap dancer on steroids. "Ma'am, there is a gas station over the Bight."

"Roger that. Hammer, head south. I'll take care of the rest."

"Understood."

The C-17 came up off the runway, its turbines screaming. Reaching the right altitude, Reggie turned the bird and pointed it south.

ZURICH, SWITZERLAND

The four screens came on in front of Sofia Meier and she waited for everyone to log on. Tall, with long legs, blond hair, and sultry eyes, Sofia more resembled a model than an executive banker. But she was exceptional at her job. Tough and wily.

The first one to appear was Jin-Hyun Park, the electronics mogul. He looked like your typical nerd. Bowl haircut, glasses, babyface.

"Hello, Jin."

"Sofia."

"I trust you are well?"

"Thank you, yes."

Next to appear was Viktor Petrov. An older man, he was a former Russian general who'd found it more profitable to sell arms to those who needed them.

"Viktor."

"Sofia."

The words were clipped. There was no love lost between them. Petrov didn't like the power she wielded in the banking world, and she didn't appreciate his misogyny. "I hope this meeting won't last too long, Sofia."

"As long as it takes, I'm afraid, Viktor."

The third screen blinked, and Khalid's face came on. "Sofia, looking lovely as always."

Khalid was at the outer extent of his country's limit of four wives. A fact, however, that didn't stop the smooth-talking playboy and oil billionaire from exploring other possibilities each time he flew to Europe. "How are your wives, Khalid?"

"Boring as always," he replied with a grunt.

"You should show them more respect."

"I treat them exactly as they deserve."

As usual, the last to appear was Adrian Tan Wei. The logistics man had been distracted by work, forgetting about the meeting time. "Adrian, late as always," Sofia admonished him.

"I was working," he replied. "My apologies."

"Right," Petrov growled. "Now that we are all here, why did you call the meeting, Sofia?"

"We seem to have a problem," she replied.

"You are the one to take care of problems, Sofia. Not bother us with the minutiae."

Generally, she would but considered the current situation worthy of their attention. Not only was she their banker, but she was also their troubleshooter. On lower floors of her office building was a hub full of computer techs who could do just about anything she asked of them. Except fight.

"I felt you should know," she replied.

"Know what?"

"There have already been two attempts to terminate the target, and both have failed," Sofia explained.

"Who?" Khalid asked, raising an eyebrow.

"Sergei Andropov and Richard Carmichael of the Australian SASR. Andropov hit the mercenaries at Ali Al Salem Air Base. He lost a good deal of his force but from what I can gather, he's regrouping and getting ready for another try."

"What is the Australian SAS doing involved?" Petrov asked.

"They were deployed by the Australian Minister of Defense. Apparently fifty million was too much to pass up."

"And they failed?"

"Yes. Carmichael was killed in the attack."

"It is obviously hard to get things done these days," Park said matter-of-factly. "Where are they now?"

"They have been tracked to Antarctica. The British have a not-so-secret facility there. I have people reaching out to the Argentinians and French."

"The French?" Wei was curious.

"French special forces have a base there too. It's where they do their winter warfare training at different times. Again, it's not so secret; there are a few. My people are issuing them with orders to attack the facility and capture or kill The Persian. They will think it came from their own government."

"That will incite an international incident," Khalid pointed out.

"Nothing will be traced back to us."

Sofia's phone beeped. She checked the screen and saw the message. "Good news. The French are moving. They are sending two teams, it would seem."

"What about the Argentinians?" Wei asked.

"I have just paid a million Euros into the account of General Alberto Moreno. He will dispatch a force of *Agrupación de Fuerzas de Operaciones Especiales*, or AFOE as soon as possible. It will be a race to see who gets there first to collect the bounty."

AFOE were Argentinian Special Forces.

"When will we know?" Park asked.

"I will monitor things from this end and keep you informed. With luck it will all be over in twelve hours or so."

"The Persian can't be allowed to be questioned by anyone, Sofia," Khalid said. "If he is, everything will be exposed."

"I may already be."

"What do you mean?"

"Someone was digging around, and they may already have certain information," Sofia explained.

"I thought your people were good?"

"They are, but whoever it was, is good too. If they know who we are, and I mean myself included, then you might want to have extra security."

"Just get rid of the problem, Sofia," Petrov growled.

"Don't I always?"

————

IN THE AIR, 30,000 FT

"So, we've got Russians and Australians after our asses," Knocker said. "It's Team Reaper Lottery. Take a ticket and go in for the kill."

"Our friend isn't a well-liked man," Jorgensen reminded him.

Kane turned to Slick. "Can you help us out? Where is our next threat coming from?"

"Take your pick. It's a global bounty."

"Bollocks."

"We should be right once we get to the base," the MI6 man said.

"I hope so," Kane said.

The tanker was waiting over the Bight as was organized. A few strings pulled and everything was set. With the refueling done, Cara went up to the cockpit. "Regie, how low can you fly this beast?"

"I can make her surf if you want, ma'am."

"Put us on the deck, I want to be off radar all the way."

"Don't forget we have stealth capabilities, ma'am."

Cara nodded. "I know, but they're finding us somehow."

"Heading to the deck, ma'am."

Returning to the rest of the team, Cara checked in with Rani first. "Once we drop at the base, I'll be staying with the team. You and the rest will fly back to Hereford. I'm placing you in command in my absence."

"What if you need us?" Rani asked.

"Having a C-17 sitting on the ground surrounded by snow and ice will stick out like dog's balls. It's a signal fire we don't need."

"Yes, ma'am."

From Rani, she moved to Kane. "Reaper, make sure the team has all they need, including warm clothes."

"Yes, ma'am."

"You can still send the MPs home," Cara reminded him.

"I was figuring on using them," Kane replied. "If we have them watching Roman, it'll free up the rest of us."

"Okay."

Cara went off to talk to Jorgensen. Watching her walk off, Burner came over and sat next to Kane. "So, care to tell me about where we're going?"

"Secret facility in Antarctica utilized by your politicians to house the worst of the worst."

"No shit," she replied. "What do you want me and my people to do when we get there?"

"You will be security on Roman. It'll free the rest of us up to do our thing."

"We'll wear him like a glove, sir."

"Don't call me sir. Kane or Reaper. Knocker over there you know, Kagiso sitting next to him. Lofty across the way and Brick there is our medic. Cara is our boss. We'll all be the ones staying behind. The rest are going back to England."

"Sounds like you've all got it planned out."

The expression on Kane's face was grim. "Not hardly."

After six hours flying time, they reached their destination. The runway was long enough to accommodate the C-17 and the weather was fair. An incoming front gave the plane and crew a mere thirty minutes to get turned around and into the air again.

When the ramp came down, there were five men waiting at the bottom, dressed in white snow suits and armed. The Team Reaper members were dressed the same. However, Burner and her people weren't prepared. Kane turned to her and said, "Get Roman. Make sure he's chained."

Kane and Knocker escorted Cara down the ramp along with Jorgenson. The man in the center of the five awaiting them stepped forward. "John Morris, I run this facility."

"Cara Billings, John Kane, Ray Jensen. This here is Jorgensen from Six."

"They let us know you were coming, Billings. They also said you had a special passenger on board." Heads turned as Burner and her people appeared with Roman. "I take it that's him."

"That's him," Jorgensen said.

"How long can we expect your company?"

"That depends," Cara replied. "The plane needs to be wheels up in thirty minutes. The rest of us are staying."

Morris nodded. "If there is anything we can do to help, then just ask."

"Will do." Kane turned to Burner. "We'll put Roman to bed, you can organize a watch."

"Roger that."

Morris said, "Right, now, let's get your package locked away."

ANTARCTICA

The facility looked like a research station from the outside but upon entering one of the huts, the team stepped into a large elevator which took them down into the ice and rock below.

"Four levels," Morris had told them on the way down. "The first two house the command center, barracks, and other amenities that all the contractors need. The bottom two levels are home for our guests."

"Is this the only way in and out?"

"No, we have three entry and exit points plus the emergency escape pods on the fourth level. When activated, it rockets to the surface in a matter of seconds."

"How many guests do you have?" Cara asked.

"Fifty. Anyone from serial killers, to terrorists, and people whom our government want disappeared."

"All legally of course," Kane said.

"By the book." Morris looked at Roman. "So, what's so special about your friend?"

"They didn't tell you?" Cara asked.

"No, just asked for emergency accommodation."

"Morris, meet Roman Lang. Otherwise known as The Persian."

"Shit, he doesn't even look Middle Eastern."

"You noticed that too, huh," Kane said. "He's German. Done a lot of things for a lot of people. Some of them don't want him to tell what he knows. Which is why there is a fifty-million bounty on his head."

Morris whistled softly. "That's a big lump."

"Don't we know it," Cara said.

"What's your security like up top?" Knocker asked.

"We have ten people up there at all times

pretending to be scientists," Morris explained. "Below the ground, we have another ten. Are you expecting trouble?"

The elevator stopped and the door hissed open. Kane said, "You could say that."

As they stepped out of the car, the chill air of the bleak corridor hit them. Every so often there was an alcove with a door leading into a cell. When they reached the one for Roman, the door stood open. The interior was almost as bleak as the corridor, containing only a toilet, basin, and a bunk. Other than that, the room was bare. No books, nothing for entertainment.

Kane and Knocker ushered him inside and removed his chains. Roman faced them and said, "They'll find me here, have no doubts, John."

"If they find you here, they're better than I give them credit for, Roman. Get some rest. Once we find a home for you, we'll be on the move."

The door shut and the lock worked automatically. Knocker said, "What happens if the power goes down?"

"We have a backup that kicks in automatically. Everything is operated from the central command post on the level above us."

"And if someone takes it?" Knocker asked.

"They can't," Morris assured him.

"If they do?" Knocker persisted.

"Then we're all screwed."

Kane turned to Lofty and Kagiso. "Stay here until Burner takes over."

"Roger that, boss," Lofty replied. He glanced at Morris. "You want to turn the heat up?"

"Everything is set to a specific temperature. Can't have the guests getting too comfortable." He turned to

Cara. "Right, let's get you settled and something to eat."

"Food," Knocker said, grinning. "I could eat a horse."

"Best menu at the South Pole."

"Beer?"

"Of course."

The Brit grinned. "Reaper, I could get used to this."

"Yeah, don't."

"I swear, the older you get, the less fun you have."

"I have fun."

"When was the last time you had fun, Reaper? Tell me that."

"In Australia."

Knocker laughed. "That was work, not fun."

Kane nodded. "Work is fun."

"Work is work. Fun is going out and having a good time, maybe even get laid."

"That's your fun," Kane threw back at his friend.

"Are you two done?" Cara asked.

Kane nodded. "Yeah, I'm hungry."

———

HEREFORD, ENGLAND

Mary Thurston waited for the call to connect and then for it to be answered. She looked at her watch and muttered a silent curse. It was 04:00. After a handful of rings, a tired voice answered on the other end, "This better be good, Mary."

Thibaut Doku was the commander of an Interpol Crime IRT, or Incident Response Team. He was in his mid-forties and knew Thurston from one of her sojourns to Lyon. "I'm sorry about the time, Tib, but I need help, and you are about the only one I can talk to."

"Why do I—" There was a moment of muffled speaking. Most likely to his wife. Then he said, "Why do I get the feeling that this is going to be trouble?"

"Because it probably will be."

"Wait a moment while I go somewhere we can speak."

She waited for a minute or so and finally Doku came back to her. "Okay, tell me what you need."

"You would have heard by now that we picked up The Persian? Roman Lang?" Mary asked.

"I did. I also heard there is a sizable bounty on his head."

"My team found that out the hard way. They were in Kuwait."

"I see." His voice was grim.

"They also got hit in Australia."

Doku sighed. "Come to the point, Mary, I need to go back to bed."

"Can Interpol take Roman?" she asked.

"No—I don't know. I would need to talk to my superiors."

"If they don't take him, I will have to instruct my man to put a bullet in his head and leave him."

"You can't do that," Doku said.

It was Thurston's turn to sigh. "No, I can't. Listen, have you heard of The Syndicate?"

"I have heard whispers."

"Roman worked for them on different jobs. He can give you any amount of intel."

"On The Syndicate?"

"On that and more," Thurston said.

"Where can I find this syndicate?" Doku asked.

"You won't. You see, for my team to be safe, I have a man taking care of them as we speak."

"An assassin?" There was surprise in his voice.

"Put it this way, if there is no one around to pay the bounty, then the hunters will stop. I have to keep them as safe as I can."

"I understand."

"You can't tell anyone, Tib," Thurston stressed.

"Don't worry, I will keep it to myself." There was a yawn. "Give me an hour and I will call you back."

"Thank you, Tib."

"And I thought I was going back to bed."

The call disconnected.

CHAPTER 5

SINGAPORE

It had been a while since Hunt's last foray into Singapore. That had been working a security detail for a British parliamentarian. Sent by Mary Thurston, she'd said there was no one else she could trust to do the job. He was certain she was blowing smoke up his ass, but it still felt good to hear.

Arriving in Singapore at noon, a young MI6 officer was waiting for him at Changi Airport and escorted him to a safehouse downtown.

"We have everything you need, sir," the man had told him.

"What's your name, son?" Hunt asked.

"White, sir," the officer replied.

"Your other name," Hunt said.

"Best you don't know, sir, just in case."

Hunt nodded. "I can live with that."

"Nothing against you, sir, but with operations of this nature, the less you know about me the better."

"By the book, huh?"

"Yes, sir."

"Stop calling me sir, damn it," Hunt growled. "My name is—"

"Don't tell me, sir."

"Fine, call me Scimitar."

White glanced at him. "Scimitar?"

"That's right. Or Hunt."

"Damn it, sir, why did you do that?"

"Lighten up, kid. I'll be in and out before anyone knows I was even here."

The safehouse was in the middle of an apartment complex on a busy street. MI6 had two apartments side by side with an interconnecting door. When they arrived, Hunt found two additional officers. A woman in her thirties, and a man slightly older in his forties. Hunt introduced himself to the older man. "Hunt."

"Clark, station chief. Over there is Millie. You already met Keller."

"You mean White?"

Clark stared at Keller. "Shit, you still doing that crap?"

"Rules state—" Keller started trying to defend his actions.

"Stuff the rules."

"Yes, sir."

"Now, Hunt," Clark said, turning his attention back to the former SEAL. "We did a full workup on the person of interest as requested. Mind telling me why?"

"Our friend has been a bad boy." Hunt went on to elaborate.

"I see. This sounds intense."

"It will be if I fail to complete my mission."

Millie walked over and handed him a folder. "Everything you need to know about your target is in there."

Hunt opened it and gave the contents a cursory look. Adrian Tan Wei. Thirty-six, logistics. Owned himself the third-largest shipping company in the world. Liked dining out, holidays in Europe, and had a thing for the ladies.

"This lady thing could help," Hunt said.

"How so?"

"Is there anything on in the city at the moment. Plays, theater, opera, things like that?"

Millie checked her smartphone. "There is an opera on tonight."

"This penchant he has for the women. Is he on dating sites?"

"Yes, several."

"Good, I need a date for him for tonight," Hunt said.

"I can do that," Millie replied. She glanced at Clark.

"Set it up, Millie."

"Yes, sir."

———

HEREFORD, ENGLAND

It took substantially longer than an hour before Thibaut called back. It was closer to four. Mary answered and he said, "That took some doing."

"What's the verdict?"

"Interpol will take Roman," he replied. "We just need your people to get him to Buenos Aires."

"I'll see what I can do."

"We have a facility there, Mary," Thibaut explained. "We can fly him to Europe from there."

"Thank you, Tib."

"Don't thank me yet. You still have to get him there."

Mary hung up and immediately dialed Cara.

"Hi, boss."

"Buenos Aires."

"Yes, city in South America."

"You need to get Roman there. Interpol will then take him off your hands."

"Roger that."

"Good luck."

"Yes, ma'am."

———

ANTARCTICA

The call disconnected and Cara went in search of Kane. In any normal building, she would just have followed the noise, but this facility was somewhat soundproof and gave no hint of where he was hanging out. She located him in the rec room playing eight ball with Knocker.

"We need to get Roman to Buenos Aires."

"Do we walk or swim?" Knocker asked, taking his shot, putting his red ball in a side pocket.

Cara turned her attention to Jorgensen who was sitting reading on a sofa in the corner. He'd found a book on the shelf and was learning about penguins. "Well?"

"I will need to make a couple of calls." He took out his cell.

"What happens in Buenos Aires?" Kane asked.

"We hand Roman over to Interpol."

"And that's it?"

"That's it."

The door to the rec room opened and Lofty and Kagiso walked in. "So this is where you all hang out," Lofty said.

Knocker held up his beer. "We've been busy."

Kagiso grinned, showing off white teeth against her dark lips. "Are you any good with that?"

"You mean the cue?" Knocker asked.

"Yes."

"I'm fair."

"What about you, John Kane?" She was mocking him.

"I can hold my own."

"Then me and Lofty will play you. If you have the heart."

Off to the side, Cara was smiling. Kagiso had just challenged their manhood, and she knew what the reaction would be. Knocker said, "Get ready to be spanked, Reaper Five."

"I like to be spanked."

A look of alarm flashed across Knocker's face. "Oh shit, Reaper, we're in trouble."

They set the balls up and tossed a coin to see who went first. Kagiso and Lofty won and the Brit said, "All yours, Kagiso."

"Shall we make it interesting?" she asked. "Twenty dollars?"

"Okay," Kane replied.

"Damn it, Reaper, I have a bad feeling about this."

"It'll be right," Kane replied.

Ten minutes later they were both handing over their money. Kagiso had a broad grin on her face. "Just because I am a woman, does not mean I cannot play eight ball."

"You two got had," Cara said, laughing.

"Shut up," Knocker replied. "I told him it was a bad idea as soon as money was mentioned."

Suddenly everything went red, and an alarm started blaring throughout the complex. Kane looked up as though he would see something. Lofty said, "That can't be good."

Kane reacted instantly. "Gear up. I want everyone on comms. The shit is about to hit the fan."

———

A PAIR of hovercrafts floated across the harsh landscape. Inside were French special forces. These were 2 SAS Company, specializing in extreme environments. Two teams of ten, the first was led by Capitaine Kylian Giroud, the second by Lieutenant Lucas Varane. Both men were experienced operators. North Africa was their last posting before being sent with their teams to the Antarctic for extreme weather training.

"Lucas, copy?" Giroud said into his comms.

"Copy, Capitaine."

Giroud was a solidly built man with dark hair. All of which was hidden under the specialized warfare suits the men were currently wearing. "We are two minutes out. Remember the plan?"

"Yes, Capitaine."

It was a simple plan. Varane would secure the top of the base while Giroud would take his team inside to secure and kill the target. Every one of the forces on site was to be treated as a terrorist and terminated.

In his headset, Giroud heard the pilot say, "One minute."

Giroud looked over his weapon. It was a SIG MCX VIRTUS. He checked the current magazine, charged his weapon, and now he was ready to go.

"Thirty seconds!"

———

"KNOCKER, you come with me. Kagiso, Lofty, reinforce the MPs. Brick, Cara, roving patrol on the second level. Remember, the MPs don't have full body cover like us."

Just then, Morris appeared through the doorway. Like the team, he was kitted for war.

Cara asked, "What's happening?"

"We have two assault craft coming in. No response when hailed. We treat them as a threat until otherwise ascertained."

"Do you know who they are?"

"French. And the only French forces down here are the French SAS."

"Bollocks," Knocker growled. "These bastards are getting serious."

He and Kane went up in the elevator and broke out onto the surface. By the time they arrived, the surface force was already engaged. "We're late to the party, Reaper."

"Yeah, but I intend to have the last fucking dance," Kane replied.

A white clad figure appeared in front of them. Kane immediately opened fire and the man fell. Knocker said in a surprised voice, "Fuck, Reaper, how do you know that wasn't one of Morris's guys?"

"Red arm band."

"That'll do it."

"All callsigns this net. The bad guys have red armbands, I say again, red armbands."

Knocker took point, pushing forward. Gunfire sounded close by. He turned the corner of a building and found a dead security specialist. He kneeled and checked him to make sure. Kane covered him. "He's done, Reaper."

The problem with the enemy having red armbands, you hesitated every time to make sure you weren't killing one of your own. This time, it almost got them killed.

A French specialist appeared, and Kane hesitated. The Frenchman fired and a bullet ripped part of the snow suit along his side. Knocker opened fire at the same time as Kane did. The Frenchman lurched and fell into the snow.

"That was close," Kane said.

Suddenly the net came alive. "All callsigns, we have a breach. I say again, we have a breach. We have shooters inside the complex."

Kane shook his head. "Now the shit has hit the fan."

———

THE FRENCH SAS shooters of the second team split into two smaller teams. The first under Giroud took the first level to secure the control room. The second team under a sergeant went lower to secure the two prison levels.

Almost immediately, Giroud and his men came under fire from two security specialists. However, firing too quickly they missed the infiltrators.

The Frenchmen fired back, and the two security men died where they stood. Giroud turned to the men closest to him. "You with me. The rest of you, secure this floor."

As Giroud pressed forward along the walkway, his men close behind, the second team took the stairs down to the next level. With the appearance of a security guard ahead of them, Giroud fired and the man cried out in pain. He dropped to the floor, writhing. As Giroud walked past, he shot the man dead.

Ahead, the control center loomed. Inside, surrounded by bulletproof glass, three men watched the French SAS operators come at them. Giroud fired but the bulletproof glass held. The commander stood staring at the three men inside. They stared back. Giroud signaled to one of his men who came forward and placed a device on the glass.

The Frenchman stepped back and waited. Instead of an explosion, the device used sound to shatter the glass. It was so high-pitched that it was beyond human ears. The glass fell like rain to the floor. From inside, a voice could be heard. "The control room has been breached, I say again—"

A burst of gunfire removed any resistance that the three security guards might have mounted.

Giroud looked at the man beside him and said, "Open them up."

CHAPTER 6

ANTARCTICA

"The control room has been breached, I say again—"

The voice stopped abruptly. Burner looked at Lofty. "Fuck, fuck, fuck."

"Easy, Burner," the Brit said. "Let's just wait and see what comes our way."

Kagiso checked her weapon and said, "A cornered lion fights with the fury of ten."

Suddenly there was a loud buzz and all of the doors along the hallway popped. Lofty said, "That can't be good."

"Damn it," Burner said. "Shorty, Ralph, secure the prisoner."

"Ares from Reaper Three."

"Go ahead, Reaper Three."

"We've got a problem. Someone just popped all the cell doors."

"Roger that. Secure the prisoner and hold."

"Copy, ma'am. Out."

Slowly, prisoners began to emerge from their cells. Burner called to Gomer who was behind her. "What's it like to our rear?"

"Same, Sarge."

Kagiso turned to face their rear, her 433 coming up to her shoulder. "This isn't good, Lofty."

"Is the prisoner secured?" Lofty called out.

"Roger that," Shorty replied.

Lofty thought for a moment. What to do? "Ares, Reaper Three."

"Send, Reaper Three."

"Ma'am, we cannot stay here."

"Okay. Try to get to the second deck. Brick and I are still here."

Lofty was satisfied with that. "Roger that. ROEs, boss?"

"Do what you have to."

"Burner, we're moving. Get Roman out here."

Burner entered the cell. "We're moving, Shorty. Put Roman in the middle where we can keep an eye on him."

"Roger that," Shorty said.

Once assembled outside in the hallway, they were ready to move but had an issue. The prisoners were closing in on them, walking like zombies. "Back the fuck up," Lofty snarled.

Non-responsive, they kept coming.

"Last chance," he growled. "Back up and get into your cells."

"Fuck you," a prisoner snarled.

Lofty fired a round over their heads. The prisoners paused but did not retreat. It was then he noticed that all had dark rings around their eyes and none wore shoes. But they didn't seem to notice the cold.

Behind the one who had spoken stood a man of Middle Eastern appearance. He was twitching uncontrollably. Behind Lofty he heard Kagiso call, "What is the hold up?"

Lofty raised his weapon again. The man who had spoken smiled, showing yellowed teeth. But there was something wrong with them. They looked like they had been filed to points. "Ah fucking bollocks," Lofty said out loud.

That was when the prisoner started to move and move fast."

"Put them down," he snarled as he opened fire with the 433. "They're drugged."

The prisoner hurtling at Lofty took three rounds to the chest but kept coming as though nothing had happened. The Brit shifted his aim and put a round into his head. This time he went down. "You need head shots! All callsigns, this is Reaper Three, you need headshots for the prisoners. They're drugged. Fuck, what have they done?"

The prisoners rushed forward.

———

"YOU NEED HEAD SHOTS! *All callsigns, this is Reaper Three, you need headshots for the prisoners. They're drugged. Fuck, what have they done?"*

A look of horror came across Cara's face. "Reaper Three, talk to me."

Nothing.

Reaper Three, this is Ares, talk to me."

Still nothing.

She whirled on Jorgensen. "What is fucking happening?"

"Ah, yes. The station's dirty little secret I'm afraid. They call it drug rehabilitation. They try to rewire their brains by using something I can't even pronounce. Instead, it made them some kind of superhuman beings."

"Like zombies?"

"Come now, Miss Billings, there is no such thing as zombies."

"But these come close."

"Yes. The good news is, if they bite you, you won't turn into one."

Cara rolled her eyes. "Oh, yeah, fucking wonderful."

She hit her transmit button again. "Reaper Three, copy?"

"Sorry, ma'am, we're a little busy right now."

"Get to the escape pod. Now."

"Roger that."

She still had one more call to make. "Reaper One, we have a big fucking problem down here."

———

"REAPER ONE, *we have a big fucking problem down here.*"

"Read you, Lima Charlie, Ares. Send traffic."

In front of him, Knocker killed another French SAS shooter. He had been out in the open and collapsed beside two security officers.

"Reaper, the prisoners are part of some drug

program. They're like damn zombies without actually being any."

"Bollocks," muttered Knocker.

"What's your status?"

"We're okay. No contacts as yet. But Lofty and the others are in a bind. They're trying to make it to the escape pod."

"Roger, we'll keep an eye out for them." He had an idea. "Get to the surface if you can, Cara. I have a plan."

"Copy, on our way."

"Can you believe that, Reaper?" Knocker asked. "Fucking zombies."

"No such thing," Kane replied while changing out his magazine.

"Tell that to the poor blighters down there." He hesitated. "I'm loath to ask, but what's the plan?"

"Knocker, old chap, we're going to steal a hovercraft."

"Of course we are."

————

Kagiso snarled like a lion as she fired her SIG P320 three times into the guts of a prisoner. As he staggered back, she lifted the weapon and shot him in the head. Another came at her, and she fired three more times until the target was down.

Still another prisoner came on. Kagiso fired once before her magazine ran dry. With muttered profanity, she hit the prisoner between the eyes with the butt. "I'm out!" she cried.

Burner stepped in beside her, a Glock firing twice.

The prisoner lurched back with a bullet in his brain and fell to the floor.

Kagiso dropped out the spent magazine and slapped a fresh one home. She glanced at Burner. "Thank you."

Ahead of them, Lofty was staring at another four prisoners. They were coming on in a relentless push. His 433 was hanging by its sling and he was firing a SIG rapidly when it went dry. "I'm out. Gomer, cover me."

Gomer stepped into the lead position and opened fire. However, one of the advancing prisoners reached him, a big guy from Surrey. He was a serial killer who had chalked up fifteen kills over a ten-year period before eventually being caught. His name was Farrell, but the police had nicknamed him 'Dinner for Two' because he would eat dinner at his victim's home; but they were the ones on the menu.

The snarling monster took two to the chest but was undaunted. Gomer snapped a hurried shot at his head and missed. Then he was upon him.

Teeth gnashing, Farrell went for the MP's throat. Gomer tried to fight him off, but the killer's strength was overpowering. Gomer fired again but couldn't get a shot at his head. Farrell's teeth closed on the MP's flesh and began chomping.

Gomer cried out in pain and fear. Farrell pulled his head back releasing a large fountain of arterial blood which sprayed the killer's face. Lofty, weapon now reloaded, placed the barrel of his P320 against the killer's head and fired.

Farrell's head snapped to the side, and he dropped like a stone. Meanwhile, Lofty crouched beside

Gomer who was bleeding out on the floor. "Gomer's down!"

Blood pooled quickly around the MP and Lofty tried to stanch the bleeding while trying to shoot at oncoming prisoners. It took only a moment to realize that Gomer was dying. "I'm sorry, kid."

Lofty turned his full attention to discharging his weapon accurately, leaving the MP to his death.

At that moment, automatic gunfire ripped through the carnage. Prisoners began to fall, and Ralph went down as well. "Back into the cell," Lofty growled.

Retreating back into the cell where Roman had been taken from, Burner snapped, "What the hell was that?".

"Has to be the French," Lofty stated. "Ares, this is Reaper Three. We're pinned down and have two KIA."

"You don't know that Ralph is KIA," Burner said.

"He got shot in the head," Roman said. "He's done."

"Shut your filthy mouth," Burner snarled, getting into his face.

Roman ignored her. "Give me a weapon. I can help."

"Like fuck," Lofty said. "Fort up. Hold this position."

"Reaper Three, this is Ares. We're coming."

———

KANE AND KNOCKER managed to catch up with Fletcher who was in control of the above-deck unit. "How are your men?" Kane asked.

"We've taken heavy casualties, and I've got two men left holed up in building C."

"And what's with the fucking zombies?" Knocker growled as he reloaded.

"They're not zombies," Fletcher snapped back. "They can be killed."

"So can zombies."

Kane intervened. "Knocker, keep a watch out. Fletcher, tell me what the hell is going on."

"Can't it wait? I have two men trapped and hanging on by the skin of their teeth."

"I need to know what is happening so I can deal with it."

"Fine. The prisoners were shipped here in one group. The government decided that if they could be reprogrammed it might work out for future criminals to be released back into the population. Originally, we started with sixty prisoners. Every one of them was given the drugs. Five died, five more we killed while they attacked guards. The other fifty showed remarkable changes. They adapted and learned to overcome."

"Not for the better, I'm guessing," Kane said.

He shook his head. "They became stronger and faster. It was like they evolved."

"What the hell did you give them?" Knocker asked without looking.

Fletcher shrugged. "No idea. We were just told to administer it."

"Now we have the French and fucking zombies to deal with."

"They're not zombies," Kane growled.

A shooter appeared around the end of a building and opened fire. Fletcher's head snapped back with a hole dead center. Knocker fired back and the shooter fell.

"I guess he won't be going home, except in a body bag," Kane said. "Right, Knocker, let's find building C and get us one of those hovercrafts."

———

BRICK WAS on point as the complex rang with gunfire. Lofty and the others were in trouble and between them and any assistance were French SAS and the super prisoners. Brick poked his head around a corner in the hallway and saw a door with a red sign saying: STAIRS.

"This way, boss," Brick said, leading out cautiously.

Cara followed him around and he had only gone a couple of steps when he called out, "Contact front!"

Opening fire with his 433, bullets ripped into a shooter who appeared in the doorway. Another Frenchman stepped into the breach and took his place.

Brick saw him throw something and instantly knew what it was. "Grenade!"

He and Cara backpedaled around the corner to where Jorgensen was waiting, throwing themselves to the cold floor just before the deadly explosive detonated.

Feeling the warm wave from the detonation wash over them, Brick was the first to react. He rolled onto his back, drawing his P320, firing twice as a figure rushed around the corner. The first round tore through the Frenchman's neck while the second hit him in the head.

Brick climbed to his feet and helped Cara up. While he peered around the corner to make sure it was clear, he checked on her. "Ma'am, are you okay?"

"I think so."

"No blurry vision?"

"No."

"Lightheaded?"

"I'm good."

"Let me know if you start getting a headache."

"What about you, Six man?" Brick asked.

Jorgensen brushed himself off as though nothing had happened. "Lead on, old chap."

They pressed on to the stairwell and started going down. In the distance they could hear gunfire becoming louder. Two prisoners appeared on the stairs ahead of them, climbing at an incredible pace. "Shit," Brick growled and brought his P320 up, his 433 hanging by its strap. There was little time to react.

The handgun roared to life, Brick recalling what Lofty had told them. The first shot missed completely, being off balance. The second found a target and the prisoner fell back down the stairs. Then the second prisoner was on top of the big man knocking his gun away.

A loud snarl escaped his attacker's lips, his teeth gnashing, trying for the throat. Brick could feel the man's unbelievable strength and tried to hit him in the face with a fist.

On the stairs above, Cara knew she only had moments to react. She bounded down to where the two men struggled and placed her handgun against the killer's head, squeezing the trigger.

She helped Brick up. He grabbed his weapon and brushed himself off. "That was close. Thanks."

"Let's keep going."

Suddenly their comms lit up. It was Kagiso. *"Reaper Three is down. He is KIA."*

———

KAGISO AND BURNER dragged Lofty back from the doorway. He'd grunted as he went down. When they rolled him over, they saw a hole in his head. "Travel well, my friend," she muttered and then called it in.

Burner took her turn at the doorway, trying to keep the French back. The prisoners that had been attacking them were all dead, but one of their own had paid a hefty price. Three Frenchmen had also died under the onslaught, taken care of by the team. But there was still enough coming through to cause a problem.

Burner ran her magazine dry. "Reloading."

Shorty stepped up as Burner moved back. He kept up a steady rate of fire. Then once he was done, Kagiso took over at the door.

"I'm low on ammo," Burner said.

"Divide up what Lofty has," Kagiso called over her shoulder.

"Two mags and what he had for his sidearm."

"You and Shorty divide it."

Kagiso kept firing until her second last magazine was empty. "Changing!"

Burner took up position and was about to open fire when gunfire ripped through the attackers. All of them fell as Cara, Brick and Jorgensen appeared. Cara hurried up to Kagiso. "Are you okay?"

"Yes, but we have lost three. Lofty is dead."

Cara nodded. "We can't worry about that at the minute. We need to secure this facility. To do that, we need to get topside. The only way out is the pods. Get Roman and let's go."

––––––––

GIROUD and another soldier were the last two of the French team below the surface. Right at that moment however, the commander regretted his decision to release the prisoners. Low on ammunition, they found themselves surrounded. "Hawk Two, do you hear me?"

There was no response.

"Any callsign this network. Do you hear me?"

Something must have gone wrong because there was no answer. Yet the prisoners kept coming. Both soldiers kept shooting until they were out of ammunition. The bodies were mounting up, but others climbed over them to get to the two SAS men. Then without any more ammunition, the prisoners overwhelmed them. The last thing that went through the SAS commander's mind was, *Who the hell were these people?*

––––––––

As IT STOOD, Team Reaper was down one man, the MPs two. The on-site security force had been hit hard; they had two men left. Morris and Fletcher were both dead, Fletcher by the hand of a Frenchman. Morris had suffered the same fate as Giroud. The French were down to five while there were still about ten prisoners below deck.

Kane and Knocker were making their way toward the hovercrafts. They arrived just as the remaining

French operators were retreating in the second of the two. "There goes the fight," Knocker said.

Kane looked around. A lot of the buildings were on fire, some giving off thick black smoke. Then there were the bodies lying in bloody patches of snow. It was a war zone on ice.

Kane toggled his talk button and said, "Ares, sitrep, over."

"Wait one, Reaper."

Suddenly there were two explosions. The sound caused both men to look up. Two square box-like objects flew into the air, propelled by small rockets. Then the rockets cut out and two parachutes were deployed. Knocker said, "That looks like fun."

The pods landed and the doors were blown off by small charges. Cara and the others stepped from their escape pods. She saw Kane and Knocker coming toward them.

"What's happening?" she asked.

"The French have bugged out." He stared hard at her. "Casualties?"

"Gomer, Ralph, and Lofty."

"Damn it," Kane muttered, shaking his head.

"Where are they?" Knocker asked.

"We had to leave them in situ."

Knocker dropped out his partially spent magazine and reloaded it with a fresh one. "Fuck it, I'm going to get him."

Cara stood in front of him and held a hand to his chest. "No. We need to get out of here."

"But—"

"Raymond, they knew we were here. Think about it."

"Bollocks," he muttered.

Cara turned to Jorgensen. "Any ideas?"

"There is an icebreaker off the Goulburn Shelf sea ice. All we have to do is get there and they'll pick us up."

Kane nodded toward the hovercraft. "Well, we've got a ride."

Cara nodded. "Get everyone aboard—wait. Who is going to drive?"

Knocker grinned.

"No. No way. We'll end up in a crevasse somewhere."

"You can always stay here, boss," Knocker said.

She shook her head in dismay. "I just know I'm going to regret this. Before we get everyone aboard, walk around and grab all the weapons and ammo you can find."

As they began to gather weapons, Kane noticed Burner. He pulled her aside. "Are you okay?"

"This is shit," she replied.

"Losing people always is," he replied. "You ever lost anyone before?"

"No."

"You need to compartmentalize it. Keep it there until the mission is over. Then, once that's done, grieve for your friends."

Burner nodded. "I hate leaving them there."

"Can't be helped. Cara will radio our situation, and someone will come and get them."

"Where to now?"

"Buenos Aires. To get rid of Roman."

"I heard that," Roman said. "The problem is, John, you have to get me there."

"We'll get you there, Roman," Kane said. "Rest assured of that."

Ten minutes later, they were loaded into the hovercraft, including the two remaining security men, and racing across the ice.

———

IT NEVER REALLY GOT DARK at this time of the year in Antarctica. Every now and then a severe snowstorm would come through but so far, the weather had held. Cara had got through to Thurston and informed her of what had gone down. "They knew where we were."

"I'll reach out to Slick and see what he can find," Thurston said grimly. "I'm sorry you lost Lofty, Cara."

"I'm just sorry we had to leave him."

"I'll send some strike teams down there to clean it all up with the help of the security company."

"It was just a big shit show, Mary. The prisoners were like super fucking zombies."

"I'll take care of it."

The call disconnected and the hovercraft pushed on. They were now out on the sea ice and closing on their destination. Progress had slowed but Cara figured they would be in position in another hour.

———

ZURICH, SWITZERLAND

Sofia was at her console in the hub. She was waiting patiently for news about the Antarctic mission.

"Ma'am," said one of her female techs. "The new satellite is in position. The feed will be through shortly."

"Thank you, Mila."

The big screen came to life. "That's it, ma'am. The facility."

Dark smoke rose from the burning buildings. Bodies could be seen on the ice. "What am I looking at?" Sofia asked, not wanting to hear the answer.

"That is the facility, ma'am," Mila replied. "The French SAS have been defeated. We caught this image a while ago."

The screen opened a smaller box. It was a picture of people climbing into a hovercraft. "Is that them?"

"It appears so, ma'am."

"Where are they going?"

"They are taking a direct route toward the ice shelf."

"Why?" Sofia asked.

"Ma'am?"

"Why are they going to the ice shelf? There is nothing there."

Another picture appeared. "Maybe this, ma'am. It is the *South Sea Explorer*."

Sofia nodded slowly. "Where are the Argentinians?"

"About five minutes out, ma'am."

"Give them coordinates to intercept that hovercraft. They mustn't be permitted to get off that ice."

———

ANTARCTICA

Knocker had slowed down as he picked his way through a pressure ridge field. It wasn't impassable, but it was tight in places. Kagiso sat beside him in the copilot seat. "Has anyone asked how you're doing, lass?" Knocker asked her.

"I am fine," she replied.

"It's always hard to lose friends."

"I have lost friends before," she replied. "Like those his spirit will graduate into another form."

"What form do you figure Lofty is bound for?"

"The hyena," Kagiso replied without hesitation. "His laugh was infectious. Now when I return to Africa, I can hear him all the time."

"I think Lofty would like to return to Africa," Knocker replied. He looked at his watch. It was 23:00. "Good Lord, it's almost midnight and not even dark. Well—"

Suddenly an AS332 Super Puma flew low across in front of them. Knocker stopped and cursed. "Bollocks. This isn't good. Reaper, Cara, you'd better get up here. On second thoughts, just look out your window."

Moments later he heard Cara say, "Argentine?"

"Yeah, I'd say so. You can guess what they're doing here."

There was a moment's silence before Cara said, "Everyone out. Take up defensive positions in the pressure ridges."

Taking weapons and ammunition, the weary band exited the hovercraft, settling into various positions in the vicinity. While waiting, they watched the helicopter land out on the flat. Then the Argentine soldiers climbed out.

"I make it fifteen," Kane said over his comms.

"I concur," replied Cara.

Burner turned and looked at Roman. "These people really want you dead."

"I guess I'm just likable."

"Shorty, keep an eye on him."

"Permission to shoot him if I need to, Sarge?"

"Don't forget to smile when you do it."

The Argentines soon gathered themselves and started to approach in a skirmish line. Kane and the others watched them come on. He said, "Hold your fire until they get close. That way we don't waste ammunition."

A few moments later, the Argentines stopped. Three men stepped forward. Kane frowned wondering what they were up to. Then they fired.

Two smoke, one explosive. The smoke landed short of their position but the explosive round hammered into the hovercraft, blowing it up.

A pall of silence descended over the small group until it was broken by Knocker. "That'll put a fly in your porridge."

Kane nodded grimly. "Get ready. Here they come."

CHAPTER 7

SINGAPORE

Meanwhile in Singapore, Hunt was preparing to leave the safehouse to attend the opera. Smartly attired in black suit complete with handkerchief in his top pocket, he was in the briefing room with three others including Clark and Keller. The latter said, "You look like you're going somewhere."

"I feel out of place," Hunt replied.

Keller said, "You won't get in there with a weapon. Terrorism kind of screwed that. But we have an alternative."

Clark handed over a pen. Hunt looked at it. "I can make this work."

Keller held up one that was identical. "A wolf in sheep's clothing, my friend. Click it once and it is just a pen. Three times fast and..."

A long thin needle ejected from within. Hunt nodded. "Straight to the brain, huh?"

Keller shook his head. "No. The needle you have is

coated with some kind of toxin that the boffins thought up."

"Boffins?"

"Scientists," Keller elaborated. "Death is almost instant. It'll look like a good old heart attack. So, for God's sake, don't jab yourself with it."

"I'll try to remember it," Hunt replied.

At that moment, their attention was drawn to the door as Millie walked in. She was wearing a form-hugging red dress cut low in the front and stopped just above her buttocks at the back. She did a circle and said, "What do you think?"

"You look lovely," said Keller.

Hunt nodded appreciatively. "You do at that."

"Nice tattoo," Clark said.

Keller gave him a scolding look, but Millie was on top of it. "Is that all you can see? The tattoo above my ass?"

"Ah, sorry."

Millie looked at Hunt. "So, what's the plan?"

"You're doing it," Hunt said.

"No, seriously. I've heard about playing cards close to your chest but I'm flying in the dark here."

Hunt smiled. "Your part is to get him there. I'll take care of the rest."

"How?"

"At intermission everyone goes to the bathroom. I'll take him there."

"That's it? No great car explosion, no assassin's bullet?"

"Afraid not."

Millie pouted. "You are no fun. I get dressed for a party and you give me a wake."

"That's the idea."

"Fine." She looked at her watch. "I need to go. See you there."

She started walking away when Hunt said, "He was right."

Millie turned. She gave him a frown. "What?"

"Nice tattoo."

Smiling, she flipped him the bird and kept going.

Keller stepped close to Hunt and said in a low voice. "Whatever you do, don't get her killed."

THE OPERA WAS BEING HELD in the Singapore Ramada. It was a large theater building with a five-star hotel attached. Hunt had made his way through the line and inside. He was close behind Wei and Millie. The logistics man had arranged to have her picked up at an address two blocks from the safehouse. Millie had been waiting outside.

Wei and Mille were directed toward the stairs. Hunt began following them up but was stopped by an usher. "Can I see your ticket please, sir?"

Hunt showed him. "I'm sorry, sir, but this is for the main floor. Only the members are upstairs."

Hunt nodded. "Thank you."

After the usher had left, he said quietly. "Millie, I'm stuck on the ground floor. You'll have to direct me."

Up until that point, they'd had no contact. But by way of response, she made barely discernible clucking sound with her tongue. Her initial meeting with Wei involved a lot of small talk as the couple got to know each other. When asked what she did, Millie admitted to lying. "Don't they all do it?" she said. "I'm actually a secretary for a merchant business. I'm sorry."

Wei had responded by answering, "I guess I should come clean too. I'm not a lawyer."

"No?"

"No, I own one of the biggest shipping companies in the world." It was a boast designed to impress.

However, Millie had chuckled and said, "I guess I was right."

"Indeed, you were."

Most of it was small talk.

Hunt found his way to a seat and waited patiently, watching the performance. It didn't take long for him to conclude that opera was not his thing.

Intermission came after an hour. Those who needed a bathroom break or just to stretch their legs did so. Over the open mic Hunt could hear Wei talking to Millie. For a long time the former SEAL thought that he wasn't going to go. Then just before the singers were to come back on stage, he went.

"He's gone, Bord."

Hunt got up from his seat and squeezed through to the aisle. Once there he hurried toward the foyer against the incoming tide of well-dressed humanity. There were still a few people outside, so he was rather inconspicuous as he made his way upstairs.

At the top was a long, carpeted hallway lined with gaudy wallpaper and works of art. He hurried along it until he reached the bathrooms. Wei was already in there along with two other gentlemen. All three finished their business at the same time which meant Hunt needed to keep Wei there just a little longer until the others left.

As usual when men go to the bathroom, there was an unwritten code to keep a fair amount of distance between each other. This gave Hunt his opportunity. He squeezed in at the spare basin beside Wei and another man. Hunt started to wash his hands and accidentally splashed water down the front of Wei, wetting his pants.

The shipping magnate reeled back. "What are you doing, man, be careful."

Hunt stared at him. "I'm sorry, what did you say?"

"I said watch what you are doing," Wei hissed in English. "You made me all wet, you clumsy oaf."

"No need to be like that, pal. It was an accident."

The others left the bathroom while Wei reached for several paper hand towels and began wiping himself down. While he was concentrating on that, Hunt took out the pen. A double click and the needle appeared. Then he walked up behind Wei and stabbed him with it. Down low. This wasn't a movie.

Wei wheeled around and stared at Hunt. He opened his mouth to speak but no words came out. Instead, he staggered, clutching at his chest. Moments later he fell to the bathroom floor. Hunt checked him to make sure, then he walked into a stall and dropped the pen into the toilet before flushing.

As he left the bathroom he said, "Target down. Meet you in the foyer."

"On my way."

As they approached each other in the lobby, Millie asked, "Any problem?"

"No."

She said, "You know, I hate to be all dressed up and go home this early."

Hunt looked down at his suit. "I feel the same way."

Millie took out her cell and dialed a number. Hunt heard her say, "All done. Now we're going to dinner."

She listened for a moment and then said, "Yes, see you in the morning."

Hunt held out his arm. "Shall we?"

Millie smiled. "Let's."

ZURICH, SWITZERLAND

While Sofia was watching events unfold in her ops room, a call came through informing her that Wei was dead of an apparent heart attack. She hung up and thought about the man. "No, I don't believe it."

Speaking into her headset mic, she asked Mila to come and see her.

"On my way."

Rising from her desk, Mila walked to the back of the room where Sofia sat. The room itself was set up in terraces where individuals had their workstations. Sofia sat right at the back in a large leather chair. From there she could see each workstation and the wall of large screens. "Yes, ma'am."

"Adrian Tan Wei has been found dead in a bathroom at the opera. Supposed heart attack."

"Oh, no," Mila gasped.

"I don't believe it," Sofia continued, swinging sideways in her chair to look at Mila. "I want to know what happened at the opera, understood?"

"Yes, ma'am."

Returning to her console, Mila went to work. Meanwhile Sofia concentrated on the central screen and watched the unfolding battle.

———

ANTARCTICA

A continuous onslaught of bullets hammered their positions. Team Reaper and those attached to them had been forced back into the jungle of pressure ridges. The hovercraft burned fiercely, staining the air black against the stark white of the ice and snow.

Kane looked over at Knocker and said, "We're running low on ammo."

Knocker grinned and said, "Oh well. Still, could be worse."

A round hit his body armor, and he fell back. Kane looked down at his friend. "You had to say it, didn't you?"

Knocker winced and scrambled to his feet. "Remind me to keep it shut."

"Knocker, are you okay?" Cara asked, having seen him go down.

"I'm apples, boss."

"Just don't become the fermented kind."

More rounds buzzed angrily around them. The team had made little impression on their attackers but at least they were still all in one piece. "Fuck this," Knocker growled and sat down behind a lump of ice. Kane frowned at him as he reloaded. "What are you doing?"

Knocker reached for the satphone he carried. "Phoning a friend."

"This isn't fucking Millionaire, Raymond."

"Don't fucking call me Raymond, John." A pause. "Hey, Slick, how're they hanging?"

"Is that gunfire I hear, Knocker?" Slick asked from thousands of miles away.

"Yeah. We're a bit pinned down and need some assistance."

"You don't want much," Slick said. "Wait one."

A few moments later he said, "You're in luck. I might just have something for you. Monitor your traffic."

"What?"

But Slick was gone.

Knocker looked over at Kane who had begun firing again. "He hung up."

"What did you expect? The hand of God?"

"Reaper Three, this is Sword, copy?"

The Brit grinned. "Hold that thought, Reaper. Copy, Sword, this is Reaper Three. Send traffic."

"A friend told us you were in trouble, Reaper Three. Said you might need some help."

"What have you got, Sword? We'll take whatever you have to spare."

"Can you hang on for fifteen minutes?"

"Yes, why?" Knocker asked.

"That's how long it will take the Tomahawk to get there," the voice replied.

"Roger that, Sword, am setting time now."

"Missile away. Good luck."

Knocker said, "All callsigns from Reaper Three. We have a Tomahawk in the air, fifteen mikes out."

"How the hell did you manage that?" Kane asked.

"Don't ask. That's one for Slick to answer. He's the driving force behind it."

Knocker rose up and was about to fire when he saw a shooter fire a HE round. "Incoming!"

The whole team got low as the round landed and blew up chunks of ice from the ridge in front of them. Coming to his feet, the Brit opened fire and grunted in satisfaction as his shot found its target and the man fell.

"This is Reaper Five, I'm pinned down. I have two shooters trying to flank on the right."

Kane came into a crouch. "I'll go."

Keeping low he ran through a storm of bullets until reaching Kagiso's position. "Where are they?"

"At our two o'clock."

Kane edged up the small ice ridge and looked. His head drew a sudden fusillade, and he slid back down. "Okay. I need you to unload on their position to keep their heads down."

Kagiso nodded. "Just tell me when."

Kane nodded back, drew in a deep breath and said, "Now."

Kagiso opened fire and Kane started running. She fired in rapid bursts and before long the magazine in the 433 was empty. But her actions had the desired effect.

Kane had managed to outflank the flankers. Maneuvering around an ice outcrop, he stepped out and there they were. He opened fire and the two men died where they were.

However, with his task done, Kane didn't retreat. He moved to the men and picked up their weapons and grabbed all their spare ammunition. Only then did he fall back. Upon reaching Kagiso once more, he stopped. "How are you off for ammo?"

"I have enough."

Patting her on the shoulder, he said, "Keep your head down."

When he reached the others, he tossed one of the weapons to Knocker. "Here."

Knocker looked at the Brügger & Thomet APC submachine gun and his lip curled with disdain. "What is this? A bloody gnat's dick?"

"You don't have to use it," Kane replied. "How are we for time?"

"Five minutes."

"Okay, let's hope it does the job."

Suddenly over the comms came Cara's voice. "I'm out."

Kane and Knocker looked over at her position and saw four Argentine soldiers leapfrogging toward her position. Knocker came to his feet. "My turn, Reaper. Hold my beer."

———

CARA HOLSTERED her P320 and drew the combat knife she always carried. Muttering a curse she readied herself to die. But by hell if she went, she'd take some of them with her.

The first of the Argentines appeared and she threw herself at him. Her shoulder hit him in the chest and made him stagger. As he tried to regain his balance, she brought the knife around in a sweeping arc.

The blade in Cara's fist found flesh and opened the throat of her attacker deep and wide. Blood sprayed across the snow and ice like a macabre Pro Hart painting.

She let out a scream as she turned to face the next attacker. The sight of his dead comrade gave him pause and it was enough time for Cara to react. She went low just as he pulled the trigger on his weapon, and the burst went high.

Cara slid along the ice and brought her knife up, stabbing the soldier in the groin. Once more blood sprayed and the man let out a shriek of pain. He slumped to the ice and Cara slashed his throat, opening it wide. Blood splattered her face as she pushed him away, not taking his weapon for herself.

Coming into a crouch she looked like an animal fresh from dining on a kill. Cara turned and came face-to-face with the two remaining soldiers. This was it.

Suddenly a snarling form came from nowhere and landed on top of both men. Knocker had arrived just in time. His P320 hammered twice, and the first of the two soldiers lost his brains.

Knocker turned on the second and repeated the dose. Then he turned to Cara. "You okay?"

She nodded. "I had them."

He grinned. "Of course you did."

The Brit grabbed their weapons and passed one to Cara. "This'll have to do."

She took some spare ammo and took up her position. Knocker glanced at his watch. "Shit. Down! Everyone get down!"

His words were transmitted across the comms network, and everyone hit the ice just as two Tomahawks came in.

The impact of the warheads was shattering. The helicopter and the Argentines disappeared in the explosive inferno. The ice shook and Kane felt the heat wash over them. It was so close that had there not been ridges between the team and the blast, they would have suffered the same fate as their attackers.

An eerie silence descended over the ice and Kane wondered for a moment if he was in fact dead. Then he said, "All call signs check in."

One by one everyone called in. Knocker was the last. At the end of his brief reply he said, "Reaper, you'd better get over here. We could be fucked."

KANE ALMOST HAD a bout of vertigo as he looked down into the yawning fissure. "Shit," he muttered. He looked to the left and then turned his head to the right. The chasm stretched as far as the eye could see. "The Tomahawks did this?"

"The crack must have already been there," Knocker replied. "The missiles just opened it up."

"That puts a damper on things," Cara said.

"There is no way we can cross it," Kane said.

"No."

"We'll have to walk around it."

"That could add an extra day to our schedule," Knocker pointed out. "Does that icebreaker have a helicopter?"

Kane turned and sought out Jorgensen. "Jorgensen, does that ship have a helicopter?"

"Yes, that was how they were going to get us off."

Kane nodded at the bleak icescape around them and said grimly, "You'd better call them and tell them to come and get us. We're going no farther."

CHAPTER 8

ZURICH, SWITZERLAND

Sofia watched everything unfold right up to the fiery ball at the end. "*Damn it!* What just happened?"

"Two Tomahawk Missiles just took out the Argentine force," Mila said.

"What? Where did they come from?"

"We can only assume there was a submarine within range."

"I picked up a transmission about fifteen minutes ago, ma'am," another operator said.

"Play it for me, Lukas."

Sofia listened to the transmission, and her face grew dark. "You only bring this to my attention now?" Her voice was low and held menace.

"I was busy at the time and thought nothing of it. I'm sorry."

"Busy? You were too busy to report this to me? With what may I ask?"

"I had him working on the Wei case, ma'am," Mila said.

"And did he find something? I pray that he did because if he hasn't..."

"Yes, ma'am," Lukas replied. A smaller screen opened in the bigger one. "I think these are the two who killed Mr. Wei."

Sofia squinted. "Make it bigger."

The picture enlarged. A man and woman. The man in a suit, the woman in a red dress. "What makes you think they are the ones?"

Two more pictures. The man was seen to be entering the opera on his own and the woman was with Wei. "The picture of the two together. Was that after?"

"Yes, ma'am."

Sofia nodded slowly. "I want to know who they are, where they came from, and where they went. Mila, find me a team in Singapore we can use. I want them operational as soon as we find out."

"Yes, ma'am."

Sofia stared at the picture of Hunt and Millie. "Who are you?"

———

THIRTY MINUTES later Mila came to Sofia who was seated in her chair contemplating the reasons these people might want to kill Wei. "Ma'am?"

Sofia looked up. "Yes?"

"We know who they are. The man is Borden Hunt. Former Navy SEAL. Now in the private sector. The woman's name is Mille Rogers. She is MI6."

"Why?"

"Why what, ma'am?"

"Why did they kill Wei?"

"I'm afraid I don't know."

"Where are they?" Sofia asked.

"At the hotel. The Singapore Ramada."

"The one where they killed Wei? Those cheeky fucks. Where did they come from?"

"We were able to back trace them to an address we think is a safehouse," Mila explained.

"Do we have some resources on the ground?" Sofia asked.

"Yes."

"Enough for two teams?"

Mila shook her head. "I'm afraid not."

Sofia thought for a moment. "Send the team to the safehouse. Then the hotel if they are still there."

"They will be," Mila said knowingly. "They got themselves a room."

———

SINGAPORE

Their first coupling was like a pair of wild animals rutting, coming down from the high of their successful mission. The second time was more sensual and slower. Now Hunt and Millie slept the sleep of the exhausted. Both were naked with only a sheet draped over them.

At the sound of the beep, Hunt's eyes flicked open. His hand went immediately under his pillow to where he'd hidden the knife he'd taken when they'd eaten dinner. He withdrew it then clamped a hand over Millie's mouth.

In the light filtering through the thin curtains he saw her eyes open. "Get on the floor. We have company." His voice was almost inaudible.

Hunt slipped from the bed and silently placed pillows under the sheet so that it looked like there was someone sleeping. He then hid behind the bedroom door and waited for their visitors to come.

At first there was silence. Nothing moved. Then the suppressed muzzle of an MP5SD slid past the end of the door and opened fire.

Bullets hammered into the bed, successfully killing the pillow. That was the cue for Hunt to react. He slammed the door forward, knocking the shooter off balance. He then stepped into the room and knocked the MP5 aside, bringing up the knife and driving it home just under the chin.

With his left hand, Hunt grabbed the weapon. As the man staggered, Hunt tore the weapon free of the shooter's grasp and turned it, reversing his grip, and opened fire.

The rounds from the weapon tore into body armor and flesh, stopping at the head. The shooter fell, revealing two additional assailants behind him. Hunt fired another burst then threw himself across the bed. He landed on Millie, making her cry out in pain.

More bullets ripped through the room and the bed shuddered under their impact. Others punched holes into the thin walls. Hunt came up from the floor and opened fire in short bursts. Nothing more confronting than a naked man with an MP5.

The shooter jerked as a bullet tore out his throat. He shuddered and fell to the floor next to his friends.

Then came the silence. Hunt stood up. "Get dressed. We need to leave."

A quick check told him that all three shooters were down. One was almost dead but not quite. Hunt crouched beside him. "Who are you?"

The man was Asian. He muttered something that sounded like he was telling Hunt where to go.

The former SEAL shot him in the head.

Moments later they were dressed and hurrying along the hall. "What was that?" Millie asked aloud.

"Someone knew where we were and what we did," Hunt replied.

"Chrysalis?"

"That would be my guess," he replied.

"Oh, no," Millie said. "If they found us, they know about the safehouse."

"Exactly what I'm thinking."

Millie grabbed her cell and dialed while they were on the move. After two tries she said, "They're not picking up."

The pair started to move faster.

ZURICH, SWITZERLAND

"What is with all the fucking incompetence," Sofia snarled and threw the coffee cup to the floor. The ops room had been watching on through the body cams of the operators. "Are any of them alive?"

"No, ma'am," Mila replied. "They are all down hard."

"Do we have anyone else we can call on?"

"The Xiang Triad."

"How fast can they get people to the safe house?" Sofia asked.

"Do you figure that's where they will go?"

"I'd put money on it."

"I'll find out."

"Tell Xiang if they succeed, I will pay ten million."

While Mila made the call, Sofia touched her headset to talk. "Have we eyes on them?"

"Just trying to locate them, ma'am," a man said.

"Thank you, Finn. I have faith in you."

That was Sofia's way of saying don't fuck it up.

"Ma'am, I have them."

"Show me."

Four small feeds came up revolving constantly. Sofia's eyes tried to keep up. "What am I seeing?"

"Traffic cams, ma'am. The feed goes the same way as the clock. Each time they pass one the next one takes over."

Sofia watched and nodded. "Well done, Finn. Now where are they headed?"

"As you thought, ma'am. It looks like they are going to their safe house."

She watched the changing screens for a while longer and cast her gaze to Mila who was just finishing the call. "Xiang will mobilize his people immediately."

"Good. Let's hope they are successful."

———

SINGAPORE

"Oh, good Lord," Millie whispered hoarsely. "They're all dead."

Clarke and Keller lay on the floor in the ops room, their weapons beside them. Two other MI6 operatives had also been killed. "Is that everyone?" Hunt asked.

"Y—yes," Millie managed to get out.

"Right, we need to leave."

"Okay."

Hunt moved to the window and looked down at the street below lit by regularly spaced streetlamps. While he watched, two black BMWs pulled up disgorging four men from each. Hunt turned back to Millie. "Too late. Where is your armory?"

"This way."

She took Hunt into a second room and pulled on a wall hook. A partition slid open and revealed another room lined with weapons. Hunt took down a suppressed HK 433 and some magazines. He grabbed a couple of flashbangs and grenades. Then he grabbed two lots of body armor. Hunt tossed one to Millie who'd selected an MP5SD. "You might want to change out of that dress."

She shrugged and grabbed a knife, cutting the dress off just below her buttocks. "That will do for the moment." She did, however, slip out of her heels and put on her comfortable gym shoes.

Hunt slapped home a full magazine. "I guess it will."

The former SEAL took down some NVGs and handed Millie a pair. "Let's go."

They met them in the hallway to the elevator. Hunt had said to Millie, "Stay behind me until I run dry."

As soon as he heard the ding, Hunt used his weapon to shoot out the lights. Now in darkness, he had the advantage. The killers stepped out of the lighted elevator, and Hunt opened fire at everything his laser sight touched. In no time at all, the triad men were whittled from eight to five with dead men dressed in suits lying in the hallway.

Hunt grabbed one of the flashbangs and pulled the pin. He threw it along the hallway and tried his best to protect himself from the blast in a doorway. The grenade detonated and two men staggered out from cover, trying their best to rebalance their equilibrium. The 433 erupted four more times. Two rounds each for the triad killers.

That left three.

One appeared with an Agram 2000 submachine gun. He let rip with it on full auto. 800 rounds per minute. He sprayed the hallway like he was holding a garden hose.

Hunt hit the carpeted floor, taking Millie with him. Bullets punched holes in the walls and the floor all around them. It was an absolute miracle they weren't hit. Then when the magazine ran dry on the Agram, Hunt came up and put two well placed rounds in the gunman's head.

Two remaining.

Hunt didn't wait around for them to respond. Instead, he came to his feet and pressed forward. A shooter appeared and died. The final one appeared and fired. Hunt felt the tug of the bullets on his clothing just before he sent the son of a bitch straight to hell.

He turned to Millie. "Are you okay?"

She nodded. "I'm fine. But you, you're fucking crazy."

"Let's get out of here."

The pair moved swiftly down the stairwell to the basement garage where the SUV was parked. He tossed Millie the keys. "You drive."

"Where?"

"I'll tell you once we're moving." Pulling out his cell, Hunt dialed a number.

Slick answered. "How can I help you, Mr. Hunt?"

"I need you to make me invisible, Slick," Hunt said.

"Your wish is my command."

———

ZURICH, SWITZERLAND

Two hours after the fight in the safehouse the news came through. It was Mila who broke it to Sofia. "The team was wiped out, ma'am."

"Damn it. Why can't they just die?"

"Yes, ma'am."

"Where are they now?"

There was a pregnant pause before Mila said hesitantly, "We don't know. All the traffic cameras are down."

"All?"

"Yes."

"What about our satellite?" Sofia asked.

"Someone has hacked the feed and put some old television show on it."

"What show?"

"F-Troop."

Sofia shook her head. "What about the others who have Roman?"

"They were picked up by a helicopter and taken to an icebreaker off the coast. The satellite was out of range just after they landed."

"Find out where it is going. I want them located and Roman terminated forthwith."

"Yes, ma'am."

BUENOS AIRES, FIVE DAYS LATER

The anger in Sergei Andropov had been building since the incident at Ali Al Salem Air Base. He'd lost some good men there and he meant to avenge them. The intel from Sofia had those responsible aboard an icebreaker headed north. Destination unknown.

Andropov figured that there would be two possible destinations for the ship. Montevideo or Buenos Aires on the other side of the bay. That was the unknown. So hedging his bets, he dispatched a team to each and waited for news.

The ship itself was still five days out. He tossed around the possibility of a sea interdiction but passed on the idea. He'd wait until it came into port. Meanwhile they were set up in a warehouse on the outskirts of the city.

His sat phone rang. It was Sofia. "Are you in position?"

"I have been in position for two days," Andropov growled. "Where are they?"

"We assume they are still on the icebreaker," she replied.

"Is there not a way you can confirm it?"

"Not until the ship docks at its destination." There was a muffled conversation and Sofia came back, her voice revealing more than a hint of concern. "It seems the icebreaker has turned around and is headed south again."

"Shit," Andropov said. "You know what that means, don't you?"

"That they're not on the damn thing."

"Exactly."

"What will you do, Sergei?"

"I'm going to stay put. They have to come ashore somewhere. I'm guessing this is it."

"Good luck."

———

ZURICH, SWITZERLAND

The past days had been full of bad news, and it was wearing. Sofia's team of techs had lost the assassins and now Roman and his protectors. Someone was running interference for them and whoever it was, was damn good. So good, that they couldn't even track him down.

Sofia was at home eating her dinner and drinking a bottle of champagne trying to wind down a little. It was hard waiting for results when things were beyond her control. Especially when her partners were breathing down her neck for results.

Her computer pinged. She opened it and read the message left by Mila. There was also a voice file.

"Interpol will take Roman. We just need your people to get him to Buenos Aires."

"I'll see what I can do."

"We have a facility there, Mary. We can fly him to Europe from there."

Sofia lowered her glass of champagne and listened to the voice file again. Once that was done, she smiled and made a call. "Sergei, I know where they are going to be."

USHUAIA, ARGENTINA

After a couple days of rest and regrouping, their ammunition replenished, Team Reaper, along with Burner and Shorty, were ready to go again, with Jorgensen from Six.

They had transferred from the icebreaker to a British submarine while at sea, which had delivered them to Ushuaia where they disembarked.

The plane organized by MI6, a C-130, was on the tarmac waiting. Its hold contained all the equipment the team would need to accomplish their mission. Once in Buenos Aires they would hand Roman over and then head home.

Taking no chances, they were all dressed in kit and had Slick watching over them. That didn't help with the cold and wind though.

"Are we clear, Bravo Three?"

"Roger that, Reaper One. Load them up and move them out," Slick replied, trying to imitate an old west movie he'd seen.

"Your American West accent sucks."

"Yeah, sorry about that."

"What are our friends up to?" Cara asked.

"Well, they're persistent, ma'am, I'll give them that. So far, I've been able to hold them off. However, your old friend Sergei Andropov is back on the scene."

"Do you know where he is?"

"No, ma'am."

"What about our friends? Where are they?"

"They're good, ma'am. They're bouncing shit everywhere and blocking every move I make. Yesterday they were in Iraq, today Egypt."

"So, they could be anywhere."

"Just like us."

"There are still other ways they can find you," Slick warned. "If they pick up any transmissions or there is a satellite I don't know about."

"Just do what you can."

"Yes—ah fuck."

"What's the matter?"

"They just hit me with some kind of virus. Oh, they're good. I'm going to have to shut the system down."

"What does that mean?" Kane asked.

"You're going to be exposed," Slick replied grimly. "Good luck."

Then he was gone.

"This just gets better and better," Cara said.

"This ought to be fun," Kane said. "Old school against high tech."

"Thank God we're only going to Buenos Aires."

CHAPTER 9

DAEGU, SOUTH KOREA

Kane and his team weren't the only ones exposed. Hunt and Millie were also. It was 21:00 and they had just taken an international flight, landing in Daegu South Korea. Upon turning off flight mode as they reached the terminal, Hunt looked down to see an encrypted message that had come through during the flight, advising that home base had been corrupted through a cyberattack. Fortunately, there were other intelligence agencies they could rely on. This time it was the CIA. Mary Thurston had pulled some strings to get them some help.

"Our friend should be here soon," Hunt said.

"I hope so. It'll be good to have a shower."

After leaving the Singapore safehouse, Thurston had directed them to the American Embassy. From there they had been provided tickets and clean passports to use, and they then boarded a flight to their current destination. Now all they had to do was gather intel on their next target and execute a plan.

Simple.

Not really.

Once more, they were on the precipice of things turning to shit.

———

ZURICH, SWITZERLAND

"We have them," Mila said through her headset mic.

"Who?"

The one named Hunt and the MI6 woman. Her name is Millie Morris."

"Where?" Sofia asked.

"In Daegu, South Korea. They just got off a flight from Singapore."

"At least we know what they're up to," Sofia said. She reached for her cell. It rang and Park answered.

"What is it, Sofia?" he asked.

"The ones who killed Wei have just surfaced at Daegu Airport," she said.

"Are they coming after me next?" Park asked. "Is that what you're saying?"

"I'm not saying anything," Sofia replied. "It could be a coincidence or—"

"Or they're here after me."

"Yes."

"I will be ready," Park said and hung up.

"Mila?"

"Yes, ma'am?"

"Let's welcome them to South Korea."

"Yes, ma'am."

———

DAEGU, SOUTH KOREA

They were just finishing up at customs when the proverbial hit the fan. Hunt had his stamped passport in his hand when cell phones all around them started pinging with notifications. Hunt looked at his own and felt a chill run down his spine. There, on the screen, was a picture of him and Millie. It said they were wanted by Interpol for murder and for them to be apprehended at once.

Hunt glanced at Millie. Alarm was all over her face as she looked back at him, her cell in hand. This was not good.

Then it became worse. Every television screen in the surrounding area was showing their faces, giving their real names and aliases, saying they were wanted. The customs officer in front of Hunt moved his gaze from the screen nearest and looked at Hunt. It took barely a moment before recognition dawned.

"Ah, fuck!"

Turning to grab Millie's hand, Hunt told her, "Run!"

Suddenly there were shouts from behind them. Hunt shouldered his way through the crush dragging Millie with him. "We have to make it to the pickup point."

They broke out into the open and were able to pick up pace. Hunt heard the squawk of a radio off to his right and saw a security guy. He deviated to the left. "This way."

Running toward the travelator, the fugitives jumped onto the one heading away from them. Looking up, Hunt saw two security guards step into position to receive them and stopped so suddenly that Millie ran into his back. He glanced behind them and saw two more.

"Oh crap," Millie said breathlessly.

Placing his hands in the air, Hunt let the travelator take them toward the two security men. Behind him, Millie did the same. "I guess that's that then," she said.

Hunt nodded. "I guess it is."

But it wasn't. Hunt wasn't about to give up.

As soon as the security guard put his weapon away, and reached out to cuff Hunt, the former SEAL exploded into action. He grabbed the man's arm in his left hand and pulled him forward. Then he swept his right elbow around. It crashed into the security man's temple and put him down. Out like the proverbial light.

Not waiting to see the result, Hunt turned to face the second guard and went hard at him. He knocked the man's weapon up and away. The gun discharged noisily and the bullet punched harmlessly into the ceiling.

Grabbing hold of the man's wrist, Hunt twisted. The sound of bone breaking seemed loud and the man shrieked in pain. The gun dropped and Hunt hit the man in the face knocking him on his ass. He turned to Millie. "This way."

They were running once more through the throng of travelers who were scattering because of the gunshot.

Hunt and Millie ran along the length of an extensive concourse with the two other security guards in pursuit.

Up ahead, Hunt saw another security guard. Looking about them, Hunt noticed the crush of people seemed to be getting thicker.

"What now?" Millie asked.

"This way," he replied and hurried into the densest part of the crowd he could find that moved like a wave.

Bobbing up and down like birds looking for danger in a flock, Hunt and Millie kept moving with the flow. Hunt reached for his cell and sent a message to the CIA officer that was waiting for them. As the crowd passed a clothing store, the pair broke off and entered. They took hats and coats off the rack and then joined the crush once more.

———

ZURICH, SWITZERLAND

Sofia stared at the screen trying to pick out their targets among the throng of people. Her eyes darted around the screen. "Where did they go?"

"We're working on it, ma'am," Mila replied.

"Find them," she hissed vehemently.

The crowd moved like a wave across the sand as thousands evacuated the terminal. Sofia's people sifted through the footage as she waited impatiently. Finally, they came up with something.

"They went into this store in the terminal," Mila said, showing the footage. "Then they came out wearing a hat and coat each. Then—"

The screens went dark. Sofia frowned. "What just happened?"

"One moment, ma'am." Mila turned to Lukas. "What just happened?"

"The feed went dead," he replied. "Someone just brought it down."

Mila turned back and said, "Ma'am—"

"I heard. Now, do what you can, and find them."

"Yes, ma'am."

———

DAEGU, SOUTH KOREA

Hunt and Millie climbed into the car that was waiting for them. The driver's name was Jackson. When Hunt let him know what was happening, Jackson made a call and had every security camera on the grid shut down.

"Thanks for your help," Hunt said.

"Anytime," Jackson replied cheerfully.

"Your people need to know that Chrysalis shouldn't be underestimated," Millie said to him. "They will be tracking us."

"They'll have to do it some other way," Jackson replied. "Our techs shut down the whole camera grid for ten blocks. They'll have no idea where you went."

"Don't be too sure about that," Millie replied.

"We'll deal with it if and when we have to."

Hunt's cell buzzed. He looked at the screen as their SUV turned right. The message was from Slick. **Back up and running.**

Hunt turned his screen to show Millie the message. She nodded. "Thank heavens."

The former SEAL nodded. "Yes, but for how long?"

―――――

IN THE AIR, 30,000 FT

Cara's cell buzzed and she looked at it. After reading the message she made the call. "Talk to me, Slick."

"I'm basically up and running," he replied. "I can see you, but they can see you too. It's not great but it will help."

"Better than nothing," she replied.

"Yes, ma'am, better than nothing."

The call disconnected and Kane joined her. She said, "Slick is back up and is able to provide us with limited help. The bad news is our friends will still be able to see us."

"Better than nothing, I guess," Kane replied with a shrug.

"That's what I said. Interpol will meet us at the airport, and we'll go from there. They'll escort us to their facility."

"To tell the truth, this guy is more trouble than he's worth. I'll be glad to see the back of Roman," Kane said.

"Me too."

―――――

CAMPO DEL SUR AIRSTRIP, BUENOS AIRES

Sitting in the first SUV in a line of four, Leandro Cosenza was awaiting the plane's arrival. He looked at his watch. It was twelve thirty p.m. In the passenger seat beside him, Sergei Andropov sat silently. Each vehicle had two Interpol agents inside, but none apart from Cosenza was privy to the intelligence regarding the identity of their passenger.

The Interpol officer rubbed his hands nervously. Andropov looked over and said, "Just take it easy, act normally and your family will remain fine."

The truth was they were already dead. After Andropov had shown him the video of his wife and two children, they had been killed.

"How do I know you will release them?" Cosenza asked for the tenth time.

"You don't," Andropov replied. "All you have to concentrate on is delivering these people into the ambush I've organized, and my people will take care of the rest."

Cosenza nodded.

They sat in silence until the noise of the plane coming in could be heard. Then they watched it land. Andropov said, "Anything from you and your family will die."

The C-130 taxied to the apron where they were waiting and stopped, powering down the engines, lowering the ramp. The pair watched as Roman was escorted from the plane. They noticed everyone was dressed in full kit. Andropov and Cosenza got out of their SUV, and the other Interpol agents followed.

The new arrivals and their charge walked over to where they waited. Cosenza asked, "Cara Billings?"

Cara nodded. "Yes."

"I'm Leandro Cosenza, Interpol officer in charge."

Cara indicated Kane and Knocker. "Kane and Jensen, my right and left hand."

Andropov nodded at Roman. "That him?"

"Roman?"

"Yes."

"That's him," Cara said. "We'll be glad to be rid of him."

"Shall we go?" Cosenza asked. "Divide your people up between the vehicles."

Kane turned to Knocker and said, "Get Roman in the second vehicle. You and Burner ride shotgun on him. The rest spread out among the other SUVs."

"Roger that, Reaper."

There was a flicker in Andropov's eyes. He'd heard of this man. The indestructible man they called the Reaper. He and his team had taken down more bad people than he'd had hot dinners. "I am privileged," Andropov said.

"How so?" Kane asked.

"I get to meet the famous Reaper and his team of operators."

"Infamous is more like it," Cara said. "Let's go. We're burning daylight."

Once the vehicles were fully loaded, the convoy left the airstrip. From there they headed into Buenos Aires and the waiting arms of trouble.

ZURICH, SWITZERLAND

Sofia looked at the time stamp on the screen. It was 12:45 p.m. in Buenos Aires, five hours behind Zurich time. Watching the group get loaded into the SUVs and drive away from the airport, Mila said, "Andropov should have done it there."

"Let's see how it plays out," Sofia said.

Her stomach growled and Sofia remembered she'd forgotten to eat lunch. Ignoring the hungry protest she concentrated on the screen. She saw the small convoy turn.

"Where are they going?" Mila asked.

"Make the map bigger," Sofia said.

She concentrated her gaze, seeing the convoy make another turn. "They are headed to Bajo Flores."

"What is there?"

"1-11-14."

"What is that?"

"The closest thing to hell on earth."

———

BUENOS AIRES

"Reaper, something is wrong," Knocker said through his comms. "These guys back here say we're going the wrong way."

Kane remained silent.

"Did you hear me, Reaper?"

Kane glanced at Cara. "Roger, Two, you'll just have to hold it until we get there."

"Why didn't he go back at the airfield?"

Kane shrugged. "No idea."

The convoy kept on as the streetscape began to change. At first the difference was barely discernible, but the farther they went, the descent became more marked. Gone were the nice buildings replaced by high density apartments stacked on top of each other three to four floors high. Ramshackle dwellings that appeared decrepit, ready to fall down, their walls covered in graffiti. In between were narrow alleyways and the streets were plastered with refuse and piles of junk.

Kane glanced at Cosenza. The Interpol man was sweating profusely even though it wasn't that warm. Something was very wrong.

Kane eased his P320 from its holster. Cara did the same.

Just in time.

Knocker's voice came frantically over the comms. *"Ambush! Ambush! Ambush!"*

Andropov must have heard the call over the comms because he reacted instantly. He grabbed his sidearm and turned but Kane was already ahead of him. The P320 came up and fired at the Russian's head. The bullet hit the security man in the temple and his head flopped sideways like a rag doll.

Cara went to shoot Cosenza, but he cried out, "Don't shoot! Don't shoot!"

"What the fuck is going on?" Cara hissed.

Incoming rounds began to hammer the vehicles.

"He is Andropov," Cosenza said, indicating the dead mercenary. "They have my family."

"We can't stay here," Kane snarled. "Everyone out, it's a kill box. Into the alleys."

Doors were flung open, and they all tumbled from their rides. Knocker, using a door for cover, started firing at rooftops. "Burner, get that prick out and into the alley."

Burner grabbed Roman and dragged him from the rear seat. The two Interpol agents took up positions the same as Knocker. "Get the fuck out of it," he snarled at them.

The warning came too late. Both men took rounds and fell to the ground, not moving. The Brit covered Burner as she shoved Roman across the narrow street. He said into his comms, "Reaper, we're moving left."

"Roger that. All callsigns left side, left side."

Breaking away from the vehicles, the team headed left. Two more Interpol officers went down under the stream of fire and Kane muttered a curse.

A sudden cry of pain emanated from Kagiso as she stumbled and fell. Knocker muttered a curse and went to her. "Are you okay, lass?"

"Hit in my armor."

He dragged her to her feet. "Come on then. This is no time to be laying around."

As they entered the alley, Kane said, "Keep moving. Knocker, you're on point. Shorty, help Burner with Roman." He turned to the four remaining Interpol officers. "Are you boys coming with us?"

"Do you know where we are?"

Kane looked around at the dwellings that almost swallowed the alleyway. "I'm going to take a guess and say the devil's asshole."

———

ZURICH, SWITZERLAND

While most people were sitting down to their evening meal, Sofia was watching events unfold in Buenos Aires. Her people were working hard once again, and the new shift was due at any time now for their twelve-hour shift. Meanwhile, they had just observed the failure of the ambush, and Sofia was almost certain that Andropov—

"Andropov is dead," Mila blurted out. "His second in command just called it in."

"These people have the lives of a cat," Sofia growled. "What is he going to do?"

"He's pulling his people out."

"Tell him I'll put an additional ten million to the reward."

"Yes, ma'am." Mila relayed the message and for several moments argued with whoever was on the other end before saying to Sofia, "In his words, ma'am, not mine, he said stick your money. They've dead to bury. What do you want me to do, ma'am?"

"Let them go. Just try and keep track of Roman."

"We're about to lose the satellite coverage for a few hours."

"What about cameras?"

"Not where they are," Mila replied.

"Shit," Sofia snarled.

"I might have an idea," Mila told her.

"I'm listening," Sofia said.

"The slum where they are is controlled by Los Escorpiones, one of the major gangs in the city. If we can reach out and get them on side, they might do our work for us."

"Do it."

"Satellite coverage gone," Lukas said.

Coming to her feet, Sofia began to walk away, saying, "Keep me informed. I have a meeting to attend."

"Yes, ma'am."

Heading to her office, Sofia sat before her bank of

screens and waited for everyone to come online. Park was the only one who complained about the time. "Obviously your clock could be a little better."

"It's fine here," Sofia shot back at him.

"I'm happy for you."

"What is happening?" asked Petrov.

"You all need to step up your security," Sofia said.

"Why?"

"Because you have become targets of an assassin," Sofia replied.

"The same assassin that killed Wei?" Park asked. "The same one that is now in South Korea after me?"

"That's right."

"Why haven't you taken care of it?" Khalid asked. "This is what you do."

"He is good."

"What about Roman?" Petrov asked.

Sofia nodded. "He is in Buenos Aires with the mercenaries. They are locked down inside one of the slums."

"Good. Andropov and his people will take care of them."

"Andropov is dead, and his people are pulling out." Her voice was matter of fact.

"Damn it. I would have thought we'd be paying out the money by now."

"These mercenaries are not your average team. They are very good at what they do."

"Then find someone who can take care of it," Petrov snarled.

The screens went blank. "Asshole."

Sofia's cell buzzed. She picked it up and put it to her ear. "Yes?"

"Los Escorpiones are mobilizing now."

"Good."

———

BUENOS AIRES

They seemed to come out of nowhere. Dozens of armed shooters who scrambled around like ants after a scrap of meat. Knocker crouched behind an old concrete water trough used for communal laundry at the edge of a small plaza.

Incoming rounds chipped shards from the trough as they impacted it furiously. Knocker got lower as he tried to prevent himself being exposed. "Reaper One, from Three, I'm pinned down."

"Damn silly thing to do," Kane growled as he opened fire from the cover of an alley.

Shooters seemed to leap from cover to cover while others were firing from the second floor of a rundown building. Two disappeared after being shot. Behind Kane, Cara was firing in a steady rhythm picking her targets and dispatching them.

Kagiso had taken up position behind a 44-gallon drum which rang like a bell every time it was hit. Brick, meanwhile, had hunkered down behind a pile of scrap metal.

The four Interpol officers were down to three after one had taken a round to his throat. His body was an untidy heap beside Brick who'd checked him over and pronounced him dead. As for Burner and Shorty, they sat on Roman and watched their six.

Kane said, "Lay down some covering fire for Raymond."

The team picked up their outgoing rounds while Knocker scrambled back. Over his comms Kane heard him say, "Don't call me fucking Raymond."

With Knocker back from the brink, they now had to formulate a plan. Cara said, "We can always go back—"

"Contact rear!" Shorty exclaimed and opened fire.

"Nope," Kane replied, pushing past her.

When he reached Shorty, he saw the handful of shooters coming along the street they had just crossed over. Kane opened fire with his 433 and a shooter fell to the ground. The others were brave or just downright stupid because they remained in the open and returned fire.

Between them both, Shorty and Kane left numerous assailants down and bleeding out on the street.

Kane said, "Keep holding here."

Across the plaza the sudden onset of machine-gun fire opened up from the second floor of the building opposite. Kagiso dropped low behind the drum as it began to play a whole new symphony. Brick pressed himself harder against the scrap metal.

"Reaper, we need to shut that gun down if we have any chance of getting out of here," Knocker said.

"I'm open to suggestions," Kane replied.

Knocker reached into his pocket and pulled out a grenade. "Remember?"

Reaper nodded. "Yeah, never leave home without it. I hate to point this out, but you'll never throw it that far. I don't care what sort of cricketer you were in your formative years."

"I'll need to get closer."

"No," Cara snapped. "You can't go out there."

Knocker gave her his biggest grin and said, "Hold my beer, boss."

"Ah, fuck!"

Without waiting, he broke cover and set off running. Kane growled into his comms, "Friendly in the open. Cover him."

Kane, Brick, Kagiso, and Cara opened fire, trying to suppress what incoming they could. Knocker dove behind the trough and then darted left to a pile of rubbish. Bullets peppered his position, but it didn't seem as bad as before. From the garbage he ran forward, taking cover behind a stack of wooden pallets.

But he still wasn't close enough. Glancing around for inspiration, he noticed a refrigerator. It was upright and looked about the best cover he would get. Taking a deep breath, Knocker ran.

The machine gun chased him across the open space to the refrigerator as he took shelter behind it, bullets punching into it but not through. "Reaper, get ready to move when this thing goes off."

"Roger that," Kane replied. Then muttered, "Stupid bastard."

Knocker pulled the pin and threw the grenade at the second-floor balcony where the machine gun was. The explosion was catastrophic, hurling the weapon and user from the platform. Those nearby were also caught up in the blast and a bloody arm fell to the rubble-covered ground below.

The grenade had the desired effect. The incoming fire seemed to die down as Kane and the others broke from their positions and ran forward. Knocker left his shelter behind the refrigerator and pressed onward as well.

They were now moving along a narrow street, made worse by piles of rubbish, but at least it was empty of assailants. Kane came up to Knocker's shoulder. "They're taking up new positions."

"We need a new plan, Reaper," Knocker replied.

"No shit." Kane turned and looked back at the others. He noticed Jorgensen. The MI6 man was bleeding from an arm wound. "Brick, check Jorgensen."

"Roger."

Cara came over to them. "This is a right fuck-up."

"What do you suggest?" Kane asked.

Cara looked around and saw an open door of a ramshackle building. "In there."

"We'll get pinned down if we go in there," Knocker growled, then respectfully added, "boss."

"Move your ass."

"Yes, ma'am."

Once they were crowded inside, Cara said, "We need to get out of here."

Kane just stared at her, waiting.

Cara continued. "If we can get back to the airstrip, then we might have a chance."

"We'll need a plane," Kane said.

"Jorgensen?"

"Yes?" he said while Brick worked on his wounded arm.

"Can you get us a plane?"

"I'll do what I can."

"We'll need a ride to the airstrip," Knocker pointed out.

"Agreed," Cara replied. "But we won't find one here. Take a moment to regroup and then we'll go."

Knocker checked on Kagiso. "Are you okay, girl?"

"I am fine," she replied. "You are the crazy one."

"You'll get used to me," he said with a smile.

Meanwhile Kane checked on Burner. "Still hanging in there, Sergeant?"

"Fucking-A, sir."

Kane directed his gaze at Roman. "I see you're still alive."

"Don't sound so happy about it," he replied.

"I won't."

"You know, all you have to do is let me go and this will all stop."

"Yeah, not going to happen."

Knocker cursed. "We've got more friendlies closing in."

"Roger that. Shorty, find us a back way out."

"Copy."

The big man disappeared, and moments later there was a resounding crash and he called out, "Found one."

"Right, let's move," Kane said.

He took point and stepped out into a narrow alley bordered by a stinking open sewer with rubbish strewn along its length. With his 433 up at his shoulder, Kane scanned the rooftops and balconies. Behind him he heard Knocker say, "Watch the shit pit."

Traveling along the alley they emerged onto a wider street. Pausing at the mouth of the narrow lane, Kane swept both ways and was unsurprised to see that the street was vacant. Now he had a choice to make. Go along the street or to the alleyway opposite.

Cara came up to his shoulder. "What do you think?"

"The street is a kill box."

"Agreed."

Kane was about to say more when Jorgensen joined them. "I secured a ride. We just have to get to the strip."

"Then we need some wheels."

"Yes."

Kane said, "Right, let's keep moving before the police arrive."

"No, no police," a voice said from behind them. It was one of the Interpol officers. "The police will never come here. It's too dangerous for them."

"Great," said Kane. There was more than a hint of sarcasm.

"What's the hold up?" Knocker asked.

"We need some wheels," Kane replied.

"Leave it to me," he said and ran across the street.

Cara shook her head and groaned. "Oh, no."

CHAPTER 10

BUENOS AIRES

"Give me strength," Cara moaned as she looked at the bus. It was big and orange and looked like it had come out of the apocalypse.

"A double-decker bullet magnet," Brick growled. "This takes the cake, Knocker."

"It'll get us to where we want to go," Knocker protested.

"Will it *go?*" Kane asked.

"Sure, get on board."

"Shorty, Brick, pull security front and rear," Kane said. "Kagiso, up top. I'll join you shortly."

Kane looked around at the buildings. They were still in the slum and every fiber of his being warned him they were making a mistake with the bus. They all climbed on except for Shorty and Brick. As Kane passed the driver's position, Knocker was pulling wires. "Do you know what you're doing?"

"Relax, Reaper, I'm an old bus thief from way back."

"Reaper One, from Five. I'm picking up movement along the street." Kagiso's voice was calm.

"On my way," Kane replied. "Knocker, get this fucking thing moving."

Knocker crossed the wires and the motor rolled over like a tired dog and then stopped. "Flat battery."

"Shit."

"Reaper One I now have a technical coming along the street with at least ten shooters escorting it."

"Get this damn thing running, Knocker," Kane growled at his friend.

"How?"

"Work it the fuck out."

Kane went up the internal stairs to the open second deck of the bus. Cara followed close behind with Burner. Jorgensen from Six watched over Roman.

The remaining Interpol officers disappeared.

"Where are you lot going?" Knocker shouted after them.

Cara heard his voice and asked over the comms, "What's going on, Two?"

"Our Interpol friends just bugged out."

"Roger that."

Up top, they had a good view of both ends of the rubbish-strewn street. Kagiso pointed at the oncoming crowd and the technical. It looked to be a Toyota pickup with a machine gun on the back.

Suddenly it shot forward with a loud roar. The machine gunner on the back opened fire and it started raining bullets. Kane, Cara, Kagiso, and Burner threw themselves flat as incoming rounds chewed into the bus, smashing windows as they went.

Inside the bus, Knocker ducked low while Roman and Jorgensen lay in the aisle. Outside, Brick and Shorty took cover behind the bus, returning fire as the vehicle came on.

Then it passed. In a roar, a snarl, and in a cloud of black diesel smoke.

Kane rose onto his knees and saw the crowd coming their way. He glanced over his shoulder and saw the technical conducting a three-point turn toward the end of the street. "Cara, Kagiso, stay here. Burner, on me."

They hurried to the front of the bus while Cara and Kagiso opened fire at the rear. "You sure give your boss a lot of orders," Burner observed.

"When it comes to operations, I'm in command," Kane said. "Even though she's in overall command, when we're on the ground like this, I'm it."

"Roger that."

The technical had completed its turn and was now on the way back. Kane and Burner opened fire at the same time. The machine gun followed their lead. With bullets flying around them, Kane and Burner stood firm.

A few moments later the windscreen of the technical disintegrated and it pulled left. The vehicle slammed into a wall, the machine gunner thrown forward. The shooter sailed over the cab and hit head-first. His skull split wide, and his brains added a dash of color to the graffiti already there.

"Knocker, there's your battery, go get it."

"A pickup battery won't start this bus, Reaper," Knocker replied.

"You don't know until you try. Besides, it's all we have."

"Damn it."

In an instant Knocker was out of the bus and running along the street. Bullets started kicking up around him. "How about fucking covering me, Reaper."

"Keep your stupid head down."

"Great," Knocker growled.

"Reaper, up high," Burner warned.

Kane looked up to the rooftops and saw a handful of shooters gathering. "Damn it. Reaper Two, they're on the rooftops."

"And you're telling me this because?"

Kane fired and a shooter disappeared. "Just thought you'd like to know."

While the rest of the team tried to keep the shooters from killing him, Knocker managed to get the hood up on the technical. But that was as far as he got. The rate of incoming fire increased, and Knocker felt two rounds impact him. He cried out in pain. "Fucking bollocks."

"He's hit," Burner said urgently.

"Knocker, you okay?"

"Yeah, I'm—argh!"

He went down on one knee and crawled into cover. "This is going well, Reaper."

"Give me a moment."

"He's been shot three times," Burner pointed out.

"He's got a suit on," Kane said, still firing.

"What suit?"

"A Synoprathetic suit," he told her. "It's bullet proof."

Burner just stared at him.

"Fuck it," Burner snarled. She turned.

"Where are you going?" Kane asked her.

"To save his British ass."

"I'll go," Kane said.

"No, you need to command. I'm expendable. I'll go."

Kane shook his head. "Don't get shot."

Burner bounded down the stairs of the bus and out onto the street. She ran over to where Knocker was and crouched beside him. From there, she started firing at the shooters in their elevated positions.

"What the fuck are you doing here?" Knocker asked.

"Saving your British ass."

Knocker came back up and started work again. "Good way to get yourself shot."

"Like you?"

"At least I'm wearing a death suit."

"A death suit?" Burner asked firing at another shooter.

"Yeah," Knocker said. "Every time you get shot in one of these it feels like you're fucking dying. Come on, I've got this thing."

They started back across the street and Knocker worked on the battery. "You figure this will work?" Burner asked.

"Not a hope in hell," he replied. "But we'll give it a shot anyway."

Meanwhile, up top, Kagiso and Cara were working their way through targets. Kagiso on the street, Cara the elevated positions. "Changing," Cara snapped as she reloaded.

Kagiso kept up her fire and blew away two more gang members. She had lined up on a third when a round thundered into her side from across the street. She let out a cry of pain and slumped down to the bus's floor.

"Kagiso!" Cara exclaimed.

"I am still here, Fierce One," Kagiso replied, her voice etched with pain. "It hurts like a bastard. Is that right?"

Cara grinned to herself. "Yeah, that's right."

"Ares, are you good?" Kane asked.

"We're good."

"Roger that."

Meanwhile Knocker had the battery in. There were two, he would leave one in on the chance it would help but he wasn't going to hold his breath. "Fuck, look for some tools in the bus."

"What kind?"

"Wrenches, sockets, anything."

Burner set about her search, all while bullets rained down upon the bus. Moments later she came back with a screwdriver. "I could only find this."

"It'll have to do."

Using it, Knocker was able to lever the battery leads off. Then he removed it. The blasted thing was heavy. A lot heavier than the one he was going to replace it with.

Using the screwdriver handle, Knocker was able to bash the leads on. He sighed. "Moment of truth."

Climbing into the driver's seat he tried to start it. It turned over, but it wasn't very encouraging. His foot pumped the gas pedal and he tried again. This time the bus fired. "Well, fuck me." Into his comms, he said, "All aboard for Piccadilly Station."

Brick and Shorty climbed on the bus as it roared off

along the street. Most of the team was on the top deck clearing the way.

"RPG! High left."

The shouted warning came from Brick. Everyone swiveled to meet the threat. They opened fire but were too late. The man with the RPG had already fired and the grenade shot across the distance between its origin and the bus.

It hit short but not by much, the blast buffeting the side of the bus. Two windows shattered, spraying Roman and Jorgensen.

The bus lurched and came to a stop.

After which, things got worse.

Roman came to his feet and ran for the open door. He jumped out and took off down an alley.

"Ah, shit," Knocker growled. "We've got a runner."

"What?" Cara demanded.

"Roman just jumped from the bus and took off down the alley."

Kane looked at Cara. "I'll go," he growled. "Get to the plane."

"Reaper, no!" Cara exclaimed.

He pulled his comms. And got rid of his kit except for the handgun and ammunition for it. "Don't wait. Get to Santiago, Chile, I'll meet you there."

"What are you going to do?"

"Kill him if I have to."

Kane bounded down the stairs and out the door. Cara had a parting gift for her team commander. "Knocker, ditch your comms and kit and go with Reaper."

"Roger that," Knocker said, losing his gear like he was in a brothel.

He leaped from the bus and followed Kane along the alley. Both were dressed in jeans and shirts so they wouldn't stand out as military. Behind them the bus roared away. Knocker caught up to Kane at the end of the alley. "What are you doing here?" Kane asked.

"Following orders," the Brit replied. "Where's our rabbit?"

Kane nodded to the left. "Down there. He went into that apartment complex across the street."

Knocker's face screwed up. "Apartment complex my ass. That's a fucking deathtrap waiting to fall down."

"Yeah, that's the part we don't want to think about."

————

DAEGU, SOUTH KOREA

While Kane and Knocker were after Roman, it was 03:00 in Daegu and Hunt and Millie were sitting in a dark SUV across the street from the apartment complex where Park had the whole top floor to himself. A light had come on inside and then gone off again a short while later.

After being rescued from their predicament by the CIA, they had been taken to a safehouse not far from where the target resided. There they had met Yates, the head of station, and Gillies, the operations boss. Both were men in their forties and had graying hair. Yates was career CIA while Gillies had come to the CIA from the Rangers.

Staring at the pair, Yates had said, "You certainly do attract a lot of attention."

"Thanks for your help," Hunt replied.

"Care to tell us what we're helping you with?"

Hunt told him.

"I always knew there was more to that son of a bitch than first thought. We've had Chrysalis on our radar for a while but come up with not much."

"Once we're done," Hunt said, "we'll need a quick covert getaway out of the city."

"We can do that. Where to?"

"Saint Petersburg, Russia."

Yates said, "We can get you there, but it might take a few days."

"Just as long as I can get there on the down low."

"Just you?"

Hunt nodded. "Just me."

"What about me?" Millie asked.

"Can you get her back to London?" Hunt asked.

"A lot easier than getting you to Saint Petersburg."

"Good, do it that way."

With that sorted, Gillies asked, "When are you going for Park?"

"The sooner the better."

———

WHICH BROUGHT them to their present position observing the complex. Hunt took out a suppressed Glock supplied by the CIA. Millie had the same. He was about to climb out and said, "Eagle Nest, Eagle One. Put that feed on a loop now."

"Roger that, Eagle One. Will let know when clear," Gillies replied.

"You right to go, Millie?"

"I'm good."

"Just stay behind me and watch our backs, okay."

"Yes."

"You'll be fine. Something to tell your boss when you get back."

"Eagle One, feed now on a loop. You're clear to go."

"Guards?"

"First one is on the ground floor near the door."

"Friendlies?"

"All in bed, Eagle One. I'll guide you through."

"Roger, moving now. Kill the power."

An instant darkness enveloped the neighborhood for five blocks.

Crossing the street, they lowered their NVGs before entering the building. The security guard was fiddling with the light switch when Hunt entered. Hearing the door squeak open, the man spun around.

The Glock fired once, and the man slumped against the wall below the switch. "Tango down."

"Roger, Eagle One. The next obstacle is in the stairwell on the first floor."

"What about the elevator?" Hunt asked. "The guards still there or have they twigged?"

"Two guards outside where you get off."

"Roger that." Hunt said to Millie, "Follow me."

Taking their time they ascended the stairs, cautiously checking each landing before climbing again. Before they took the last flight Hunt waited.

Then Gillies said, "He's coming down toward you."

Seeing the target Hunt placed a round in his head, a spray of blood and brains painting the wall behind him. The man fell and tumbled forward on the stairs. Hunt stepped over his body and kept going. Millie did the same. Reaching the top floor where the other guards were supposed to be, Hunt stopped just before entering the hallway. "What do you see, Eagle Nest?"

"Still the same, One—wait." There was a pause and Gillies said, "They're coming your way, One."

Hunt lifted his NVGs. It wasn't as dark as he'd hoped. The top floor had large windows and although the power had been killed and the lights were out, the light from the moon was something they couldn't shut off, and it spilled through the wide entry to the stairwell.

With no door to open, the former SEAL peeked around the corner. He could see the men walking side by side. They were both armed with compact submachine guns. Hunt eased back and whispered, "You take the one on the left, I'll go right."

"Copy."

"Three...two...one...go..."

Stepping into the corridor together they opened fire. Due to skill and practice, Hunt fired first. His target dropped like a stone to the carpet in the hallway, and a second later his comrade fell too. Neither man moved.

"Two more tangos down," Hunt said.

Gillies said, "Just ahead of you on the right is the entrance. The master bedroom is at the back of the penthouse. There are two in the bed. I assume that it is his wife."

"Children?"

"No."

"Copy."

Hunt and Millie moved slowly toward the door. As they reached it, Hunt tried the handle. It was locked.

He said into his comms, "Eagle Nest, I need this door opened."

"My magic wand will have it open shortly. Sorry, but I can't access it without the power on. You will need to find another way," Gillies replied.

Millie looked back along the corridor to the bodies of the two guards and had a thought. Turning to Hunt, she suggested, "Maybe we should check those guys for a passkey."

Without wasting another second, Hunt headed back down the hallway to where the carpet was soaking up the blood of the two fallen guards. Rifling through the contents of their pockets, he was annoyed to find nothing of any help on the first one. The second, however, proved more successful, and he pulled the card and stood up, moving back toward Millie with purposeful strides.

The battery backup on the locking mechanism was working, and the light went green when Hunt slid the card into the slot. The lock clicked open and he pushed the handle down to open the door.

Inside the suite was in semi darkness. Like out in the hallway, the moonlight shone through the floor-to-ceiling windows. Using hand signals, Hunt directed Milly around the sofa while he moved behind it. They were only halfway across the living room when Gillies's voice came to them again. "Eagle, hold position."

Both froze. "What is happening?"

"Someone is moving from the bedroom. They're coming your way."

Once again using hand signals, Hunt directed Millie to the one side of the doorway. He took up position on the other. The door snicked open, and a figure came through. It was a woman in a sensible nightdress. The pair acted without thinking. Millie tapped her on the shoulder so that she turned hurriedly to look at her. The instant that she did, Hunt wrapped an arm around her throat, then one of his hands over her mouth. With a slow squeeze, he cut off the blood supply to her brain.

Moments later, the woman relaxed and went to sleep. Hunt lowered her body to the floor.

With the bedroom door now open, the sound of someone sleeping filtered out through the opening. Hunt held up a hand, telling Millie to stay where she was. He disappeared into the room, walking around the bed as quietly as he could. Park was sound asleep. The former SEAL raised his weapon, pointed it at the sleeping man's head and squeezed the trigger. Park never even knew what hit him.

"Time to go," Hunt said when he reemerged. "Eagle Nest, this is Eagle One. Target is down. Time to fly the coop."

"Roger. We'll have a plane waiting for you."

"Roger that. Thanks for your assistance."

––––––––

BUENOS AIRES

The apartment complex was like a landfill site inside walls. The décor was a mix of graffiti and holes. Both Kane and Knocker had their weapons out and started working their way through the building. They hadn't gone far when Knocker picked up the cuffs they'd been using to restrain Roman. "This guy is bloody Houdini."

"Head on a swivel."

"Roger that."

They started with the first room on the ground floor. Knocker kicked the door open, and Kane stepped through first. The inside was about as bad as the outer. A man sat on a stained sofa, a woman beside him. Kane pointed at him. "Stay there."

"What the fuck, man?" Sitter replied in heavily accented English.

"Just shut the fuck up and we'll be gone soon."

Knocker covered them while Kane checked the bedroom. There was nothing else. No bathroom, no kitchen. "He's not here."

Knocker touched the brim of the baseball cap he was wearing. "Adios, amigo."

"Fuck you," the man snarled and came off the sofa with a knife.

Before he could do anything, the barrel of Knocker's P320 was pressed against his forehead. "That was your first mistake, friend. Don't make another."

The Brit winked at him. Then hit him between the eyes with the butt of the weapon. The man dropped like a stone, blood flowing from his forehead. He turned to the woman. "Los Escorpiones?"

She shook her head vigorously. "No, no."

"Where?" Kane asked.

She pointed upward. Kane asked, "Upstairs?"

"Yes."

"Are they there now?"

"No. They all left."

Kane nodded. "We don't want to be here when they get back."

Leaving that room, they were about to kick down the door to another when a scream from elsewhere in the building sounded followed by a string of shouts. Knocker looked at Kane and said, "Upstairs."

Returning to the stairwell they began taking the stairs two at a time, reaching the second floor in seconds. The pitch and volume of the yelling woman had increased, and when they were almost halfway along a narrow walkway, they found the room from which the sound was emanating, the door standing open. Stepping cautiously through the doorway, Kane and Knocker saw Roman standing with his hands at shoulder height. Opposite him was a woman holding a revolver, and she looked like she was about to pull the trigger.

CHAPTER 11

ZURICH, SWITZERLAND

"Have you found any of them yet?" Sofia asked Mila impatiently.

"We have no satellite feed, and have lost contact with Los Escorpiones," Mila replied.

"How?"

"We're working on it."

"What about South Korea?"

"No, ma'am."

Sofia's face grew hard. "So what you're telling me is that we are blind."

Mila shook her head. "Not blind, ma'am. We are just having trouble locating them."

Suddenly lights went out and screens and computers went dark. Mila winced. "Now we're blind."

"What just happened?" Sofia demanded.

A few seconds later the emergency source cut in. The computers and screens came back online, and everything was once more operational. "All stations report," Mila said over her headset.

One by one they all called in. She looked at Sofia. "Everything seems okay for the—"

"The main power is back up," Lukas said. "It must have just been a surge."

"Find out if that is all it was," Sofia said. "Until it is explained, I don't like the unexplained."

———

ZURICH, SWITZERLAND

"Are you in?" Thurston asked Slick.

"Yes, boss, and they have no idea."

"So, now you can see what they're up to in real time?"

Slick nodded. "Yes, ma'am."

Thurston turned to Rani. "Right, we're good to go. Let's take this bitch and her operation out."

"Yes, ma'am."

"Are you good, Luis?"

Ferrero nodded. "Go and knock on her door, Mary. Hard."

Alighting from the rear of a refrigerated lorry, Thurston and Rani were embraced by the stygian darkness that blanketed the alley where the vehicle had parked. Standing outside all kitted up and awaiting the order to move, was Strike Team Panther. One of a dozen strike teams that Global had operating in different areas of the globe.

Thurston and Rani were similarly dressed and

armed like those that waited. Thurston said to the team leader, "Let's go and say hello."

"ROEs, boss?" asked the team leader, Ian Ketterson.

"Treat everyone as hostile," Thurston replied.

"Roger that."

Stepping from the cover of darkness the team moved methodically toward the main entrance. The front wall, including the doors, were all made of glass. They knew the doors would be locked so there was no point in trying them. Instead, Ketterson picked out a window and fired three rounds.

The window shattered and fell like confetti to the tiled floor. On the other side, two guards were standing at a security desk. Both were armed with MP5s. Ketterson handled the first guard, and Gregson, the man beside him, took out the second. One shot each was sufficient.

"Slick, we're in," Thurston said. "Where are we going?"

"Down, boss. You can take the stairs or the elevator."

"Do they know we're here yet?"

"No."

"Roger," she replied. "Ket, two teams. Elevator and stairs."

The big man nodded. "Greg, you and Fossil take the stairs. The rest of us will take the quick way."

Rani pressed the call button for the elevator. When it arrived, she, Thurston, Ketterson, and Jean-Jaque, the other shooter of Panther, climbed aboard. As the elevator went down, Ketterson pulled a flashbang and said, "Get behind us, ma'am."

"I can take care of myself, Ket," Thurston replied.

"We're the ones paid to take the risks, boss. Now do like I ask."

Both women stepped back. The elevator arrived and the Panther team leader threw the flashbang.

———

"Ma'am, something is wrong," Mila said to Sofia.

"What do you mean?"

"I think someone is in our system."

Sofia froze. How could that be? Her security was the best. It—the power outage. "Shut it down, now."

Mila turned. "Shut everything down. Hurry."

The elevator dinged signaling its arrival. Sofia turned and as the door opened, she saw two men, both armed. One of them threw something and then the world exploded.

When Ketterson and Jean-Jaque stepped out of the elevator car, one went left, the other right. They picked out the immediate threats, those being two security men in the back corners. A couple of shots and they were both down.

Thurston and Rani entered the ops room and Thurston saw one of the techs pull a handgun. She put two rounds in his chest and when he didn't go down, she put another into his head. Rani saw a woman lurch for a drawer and pull it open. A quick burst into her desk and she stopped and threw up her hands.

And that was it. With the brief skirmish over, the room was subdued. Standing at the rear of the room where she watched over everything like a lord and master was Sofia. "Zero, this is Bravo. Ops room is secure."

"Copy, Bravo."

Thurston walked up to Sofia. "Hello, Sofia. I'd ask you how your evening was going but I'm thinking badly."

"Who are you?" Sofia snarled.

"You can call me Mary," Thurston said with a grin. "Panther One, destroy everything. And have one of your people secure the package. She's coming with us back to England."

"Roger that, boss."

―――――

BUENOS AIRES

"Ma'am, put the gun away," Kane said in Spanish.

The woman looked at him and spat on the floor. There was a tattoo on her face. That of a scorpion. Knocker said, "I guess that means she's not going to."

"Ma'am, we'll just take him and be on our way."

She turned her gun on Kane. "You will go nowhere. You can wait until my man returns."

"Your man?" Knocker asked, understanding what she was saying. "Who is your man?"

"Angel Allegri," she replied. She made the name seem larger than life itself.

"Is he part of the Scorpions?" Kane asked.

"Yes, he is El Jefe."

Knocker glanced at Kane. "We can't wait."

Kane looked at Roman. "I ought to let her fucking shoot you."

"But you won't," he replied. "I'm too valuable."

Kane closed the distance between himself and the

woman. She turned the gun back on him. He was close enough that if she so chose, it would be against his chest. "Do you really want to shoot me, ma'am?"

"Take one more step, puta, and you will find out."

"Hey!" Knocker shouted, startling her.

The woman couldn't help herself and turned her head to look at the Brit. That gave Kane all the time he needed to move. With a yelp of fear, the woman suddenly realized she had been disarmed, and the big man was holding her gun. She took a step back and waited for him to shoot her. Instead, Knocker stepped behind her and put her in a sleeper hold.

"Don't fight it," he whispered in her ear as she struggled. "You'll wake up soon."

Knocker lowered her gently to the floor while Kane secured Roman. His cell buzzed and he looked at the screen. Then he looked at Roman again. "Because of you, we just missed our flight. Asshole."

"Sorry, I got tied up."

The cell buzzed once more. "The general has taken another chess piece off the board. Things might be a little easier on the Chrysalis front for a bit."

"Things are never easy," the Brit growled.

Kane looked at him. "The others have taken off. It's time for your 'I know a guy' speeches."

Knocker nodded then grinned. "Reaper, I know a guy."

"Why am I not surprised that he owns a nightclub?" Kane asked rhetorically.

Climbing from the stolen vehicle they had appropriated just after dark, the pair walked toward the door where a line of patrons was waiting to get in. They were stopped at the door by two gorillas wearing suits. Knocker said, "We're here to see Bennett."

The pair stared at him as though he was speaking Mandarin.

"Are you two scousers fucking deaf?"

Their blank looks continued. Knocker shook his head. Kane asked, "Is there a problem?"

"No problem," Knocker replied. Then he said, "Well, I might have pissed Bennett off the last time I was here."

"How?"

"I might have slept with his wife."

"Again, why am I not surprised?"

"It's okay, I can fix it." He looked up at the overhead camera then hit the doorman on the right.

The man sat down hard. Kane shook his head in exasperation. "You call that fixing it?"

"All under control, Reaper," he said as he hit the second guy. This one went down just as hard. "Glass jaws."

Customers began backing away from the violence, several men laughing at the ease with which the doormen had been dispatched. Kane looked around to see if there were any threats. As Knocker headed inside, he called back, "Come on. Last one to the bar buys the beers."

"Shit."

Within the club, everyone appeared oblivious to what had just gone down. Apart from one man. Kane, Knocker, and Roman found a table and sat down.

A waitress walked up to them and asked, "Drinks?"

Knocker nodded. "Two beers."

"What about me?" whined Roman.

"Shut up," Kane said. Then he noticed a pair of security guards heading for their table. "You know what? Forget about it."

The waitress shrugged and walked away. The two came to a stop in front of their table. "Come with us," one of them grunted.

"Ask nicely," Kane said.

One of the two pulled his jacket open to show the butt of a handgun. Knocker grinned at him and put his on the table. "We've got them too, mate."

Concern showed on both guards' faces now. Kane said, "Relax. All we want is to see your boss."

"Fine. Follow us."

All three rose from the table and followed the security men through the crowd, toward the back of the nightclub, and then along a narrow corridor to an office. The first guard opened the door and allowed them access to a lavishly furnished office. There was a middle-aged male with graying hair sitting behind a large desk. On its corner sat a young woman, short skirt, low-cut top showing ample cleavage.

Knocker walked over to the man and held out his hand. "Good to see you, Bennett."

Bennett was former British military. The man sprang from his seat and punched Knocker in the jaw. The Brit's head went sideways but he stayed on his feet. Knocker said, "Yeah, I guess I deserved that."

"Fucking oath you did. You screwing my wife cost me my fucking marriage."

"You were doing the same thing," Knocker pointed out.

"Not the point." Bennett looked at Kane and Roman. "Who is that?"

"The name is Kane," Kane replied. "This here is Roman."

"Why is he cuffed?"

"He's a terrorist."

"Well, what is he doing here, then?"

"We had some problems," Knocker said. "We need a way to Santiago. I remembered you had a helicopter."

"No, fuck off."

"I'll pay you twenty thousand," Kane said.

"Fifty," Bennett replied.

"Done."

"Shit, I could have got more."

"We have to leave now," Kane said.

"In the morning," Bennett said. "I'm busy tonight."

He glanced at the woman.

"You don't want us here that long, Bennett," Knocker said. "Trust me."

"I don't want you here at all," the nightclub owner replied. "Yet here we are."

There was a knock on the office door and a man peered in. "We have a problem out the front."

Bennett reached for a remote and flicked a television screen on. When the picture appeared, it was divided into six partitions. The camera out the front captured a gaggle of men, all were armed. Then some more appeared in the sixth picture. "I'm guessing that's the back," Kane said.

"Yes," Bennett said. He stared at them and asked, "Who the fuck did you piss off?"

"No one special," Knocker replied.

"No one special? I have men armed with submachine guns at my front and rear doors. Now, tell me who."

"Los Escorpiones," Kane replied.

"Ah shit," Bennett growled. "Hit the fire alarm. The last thing I want here is a bloodbath."

The shrill sound of the alarm began blaring throughout the club, and people were filing out the front door. Bennett reached for a button under his desk and pressed it. A partition in the wall slid open revealing weapons.

Disappointed that the secret door wasn't an escape tunnel and their way out of there, Knocker was pleased to see the next best thing.

Bennett looked at Kane and Knocker. "Your problem, you fix it."

Kane indicated to Roman. "What do we do about him while we're doing this?"

"I'll be right here, keeping an eye on your Persian friend."

Approaching the armory wall, Knocker grabbed an MP5 with a strap and some ammunition. He tossed Kane one and said, "I'll pick for you, Reaper."

Then they picked up a couple pump-action shotguns and loaded them.

Within moments the pair was ready to go. As they walked out the door, Bennett said, "Try not to shoot up my club too much."

No sooner had they stepped out into the hallway when the rear door opened and armed men swarmed into the hallway.

"Contact rear," Knocker snapped and opened fire with the shotgun.

It boomed like thunder and the two lead shooters

went down, their bodies shredded by the blast. Knocker jacked in another round and fired again. The backpedaling shooter who found himself in the lead took the full force in the chest. He was blown back into the wall where the hallway turned.

Moving quickly out to the main bar and dance floor, Kane and Knocker found it empty, all the customers and staff having fled. Those who had ignored the fire alarm certainly moved to vacate after hearing the roar of the shotgun.

"You go right, I'll take left," Kane said. "Watch our six."

"Roger that."

Taking cover behind the bar, Kane was closest to the entrance. Knocker found a booth fit for his needs. Suddenly a group of gang members appeared, one shouting, "Come out, motherfuckers. We are here for the money."

Kane rose from behind the bar and cut loose with his shotgun. He fired and jacked then fired again. Two men went down, including the man who'd announced his presence. Two others screamed with their wounds. Those behind them spread out and opened fire with submachine guns.

Lead projectiles came Kane's way, tearing into the bar and shelves behind it. Showered with glass and alcohol, he muttered a curse, but him drawing their fire gave Knocker a chance to clear his throat.

Leaning around the end of the booth, Knocker opened fire with his shotgun. Pump and fire until it was empty and gang members were down and screaming. One had most of his leg shot away. Knocker discarded the shotgun and went to work with the MP5, firing short bursts.

Meanwhile Kane had also discarded his shotgun. Coming up from behind the bar, he opened fire. He was just firing his second burst when he felt a hammer blow to his side. Dropping to the glass covered floor as pain ripped through his body, there was no doubt that he'd been shot. However, the round had to have come from the rear hallway. "Knocker, watch your six."

"Roger that."

Kane groaned as the pain continued to throb through his body. He checked for blood but found none. The Synoprathetic suit had done its job. "Just lucky I didn't get shot in the head," he muttered to himself.

"Reaper, are you okay?"

"Yeah, I'm fine."

"Did you take a round?"

"Something like that."

"See, I always said you weren't invincible."

"Just shut up and keep shooting."

For what seemed like hours, but was actually only a couple minutes, the two Team Reaper men worked methodically to suppress the attackers. Then suddenly, their assailants pulled back and disappeared. Kane stood up and said, "Let's collect Roman and get out of here before they come back."

Hurrying back to the office they found it empty. "Ah, bollocks," Knocker snarled. "That damned scouser has bloody scarpered. Shit, I should have twigged. He mentioned Roman as The Persian."

"He knew about the bounty," Kane said.

"Yeah."

Kane shook his head then froze. At first, he thought his ears were playing up on him from the gunfight, but no, he was still hearing it. A beeping sound. Knocker started to speak but Kane snapped at him, "Shut up."

"What's wrong?"

"Can you hear it?"

"Hear what?" Knocker asked.

"The beeping."

Knocker listened, frowned, then headed for the desk Bennett had been sitting behind. He leaned down and looked underneath. Fixed to the bottom of it was a block of explosives complete with timer which was counting down. Knocker shrugged. "That'll ruin your day."

"Bomb?" asked Kane.

"Yeah."

"How long?"

"Fuck all. Move."

Scrambling out of the office they sprinted along the hallway to the rear of the building. The back door was open and just as they rushed through it, the bomb detonated.

CHAPTER 12

BUENOS AIRES

Kane and Knocker picked themselves up from the hard asphalt in the alley and brushed themselves off. Their faces glowed in the orange firelight from the burning nightclub. "You all right, Reaper?"

"Yeah, you?"

"I'll live. Not that I can say the same for Bennett when I get my hands on that grubby bastard."

"Do you have any idea where he might have gone?"

"No bloody idea, but I know someone who might," Knocker said.

"Shit, not another one."

"She will help us."

Kane raised his eyebrows. "She?"

"Yes." He started walking along the alley. "Come on, before the police get here."

"I just know I'm going to regret this."

———

SANTIAGO, CHILE

Cara was far from happy when she turned to the others. "They've lost Roman again."

"Don't you mean still?" asked Burner.

"No, again. They had him and then lost him again."

"I dread to ask," Brick said slowly. "But I have a feeling that Knocker was somehow involved."

"Don't get me started."

After arriving in Santiago, they had been greeted by the news that Thurston and the others had taken a major piece off the board. The queen, to be accurate. Sofia Meier. She was the one with all the tech that was bringing the world down around their ears. Perhaps her removal would slow things down.

Cara considered their options, tossing up whether to head back to Buenos Aires.

"My opinion," said Brick, "unless Reaper asks for help, we should wait here."

"I never thought I'd hear that from you," Cara said.

"I'm all for going back, boss, but risking the rest of the team isn't something Kane would want. If he wants us, he'll say. Point in case was that he didn't ask for it just then."

Cara nodded. "I agree. I just needed to hear it from someone else."

"Don't second-guess yourself, boss. Since you took over from the general, you've been doing great."

"I lost a man," she pointed out.

"Nature of the beast."

"Then we wait."

"Yes, ma'am."

ZURICH, SWITZERLAND

Thurston and her team were just climbing onto one of Global's C-17s when Cara's call came through. Before answering, Thurston said to Ketterson, "Get her locked away in the pod."

The team leader nodded and guided Sofia toward the small cell at the front of the cargo bay. Thurston, meanwhile, took the call. "Cara."

"General."

"I didn't expect to hear from you this quick. I've only just hung up."

"I have news, Mary. Reaper and Knocker have lost the target again."

"What do you mean again?"

"They reeled him in and then someone decided they wanted him more than they did," Cara explained.

"What are they doing to get him back?"

"Whatever it takes. Reaper seems to think they have a lead."

"Are you going back to Buenos Aires?" Thurston asked.

"No. We'll wait on the ground here in Santiago."

"Wise choice. Thank you for letting me know. If there's anything you need..."

"Enjoy the flight home, General."

BUENOS AIRES

"Hello, Paloma," Knocker said with a grin when face-to-face with the woman who had opened the door to her apartment.

She took one look at the Brit, screwed up her face, and said, "Fuck you."

The door slammed shut.

Knocker looked at Kane. "For a woman whose name means peaceful like a dove, she sure comes across like a hawk."

"Are you sure this is a good idea?" Kane asked, looking around their surroundings.

"It's the only one we have." Knocker bashed on the door again. "Come on, Paloma, open up."

The door swung open, and a handgun was poked in his face. "Go away and leave me alone."

"Is that any way to greet an old friend?"

"No, I should shoot you."

Kane said, "Ma'am, we just need a little help, and then we'll be on our way."

Paloma's eyes narrowed. "Who are you?"

"John Kane, ma'am."

"Are you a friend of this animal?" she asked.

"Never seen him before in my life."

"Thanks, Reaper."

"What do you want to know?"

"It's about your husband—"

"Ex-husband." She all but spat the words from her mouth.

"Yes, ma'am. He took something of ours and we want it back."

"Are you going to kill him?" Paloma asked.

"We don't want to, but he tried to kill us."

She lowered the handgun and stepped aside. "Come in."

Knocker made to enter. Paloma shook her head. "Not you. You wait here."

The Brit shrugged. "Fine."

Kane looked at his friend, grinned, and walked inside. Meanwhile, Paloma glared at Knocker and slammed the door in his face.

The apartment's interior was clean and tidy. It was a big room with a separate bedroom, bathroom, and laundry. The first thing that caught Kane's attention was the uniform hanging from a cupboard door on a hanger. "You are Policía de la Ciudad de Buenos Aires?"

Paloma gave a half smile. "Your Spanish is very good."

"I've had practice."

"Just who are you?"

Kane noted that she still had the gun in her hand. "John Kane, like I said. Knocker and I work for a security firm called Global."

"Why are you in Buenos Aires?" she asked, going to the refrigerator. Paloma took out two beers and handed one to Kane. He took the top off and took a pull. It tasted good. "It's not American but it is all I have."

"Tastes fine," he replied. "As for what we're doing, our team was transporting a known terrorist, and we ran into some trouble."

The beer stopped just short of Poloma's full lips. "What terrorist?"

"A man named Roman. He's more known as The Persian."

Putting her beer on the counter, she reached for her cell. "Damn it, I have to call this in."

"I would prefer that you didn't, ma'am."

"I'm a police person. It is my duty to do so."

Paloma, we have people chasing us that we don't even know about. He has a fifty-million bounty on his head, and everyone wants it. Including your ex-husband."

He saw her eyes light up. "Paloma, I can pay you for helping us."

"How much?"

"Ten thousand dollars. It can be in your account within seconds." He was hoping that it would satisfy her.

"What do you want in return?"

"To find your ex-husband."

"Money first."

Kane made the call to Thurston who was on the plane. "Have you recaptured our terrorist yet, John?"

"Not yet, General. We're working on it. I need a money transfer."

"How much?"

"Ten."

"Number?"

Kane looked at Paloma. "Account number?"

She told him and he repeated it to Thurston. "It will be there directly."

"Thanks, General."

"Find this prick, Reaper."

The call disconnected and Kane turned to Paloma. Her cell dinged and she looked at the screen. "Where would he go?"

She paused then said, "There is an old mansion on

the outskirts of the city. It is rundown and overgrown. We had big plans of renovating it but that never happened. If he wants to lay low, that's where he'll be."

Kane handed over his cell. "Address."

She typed it in and said, "He won't be alone."

"I wouldn't expect him to be. Thanks for your help."

Knocker was outside waiting. He looked at Kane after the door closed. "Well?"

"She gave me an address."

"That was easy."

"If you say so," Kane said.

"Why?"

"Cost ten grand."

"Why that much?" Knocker asked.

"Because I fucked up and mentioned the fifty million."

"You bloody pillock." He stared at Kane in disbelief. "That silly cow is going to call for help and go after Roman herself."

"No, she won't," Kane said unconvincingly.

"Don't you bloody bet on it, mate. That cow is a woman to be reckoned with. Trust me, I know."

"Then we'd better get there and find Roman before she does."

"Just knock on the door and shoot her," the Brit said.

"No."

"Fine, I will." Knocker stepped toward the door but Kane grabbed his arm.

"No, we're leaving."

"Reaper, if you don't put her to sleep, you're going to regret it."

"I already do. Come on."

As Knocker followed him, he heard the man say, "Don't say I didn't warn you."

"I won't."

"Fine, let's grab something to eat on the way. I'm bloody starving."

———

WHAT WAS INTENDED as a brief food and bathroom break morphed into something entirely different. As Kane was driving their appropriated vehicle down a quiet stretch of road, Knocker pointed out a neon sign advertising a pizza restaurant. Pulling into the lot, Kane parked, and the pair went inside.

Knocker said, "We were being followed."

Kane nodded. "We were."

"What do you figure?"

"Paloma?"

"Could have been her people. What do you want to do, Reaper?"

"Grab a pizza, use the facilities, and make them come to us."

"Roger that."

After placing their order, Kane went to use the restroom, leaving Knocker to keep watch and find them a vacant table. When he returned, Knocker rose and walked to the bathroom. Ten minutes later their pizzas were delivered by a young woman dressed in black and wearing an apron. The food was good and they were halfway through it, discussing the possibility that they'd been mistaken about the tail, or maybe their shadow was waiting for them in the parking lot, when the four men entered.

It took only a few moments to ascertain they were armed. Kane shook his head. "Leave your weapon in," he said to Knocker. "Too crowded in here for a gunfight."

"Fists?"

"Yeah."

"Great, I haven't had a lot of fun since we left—let me think—yeah, the nightclub."

The four approached their table and stood around them. Their leader, a young man with a mustache, said, "Get up and come with us."

"Why?" Kane asked, chewing a mouthful of pepperoni and cheese.

"Because I said so."

While deciding not to use their own weapons, Kane had taken a knife from the table and placed it in his lap. He had no intention of going with them, so he did what he had to do: stabbed the leader with it.

The knife swept around and buried deep into the man's thick thigh. The man staggered and screamed in pain. Knocker meantime had flicked the remains of his pizza up into the face of the man closest to him.

Kane and Knocker exploded from their seats before the other two could react. Kane hit the second man in the throat while Knocker stepped in close to pizza face and headbutted him across the bridge of the nose. The man dropped to the floor like a stone, blood running from his shattered nose.

Diners shrieked at the sudden violence as they scattered, cutlery and drinks going in every direction.

The Brit swung toward the next man. As he turned,

he grabbed a plate from the table and brought it crashing down. It shattered over the man's head causing him to stagger. Knocker moved in closer and brought his elbow around hard.

Connecting with the man's jaw, the Brit felt it give under the force. Eyes rolled back into his head and the man dropped to the floor unconscious.

Meanwhile, Kane had gone after his second target. With two hard punches, the man staggered back into a chair vacated by one of the other diners. Kane grabbed the man by the shirt and dragged him forward and hit him again. This time the lights went out.

Then from near the door came a fifth man. This one brought up a handgun and began firing. But into the ceiling to trying to scatter the few patrons who remained. Kane and Knocker ducked low and moved with the last handful of people. Knocker said, "This guy obviously didn't get the memo."

"Which one?"

"The one about no gunfighting in crowded places."

"Do you want to tell him?"

More bullets came their way. "No, fuck that."

They managed to make it outside, but the shooter was close behind. He appeared in the doorway and the diners ran off in panic, leaving the two men exposed. Gunfire erupted once more and Knocker staggered and fell. "Fuck...shit," the Brit gasped as he fell to the sidewalk.

Kane, on the other hand, twisted, rolled, and drew the P320 from his belt. The shooter came into view, and Kane opened fire, three rounds. All hit the man in the chest.

Kane lay there for a moment, in a half sitting position. Beside him, Knocker groaned.

"Are you okay, Raymond?"

"Don't fucking call me Raymond, asshole."

Yeah, he was fine. Kane got to his feet and dragged the Brit upright. Then he went over and checked the dead man. Rifling through the man's pockets, he emptied them out. The biggest thing he found appeared somewhat like a wallet, but Kane knew it wasn't. He flicked it open, and his suspicions were confirmed. Tossing it to Knocker, he said, "Here. Take a look."

Knocker caught it and screwed his face up when he saw what it was. "Ah, bollocks. The guy was a bloody cop?"

"That's what it says."

"Shit. That bitch. One guess where she is at this moment."

"Come on, let's move."

CHAPTER 13

BUENOS AIRES

When they arrived at the rundown estate outside of Buenos Aires, it was after midnight and all quiet. Too quiet. There were lights on inside the house but a total absence of movement. Kane and Knocker crouched in the darkness and watched.

"It's too quiet, Reaper," Knocker said.

"Yeah. Let's go and have a look. Keep your head on a swivel."

Coming out of their crouch they emerged from the shadows and into the moonlight. Their steps were deliberate, their movements furtive from cover to cover. The once grand gardens were now overgrown and full of weeds. When they reached the pool area they found their first body. The man lay in the bottom of it next to a puddle of stagnant water.

Using hand signals, Kane directed Knocker to the side door. It was a large sliding door, its glass now in a scattered pile on the floor and outside like confetti at a wedding. The glass crunched under their boots as they walked over it.

Moving inside, they found another body on the kitchen floor. Kane checked him and found a wallet with a police badge inside. When they entered the living room, it was apparent the area had been through a serious shootout. Bullet holes in the ceiling and walls had brought decaying plaster down on the boarded floor. There were three bodies covered in the fine dust that came with the wrecked plaster.

Hearing a low moan emanating from behind an old sofa, they went to investigate, keeping their weapons trained on a possible threat, but found Paloma. She'd been shot twice and was lying in a pool of blood. It was evident that she was dying.

"You look like shit," Knocker said, crouching beside her.

Paloma coughed and moaned again. Then she said, "Screw you."

"You already did that," he replied. "Was this Bennett?"

"Yes."

"Has he gone?"

"Y—yes."

"We'll get you some help," Kane said.

"No. I—I'm done. My own fault."

"Do you know where he's gone, Paloma?"

"W—Wakefall."

"What?" Knocker asked. "What is Wakefall?"

Her eyes drifted to the Brit, she opened her mouth to speak, and then she died. Knocker looked up at Kane. "What the hell is Wakefall?"

"Beats me."

Kane reached for his cell. Slick immediately answered the call. "Hey, Reaper, what's cooking?"

"I need you to find me anything referencing the name Wakefall."

"Anything special about it?"

"I have no idea."

"Leave it with me."

"Roger that." Kane disconnected and looked at Knocker. "Let's move out."

It took three days to nail down what they were looking for.

———

SAINT PETERSBURG, RUSSIA

During that time, Hunt arrived in Saint Petersburg thanks to the CIA. Picked up from the airport, he was taken to a hotel where the officer advised him that someone would be along later with a handgun and intel. At first, he thought nothing of the fact that he'd been put up in a hotel instead of a safehouse, and when he did think about it, he brushed it off.

Not for a second did he consider that he was about to be betrayed. Not when the queen had been taken off the board.

Millie had been returned safely to London the same day Hunt had left for Berlin. From Berlin he'd flown to Saint Petersburg. Now here he was in a two thousand dollars-a-night hotel with two bedrooms and a large bathroom.

Glancing at his watch, Hunt was surprised that his contact hadn't made an appearance yet. Surely someone should have been there by now. The cell he'd been provided buzzed. Looking down at the screen he saw that there had been a change of plans. He was now to meet the CIA man at a nearby park. The location was in the text.

Again, nothing to indicate any trouble.

Leaving the room, Hunt went down in the elevator to the hotel lobby then walked out through the main doors. Turning left, he walked for two blocks. The sun was going down and the air was cooling even more. There was snow on the ground, but the day overall had been pleasant. Hunt stopped at the curb and looked both ways. He waited for a Lada to roar past and then crossed to the other sidewalk.

On this stretch were a laundromat and a couple of cafés. He continued walking and turned right at the next corner. About five hundred meters further along was the park. It was covered with snow which glowed orange under the strategically placed lights. The entrance was a large arch that you had to walk beneath to stay on the path.

Hunt passed through and walked another hundred meters until he was at the center of the park. Marking the spot was a marble fountain, the water within it frozen over by a thin layer of ice.

Under a light there was a park bench. On that bench was a man with a heavy coat wrapped around him and a hat covering his hair. Hunt sat down beside him. "Cold, isn't it."

"Only if you are out," the man replied.

However, it was immediately apparent that the accent wasn't American. It was Russian. Hunt's blood ran as cold as the night air. Suddenly out of the darkness came six armed men. Hunt shook his head and raised his hands. "Shit."

The man beside him stood up and faced him. "Welcome to Saint Petersburg, Mr. Hunt."

The former SEAL wasn't even going to dignify the greeting with an answer. It made it sound like he was in a Mission Impossible movie. The man spoke again. "My name is Viktor Petrov. I believe you are here to kill me."

———

HEREFORD, ENGLAND

"Hunt has disappeared," Rani said to Thurston. "I just got a call from the CIA asking if we'd heard from him?"

"Have we?" Thurston asked.

"No, ma'am. They say that one of their people was meant to meet him in his room and when they got there he was gone."

Thurston nodded slowly. "Do they have any idea what happened to him?"

"No, ma'am. They're looking into it."

The former general picked up her cell. After hitting speed dial five she said, "My office, now."

A couple of minutes later, Slick entered. "You called?"

"Borden Hunt has disappeared in Saint Petersburg. I need you to see if you can locate him."

"Yes, ma'am, I'll get right onto it."

"Have you made any progress on that other matter?"

Slick nodded. "The *Wakefall* is a decommissioned

freighter that was scrapped. I'm just trying to locate where that happened."

"Once you do, get it to Reaper."

"Yes, ma'am."

"That will be all."

After he'd take his leave, Thurston turned to Rani. "Put your people on standby. If need be, I want them wheels up at a moment's notice."

Rani nodded. "Boss."

"Oh, and have Ketterson and Panther put on standby too. They can fly with you."

"Where is it we're going, boss?"

Thurston's face took on a grim expression. "I have no idea."

———

BUENOS AIRES

MI6 picked up Kane and Jensen and gave them a place to hide. It was a safehouse outside of the city on a large estate. Surrounded by lush greenery, the building had a terracotta roof. Large, fluted columns along the front reflected off the nearby pond. One way of describing it was "a grand old lady of architecture."

It was on the second day that Slick called. He informed them, "*Wakefall* was—is—an old freighter that was decommissioned a few years ago. Although intended for scrap, the vessel was bought by a business called Lancashire Holdings."

"Damn Bennett," Knocker said. "He was born in Lancashire."

"So, it was never scrapped and never reregistered."

"Where is it now?" Kane asked.

"Drifting off the coast of Brazil."

"Drifting?" Knocker asked.

"Yes. Put it this way, it's not under steam."

"Are you saying that it is a ghost ship?" Kane asked.

"It would appear that way," Slick replied.

"Keep tracking it, Slick. We need to get aboard that ship."

"Roger that."

"Hey, is the boss there?"

"No, but I can put you through to her."

"Do it."

Moments later, Thurston came on the line. "What can I do for you, Reaper?"

"I need transport to put us on board that ship," he replied.

"I'll see what I can do. I'll talk to the head of MI6."

"Copy that."

"There is something else you should know, Reaper," Thurston said grimly. "Borden Hunt disappeared in Russia."

"Shit. How?"

"We're trying to work it out. So far, we have shit."

"Do you think Russian FSB has him?"

"It's possible, but right now, we just don't know. Slick is on it."

"Roger that."

"I'll see what I can do about getting you on that ship," Thurston said. "Do you want backup?"

"Negative. If it's a ghost ship like Slick says, there will be no one there. But we might just find something to point us in the right direction. Can you have Bravo fly into Santiago?"

"I'll have them leave straight away. They are on standby."

"Roger that."

"Reaper, watch your back."

———

MV WAKEFALL, OFF BRAZIL

TWO DAYS LATER

"Reaper One, we'll have thirty mics on station before we need to leave. After that, you're on your own," the helicopter pilot said over the radio.

"Roger that," Kane replied. "We'll be back in twenty-nine."

The two men fast-roped down onto the deck and waited for the helicopter to pull away before moving. Both Kane and Knocker were armed with H&K 433s and were once again in full tactical gear. With one exception. Both wore General Service Respirators, or GSRs just in case there was a gas or biological threat.

The first body they came across put paid to that theory. The victim had been shot three times, the final one in the head. Kane and Knocker took off their masks. "Zero, copy?"

"Read you, Lima Charlie, Reaper One," Ferrero replied. Bravo were back aboard their C-17 and not far out of Santiago. They were also monitoring the operation. "Send traffic."

"It looks like there was some kind of firefight aboard the freighter. I'll send photos for analysis as I get them."

"Roger that."

Kane took a photo of the dead man while Knocker covered him. Once he he'd sent it off, he said, "Let's head up to the bridge."

Hurrying across the rusted hulk's deck the pair climbed the interior ladder to the bridge. They found three more bodies there. One of them was Bennett. It looked as though he'd been executed. Kane took more photos and sent them through. Then he heard Knocker say, "Well, well, what do we have here?"

When Kane turned, Knocker was in a crouch picking something up off the deck. He stood up and held up a bullet casing. "Ever seen one of these before, Reaper?"

Kane took it for closer examination. He held it high and turned it in his fingers. "It has something engraved on it."

"It looks like a wolf's head," Knocker said. "But it's a skull only."

"You're right." Kane took a photo and sent it through. "Bravo Three, copy?"

"Copy, Reaper One," Slick replied.

"I just sent you through a photo of a bullet casing. See what you can make of it."

"It just landed. Give me a few minutes and I'll have something for you."

Kane said to Knocker, "We'll split up. Whoever did this is long gone. We'll have a quick scout to see if we can find anything else."

"Roger that."

Ten minutes later the pilot of the helicopter called in. "Reaper One, Swordfish. This is your first and final warning. We're about bingo on fuel."

"Roger. Come in and land on the deck. We'll be there soon."

"Copy, Swordfish is inbound."

After touching down minutes later, the helicopter waited on deck as Kane and Knocker took more photos of the dead then climbed aboard. Just as the helicopter lifted off, Slick came back on the line. "Reaper, I tracked down the owner of your casing."

Kane could tell the uncertainty in his voice. "Why am I not going to like it?"

"There is only one organization across the globe that marks its rounds like that. It is one of their trademarks so that others know who was responsible."

"Name, Slick."

"Leonel Serrano's Los Lobos Cartel," he replied.

Kane looked over at Knocker. "Bollocks."

SANTIAGO, CHILE

Twenty-four hours later the gang was reunited, including Burner, Shorty, and Jorgensen from Six. They had gathered in an aviation hangar where Slick was briefing them on what he'd discovered.

"Let's get to the interesting part first," he said. "The casing that was found on the ship was traced back to the Los Lobos Cartel. A savage, savage group if there was one. Although not as notorious as some of the others, they are growing in reputation and doing everything they can to make the name even more renowned."

"They sound nasty," Burner said.

"They are. Their trademark signature is to cut a

person's guts open and then have them try to outrun the dogs they send after them. That along with public executions, car bombings, and a whole lot of other shit that gets things done."

"Why hasn't someone had a go at them yet?" Knocker asked.

"Anyone who tries winds up dead."

"And these guys have Roman?" Kane asked.

"It looks that way."

"Apart from the money, why would they take him?" Kagiso asked.

Ferrero said, "You have the world's most wanted terrorist in company with one of the world's most dangerous cartels. It doesn't take much to do the math on that one."

"Possible targets?" Brick asked.

"Any one of a dozen," Slick said.

"So let's not allow it to get that far," Ferrero said.

"What's the plan?" Kane asked.

A picture flashed up on the screen they were using. "If anyone knows what is happening, it will be this guy. Estaban Cruz. The man is a fixer for the cartel."

"Why do they need a fixer if they don't care?" asked Burner.

"This guy is a money laundering specialist," Slick said. "He moves cartel profits around through crypto and offshore accounts. Even luxury goods. He also set up a charity in Europe to run money through."

"Where is he?" Kane asked.

"Ciudad del Este."

"Great," Knocker growled. "Right in the middle of hell's bastard cousin."

"Where's that?" Burner asked.

Knocker stared at her, an incredulous look on his face. "Well, dear Rosie, Ciudad del Este is virtually on the doorstep of the Triple Frontier."

"Don't fucking call me Rosie, Raymond," Burner growled.

He grinned at her. "I can see we're going to get along just fine."

Burner frowned. "What do you mean?"

Cara said, "We have an opening on the team. The position is yours if you want it?"

She glanced at Kane and then Shorty. "What about him?"

Cara shook her head. "Only one vacancy and Reaper suggested you could fill it."

"I—I don't—"

"Just do it, Burner," Shorty said. "It'll pay more money than the shit we get now."

She thought a little more and then said, "Okay, I'm in."

"Good. We'll get you set up with kit before jumping off."

"Jumping to where, boss?" Knocker asked.

"Why, into Ciudad del Este, of course."

"Of course," Knocker said. "Why didn't I think of that?"

"We'll set up base in a hangar at the airport," Cara said. "There are only a select few that know we're coming. We're going to fly in on a Chilean C-130 so as not to raise suspicions. And a C-17 will certainly do that. Once we are settled, Knocker and Burner will do a recon of the estate where Cruz is located. Reaper will stay here with Brick and Kagiso and go over all the intel we have. Questions?"

"Any news on Hunt?" Kane asked.

"Nothing." Cara stared at Kane waiting for a follow-up question. When one wasn't forthcoming, she said, "Right, wheels up in three hours. Oh, I almost forgot. Jorgensen and Shorty will be leaving us today. That's all."

Burner sought out Kane after the briefing. "I don't know what to say."

"Don't say anything," Kane replied. "Just take the opportunity by the throat and choke the shit out of it."

"I won't let you down."

"I know. Now go and see Knocker. He'll get you set up."

"Yes, sir."

"I'm not sir. Reaper or Kane will be fine."

"Okay."

"One other thing. Everyone has an opinion. We encourage that. But when told to do something, you do it."

"Roger that," Burner replied then turned and walked off in search of Knocker.

"I hope you're making the right choice with her," Cara said.

"I have a feeling she'll be fine."

"I hope so. Just remember she's never seen the action we have, Reaper. She'll need to adjust and do it quickly. If she can't, she'll be RTB."

"There is no RTB, Cara," Kane replied.

"Then she will probably die. Just like Lofty."

Kane stared at her. "You know better than that," he said to her.

"What?"

"Lofty wasn't your fault. It could have happened to any one of us."

Cara's expression grew irritated. "Yes, but it happened on my watch."

"You'll lose more than just Lofty by the time we're finished," Kane said.

"Damn it. You need to find someone to take over the toys."

The remote-controlled weapons they took onto the battlefield with them were what they referred to as toys, such as the Taipan and the Rhino.

"Burner can do it once she's up to speed."

"Make sure she's ready to go. Until then, if you and your team have to go into the Tri-Border Area, one of the others will have to operate them."

"Roger that."

Kane found Knocker and Burner inside the C-17 getting her fully kitted. "How's it going?"

"Just about done."

"Good. Once you're finished, get Slick to set her up on a tablet where she can learn to fly the Taipan and Rhino."

Knocker frowned. "You sure?"

"Someone has to."

"That means she'll have to pack it in wherever we are," Knocker pointed out. "Lofty used to pack the ammunition too."

"Divide the ammo up among the rest of us."

"I'm stronger than I look," Burner pointed out.

Kane glanced over at Shorty. "Fuck it. Hey, Shorty, over here?"

The big guy, all six-and-a-half feet of him, sauntered over. "Yeah?"

"What is your name?" Kane asked.

"Shorty."

"Your real name."

"Byron Aloysius Jones," he replied.

"Stuff me," Knocker moaned.

Kane nodded. "Well, Jonesy, you are now known as Reaper Six. You will hump our special weapons and carry an M249. Are you in or out?"

The big guy grinned. "I'm in."

"Great. And no more Shorty horseshit. That name really sucks."

"Roger that."

"Now all I have to do is square it away with the boss. Knocker, get him kitted up too."

"Damn it," Knocker growled. "This team is becoming overrun with bloody Americans. Come on, Stretch, let's get you kitted out. Although, I don't know if we'll find a Synoprathetic suit that'll fit the Eifel Tower."

——————

SAINT PETERSBURG, RUSSIA

Hunt's body ached. For the first couple of days, he'd been left alone but on the third they had come for him. Taken to a special room, he'd been hung from a hook by chains they'd fixed to him. Then they had beaten him. Not too much, just enough. They wanted to keep him alive. Petrov was vindictive like that. However, Hunt still needed to give them a reason to keep him alive, so he gave them crumbs in the hope that Kane and the others would come for him soon.

Petrov entered the dungeon beneath the Velikaya Zvezda Palace. Everyone knew about the six other palaces in Saint Petersburg, but no one talked about the seventh because of its dark history. Back in the day it had been owned by Count Mikhail Voronetsky. In the early 1800s, the locals had called it the Torture Chamber. The count used to pick up prostitutes from the street and take them back to his palace where he would utilize their services, then satiate his other passion. He would torture them until they died.

Now it was being used again.

Petrov entered and walked around the hanging Hunt. He smiled caustically at him and asked, "How has your day been?"

Hunt just stared at him.

Petrov indicated his suit. "As you can see, I'm dining out tonight before going to the theater."

"Good for you," Hunt rasped.

"I can do that now, move about at will. Seeing as you are locked away."

The former SEAL didn't respond.

"Have you thought any more about our last conversation?"

Nothing.

"It seems your friends have taken a friend of ours. Sofia Meier. I'm guessing she was on your list? Hmm?"

"What list?" Hunt responded.

"Still denying it. Oh, well, I've come up with a plan. I have decided to ask for a trade. You for her and Roman. As much as I dislike Sofia, she is good at what she does."

"I'm happy for you."

"So, you see, your friends have a chance to keep you alive. It is up to them."

Hunt asked, "Does that mean I can stop hanging around?"

"Not just yet."

"Worth a try, I guess. Enjoy your evening."

"You too," Petrov replied and nodded to the two men with him.

Then the beating started again.

CHAPTER 14

CIUDAD DEL ESTE

"Crime asshole of the world," Knocker growled as they drove through the streets.

"You don't know that," Burner replied. "I think it's not too bad."

"If you like smuggling, organized crime, and armed robberies. Did you know that in 2017 a commando team stole $11 million using explosives and speedboats. Don't forget the street level gangs."

"What about the good stuff?"

"Show me where it is and I'll look at it."

"You sound like you've been here before," Burner said.

"Ten years ago, I was here with a black SAS team. We were looking for two kidnapped civvies. We tracked them down after a week. The girl was in a brothel run by the cartel. The guy turned up as a headless corpse hanging from a bridge along with three others."

"What happened to the girl?" Burner asked.

"They drugged her so she wouldn't struggle each time she was with a guy. When she returned to England, they cleaned her up and she went back to work. That same day she threw herself in front of a Tube Train."

"How did you get her out?"

"Hot extract," Knocker replied. "Our team consisted of five. We raided the brothel and had a plane on the runway waiting. We left a trail of bodies a blind man could follow."

"Aren't you worried someone will recognize you?"

"No. We all wore masks."

"All that just for her to take her own life," Burner said morosely.

"And I'd do it all over again," Knocker replied.

They continued driving until they crossed a river and were virtually in the jungle. Pulling off the road Knocker parked out of sight. The pair climbed from the vehicle and grabbed their weapons. Both had suppressed HK 433s. A few moments later they disappeared into the undergrowth.

It took them twenty minutes of swift travel to reach their layup position from which to observe the estate. Taking out his binoculars, Knocker lay down and began scanning the area. Beside him, Burner attempted to sketch out a map. "I draw like shit," she commented.

"Doesn't have to be an oil painting," Knocker replied. "Now, we've got two guards walking the perimeter."

"Roger that."

"Exterior surveillance cameras, motion sensors, razor wire atop the fence."

"Got it."

"Bollocks," Knocker grumbled. "The fence is electrified."

"Is it going to be an issue?"

"Shouldn't be. Just makes it a pain in the ass." He kept scanning. "I see four more guards. I'm just glad there are no dogs."

"Six guards aren't too bad," Burner said.

"We can double that for the ones we don't see," Knocker replied.

"Oh."

"Don't worry, Rosie, you'll learn. You can't just pick it up overnight. Me and Reaper have been doing this for years. So have most of the others."

"Don't—"

"Call me Rosie. I know."

They continued watching until it was almost dark and then they pulled back to the SUV. As they climbed in, Burner put her weapon in the back. Knocker said, "Hang on to your handgun."

"Why?"

"You'll see."

After the sun went down, the city seemed to transform. It went from a seemingly humming mecca to a den of iniquity. Prostitutes came out and stood corners, drug dealers stood alongside them, gangsters roamed in packs, and every now and then there could be a gunshot heard.

Then they pulled up at some traffic lights.

Knocker said, "Get ready."

"What for?" Burner asked.

Knocker pointed at the darkness on one of the corners. Five people emerged. They walked—no strutted—toward the SUV. Three stopped in front of the SUV while the other two separated, approaching either side.

The guy on Knocker's side tapped on the window. Winding it down, Knocker said, "Nice night."

"English?" the young man asked.

"Yes."

The gangster looked over at his friend and said in Spanish, "A limp-dick Englishman."

The man laughed and said, "We should feed his to him then take the woman and fuck her."

The leader grinned at Knocker who returned it as though he didn't understand. "Where are you going, English?"

"Back to our hotel."

He asked in Spanish, "Are you going to fuck the woman?"

"What?" Knocker asked, keeping his cool, the P320 in his grip out of sight. He'd understood every word.

"I said is it a nice hotel?"

"It's okay?"

The lights changed. No one moved.

The man leaned down and stared at Burner. "How are you, señorita?"

"Fine, fine."

He switched back to Spanish. "How about you come with me, and you can suck my cock."

Knocker smiled. "She wouldn't be able to find it, Mini Dick."

Suddenly the gangster realized that Knocker could understand him. He reached for a weapon in his belt, but the Brit was ready, forcing the door open as hard as he could. The gangster stumbled backward giving

Knocker all the time he needed. He lined up the P320 and shot the man in the leg.

The gangster cried out in pain and collapsed onto the street. Knocker pointed the gun at his head and looked at his friends who were standing in stunned silence.

Meanwhile, Burner had come out of the passenger seat and had her own weapon jammed into the crotch of the young guy on her side. "Move, motherfucker, and you'll be a fucking gelding before midnight."

Knocker leaned down to the writhing man and grabbed him by his greasy hair. "Listen up and listen good. You are very lucky I didn't put a bullet in your fucking head. Next time, you might not be so lucky."

He pressed the barrel of his weapon to the gangster's forehead. "Maybe I should just do it anyway."

"No, no."

Knocker eased his pressure. "I see you again. I'll kill you. Burner, back in the SUV."

They climbed back in and drove away.

———

"Before we go in, we need to know he's there," Kane said the following morning.

He looked at Slick. But it was Rani who said, "I'll set you up with a Hornet."

She meant the Black Hornet Nano drone. Kane nodded. "Slick, you'll need to kill the power which should disablethe motion sensors and the electric fence. We'll just need to cut our way through."

"Insert team?" Cara asked.

"Knocker, Kagiso, and me. Brick, Burner, and

Jonesy will be QRF if we need it." He turned to Brick. "Overwatch with the Hornet as well as recon."

Brick nodded. "Roger that."

"We get in, get the intel, and get out. We'll be wearing masks as well. Just in case. Any questions?"

"What happens if it all goes to shit?" Burner asked.

Kane nodded. "Knocker."

"Well, Reaper Five, we fight like hell and drag our asses out of there. Things turning to shit is what we're used to."

"Amen to that," Cara muttered. "Check your gear and make sure everything is in order. Burner, Jones, write yourselves a death letter and give it to Luis."

"A death letter?" Burner queried.

"That's right," said Ferrero. "We need something to send to your family back home. We all have one."

"Even Knocker?"

Knocker slapped Burner on the shoulder. "Especially me. Mine will make someone especially happy."

Burner frowned. "Who?"

"Ex-wife number two," Brick said.

"Shit."

———

KANE, Knocker, and Kagiso crept up to the fence. The location had been selected because the blind spot created by cover from trees and the garden. Kane said in a low voice, "Kill it, Slick."

Everything went dark.

"Knocker, the fence. Kagiso, rear security."

Knocker began cutting his way in, while Kagiso

turned away and stared into the darkness. Kane said, "Brick, how are we looking?"

"The guards are scratching their heads wondering what's happening. Looks like they just switched on their flashlights."

"Roger that."

"Reaper, we're through," Knocker informed him.

"Let's go."

Kane went first. He crawled through the opening, his NVGs pulled down. He slipped into the brush of the garden and paused before coming out the other side. Scanning his surroundings, he saw two guards.

Dropping his laser sights on the left guard, he waited as Knocker came in beside him and took the guy on the right. Kane whispered, "Do it."

Both men fired and the two guards dropped to the damp grass. They moved forward and checked to make sure both were dead. Kagiso brought up the rear.

"Reaper, you've got another headed your way at your three."

Kagiso turned and when the guard appeared she fired and brought him down. They pushed on, taking down each target that presented itself. By the time they reached the house, all six of the patrolling cartel soldiers were down.

Crossing the paved area at the rear of the residence, Kane sidled up to the back door and said, "We're breaching."

"Hold, Reaper." This time it was Slick who spoke.

"What's up?"

"There are six SUVs inbound along the road where you are."

"Is this their target, Slick?" Kane asked.

"It's the only one around."

"Shit. Brick, standby. Have Jonesy prepare the Taipan. Things are about to go south."

"Roger that."

"Reaper One, this is Zero," Ferrero said.

"Go, Zero."

"It might pay to get out. Your call."

"Copy, Zero. We need the intel. We're Charlie Mike."

"Continuing mission, roger. Out."

Kane looked at Knocker and Kagiso. "Change of plan. We grab Cruz and get out. We take him back to base."

"Roger that."

Entering the house, they headed along a hallway for the internal stairs. They had just started up when Slick said, "Reaper One, the convoy just crashed the main gate."

"Brick, can you fly the Taipan?" Kane asked.

"I had some training—"

"Good, you'll do."

"But I crashed it every time."

"Good, at least you know what not to do."

Meanwhile, Knocker had pushed ahead, followed by Kagiso. There were shouts from outside along with the sound of gunfire. The door at the end of the hallway was thrown open and a man stood there in his underwear. Knocker said, "Target acquired."

Then the hallway was filled with voices ordering Cruz to get on the ground. He held up his hands. "Don't shoot!"

"Get on the floor," Kagiso snarled.

Cruz got to his knees before Knocker stepped in

behind him and forced him down. Then his hands were secured behind his back.

Kane said, "Kagiso, go to the window in the main room and look out."

"Roger."

"Who are you?" Cruz asked.

"Shut up, asshole," Knocker said harshly.

Kane asked, "Brick, how's things going?"

"We're just about ready," the former SEAL replied.

"Slick, talk to me."

"Reaper, the new arrivals blew through the front gate and have cleaned up all the threats that remained in the guardhouse. They're coming in."

"How many?"

"Estimate fifteen tangos."

"Roger that."

Knocker brushed past Kane and headed for the top of the stairs. He could hear them coming. A voice said, "He'll be upstairs in his room."

The voices were distinctly American. Knocker took out his grenade—replaced after last time—and pulled the pin. He paused then rolled it down the stairs and ran.

The explosion rocked the house. Over his comms, he said, "Slick, these guys are Americans."

"I'll see if I can identify them."

Reaching Kane's position, he said, "Did you hear?"

"Yes."

Kagiso appeared. "We can go out the bedroom window."

Kane nodded. Knocker said, "You go, I'll keep them off you. Then I'll follow."

"Don't get yourself dead, Compadre."

"Not tonight."

Kane dragged Cruz to his feet and shoved him toward the bedroom. Knocker followed and took cover behind the doorjamb.

Kane said, "Kagiso, you go first, secure the ground and then I'll send Cruz down."

As they went out onto the balcony they were driven back by gunfire. Kagiso returned fire at the shooter taking cover behind the engine block of the lead SUV. Bullets bounced off the armored vehicle. A second shooter appeared. Now Kagiso had fire coming up from different directions. "Reaper Three, copy?"

"Copy, Four."

"I'm pinned down on the balcony. Two shooters at my four and seven using the SUVs for cover."

"Hold tight, Four."

Moments later, the Taipan was airborne and the small minigun on the UCAV came to life. Bullets ripped into flesh and metal. The first shooter was almost mangled. When the Taipan spun, the second tried to run but the auto tracking followed him. Now locked on, the beast of a weapon opened up again, sounding like fabric rending violently.

"Reaper Four, you are clear to move. Will stay on station to add cover."

"Copy." Kagiso climbed over the rail and dropped to the ground. Behind her, Kane pushed Cruz out onto the balcony and ordered, "Climb over and jump."

"Like this?"

The man was still in his underwear. "Jump or I'll fucking throw you."

The rattle of gunfire from behind them made up his mind. Cruz climbed over and jumped out into space.

As Kane began climbing over the railing himself, he spoke into his comms:

"Time to go, Knocker."

"Right with you, Reaper."

More gunfire sounded as Kane leaped out into space. From behind him, he heard Knocker call out, "This is a bad fucking idea."

The Brit flew over the railing and hit the ground with a solid thump. Kane hurried over to his friend while saying, "Brick, watch the balcony."

Kane dragged Knocker to his feet. "You do know you haven't got wings, right?"

"Now you tell me," he groaned.

"Idiot."

"Contact balcony," Brick said over their comms and the Taipan roared into life.

The rounds that spewed forth ripped through flesh, shattered glass, and turned the inside of the bedroom into utter chaos.

Kagiso started shoving Cruz ahead of her while Kane and Knocker followed covering their six. Meanwhile Brick expended the rest of his ammunition covering their retreat. Nothing like a compact minigun to keep heads down.

Reaching the perimeter they found the others waiting. Kane said, "Get the Taipan back here and let's make tracks."

"Are you all okay?" Brick asked.

"Nothing that can't wait until we get back," Kane replied. "I just wish I knew who these guys were."

———

"Talk to me, Slick," Cara growled. "Who the hell were they?"

"Still working on it, boss," the computer tech replied.

Cara looked at Ferrero. "Thoughts?"

He shrugged. "Given that they are American, I would surmise that they are mercenaries or a black ops team."

"I hope it's the first, otherwise we've just lit up our own countrymen." She turned to Rani. "Rani, is everyone okay?"

"As far as I know, boss."

She stared at the screen showing the satellite feed from the estate. One of the SUVs was on fire and, according to Slick, the attackers had lost around eight men. Cara slapped her leg. "This is horseshit."

"Boss, I've just intercepted a transmission from the assault team."

"Play it."

"*Saber One to Sheath. Someone else was on site. Your intel was shit. How could they miss that? It had to be them.*"

"*Steady, Saber One,*" came the reply. "*I'll talk to the Farm and see what they can come up with. In the meantime, come home.*"

"*They killed eight of our team.*"

"*Just come home.*"

"Shit," Cara hissed. "They're a CIA black ops team. Damn it."

Ferrero said, "If they're here, they're after Roman. They were doing the same as us. After intel on his whereabouts."

"But how the hell did they know he was in the wind?"

"Who knows?"

"Slick," Cara said. "Find out what they know and how they know it."

"Boss."

Moments later, after the words had barely left her mouth, her cell rang. Cara frowned. "Hello?"

She listened to the person on the other end and then the call was disconnected. She turned to Ferrero.

"What is it?" he asked.

"Our friends at the CIA want to talk."

CHAPTER 15

CIUDAD DEL ESTE

Arriving back at the hangar without further incident, they unloaded Cruz. While Knocker and Brick set him up for interrogation, Kane spoke with Cara and Ferrero. "I don't know who they were, but they were well drilled."

"CIA black ops," Cara told him.

Kane glanced at Ferrero. The former DEA man nodded. "She's right."

Cara continued. "Slick seems to think they've been monitoring our movements ever since they found out about Roman being taken."

"Damn it. Now they've made a run at us."

With a shake of her head, Cara said, "No, they didn't know you were on site. They were after Cruz the same as us."

"The lead agent wants a meeting," Ferrero said.

"Where and when?" Kane asked. "I'll have the team re-up."

"The officer is coming here. Tomorrow morning." Car looked at her watch. "This morning."

"Of course he is. Do you have a name?"

"Zack Rowe."

"Asshole."

"Is there something we should know, Reaper?" Ferrero asked.

He was about to answer when he spotted Doc Morales. "Doc, Knocker played bird off a balcony while we were out. He might need a once over."

She smiled grimly. "Why am I not surprised. I'll check him out."

"Thanks." Turning his attention back to Cara and Ferrero, he continued, "Agent Zack Rowe. Hard go-getter, all-around asshole."

"You sound like he's an old friend."

"I worked with him once in Africa. The Holman Affair." They'd heard of the Holman Affair. Jack Holman ran a team of Recon Marines, just like the one Kane was running. They had been inserted into the Congo to bring out two lots of missionaries. The rebels of the time had gotten wind of it and gone after Holman and his team. Trapped in a small village, they were twenty klicks from where Kane's team was to extract. Kane had asked to go to their aid by the extract helicopter. Rowe, being the CIA officer in command of the off-the-books mission, had denied the request. Holman had asked over the radio for help. Kane had heard him. Then he heard two words. "Request denied."

Holman, his team, and the missionaries had been killed. Upon his return to base, Kane had punched Rowe in the mouth.

"I never knew you were on that mission, Reaper," Cara said.

"It's one of those I don't like to speak about."

"Understandable." She sighed. "Let's get this interrogation done."

———

KANE PULLED the hood off Cruz's head. He was tied to a chair and still in his underwear. Staring at Cruz, Kane said, "Let's get this done quick and we can all get some sleep."

Cruz blinked his eyes furiously before looking at Kane. "Who are you?"

"You already asked that. But let me tell you who you are. Estaban Cruz. The man who moves cartel profits around through crypto and offshore accounts. Even luxury goods. You also set up a charity in Europe to run money through. How am I doing?"

"If you know I am cartel then you also know your life has been forfeited," he said bitterly. "All of you."

As he answered, Cara was walking behind him. She grabbed a handful of his hair and put her mouth close to his ear. "Be careful, Estaban. Or the last thing you see might well be a fountain of blood from your throat after I cut it."

She let him go.

Kane stared at him. "Roman. Otherwise known as The Persian. Your boss in the Los Lobos Cartel has him. Why?"

"I don't know what you're talking about."

"Yes, you do, Cruz. He was taken from a ship. I'm thinking it's not for money. Serrano has hundreds of millions. Which begs the question, why would the boss of a brutal cartel want a known terrorist?"

Cruz stared at him.

"Then I came up with an answer. Serrano is up to something. The question is what and against who?"

"I know nothing."

Kane shook his head. "No, you know something. Maybe not what they're up to, but you know where he is."

"No, I will not say anything."

"Won't or too scared to?" Cara asked.

"If I speak to you, Serrano will kill me."

"How can a man kill you from the grave?"

Cara stepped around in front of him and stopped. He stared at her. "What are you proposing?"

"Tell us what we want to know, and maybe your boss will walk into a bullet."

"You would kill him? I do not believe it."

"Okay, try this. Tell us what we want, and we take out your boss; or don't, and we let you go, then put the word on the street that you talked anyway. How long do you think you will last?"

"No one would believe you."

"It only takes one," Kane said.

"Okay. Serrano has him at his villa."

"What villa?" Cara asked.

"It is in the jungle. I will show you on a map. It is near the Río Sombraviva"

This was roughly translated to Shadow-Living River.

Cruz continued. "He has a coca plantation there where he has easy access to water from the river. He also uses it as a transport highway."

"And Roman is there?"

Cruz nodded. "As far as I know."

"Why did they take Roman from the ship?" Kane asked.

"I do not know."

"You're lying."

A painful expression came to Cruz's face. "Can you protect me?" he asked.

"Only if you're straight with us."

"Serrano has a plan," Cruz said eventually. "He wants to strike back at the Americans."

"For what?"

"Last year they sent some Navy SEALs down here. They hit one of his cocaine stores and also killed twelve of his men. Serrano's brother was one of them."

"I think I remember something about that," Cara said.

"He was very angry," said Cruz. "He blamed government officials for letting them in. But they had nothing to do with it. They didn't even know."

"What happened?" Kane asked.

"He killed the ones he thought responsible. Then he went after their families. Then their families' families."

"What does he plan to do?" asked Cara.

"There is a special package on the way."

"What kind of package?"

"A low-yield nuclear weapon."

"Oh shit," Cara said, looking at Kane. "We have to report this."

Kane nodded. "Yes, we do."

Kane went and got a map. While he did this, Cara

untied Cruz. "You try anything funny, and I'll put a bullet in your head."

When Kane returned, he rolled out the map. "Show me where it is."

Crews pointed at a bend in the river. "In there. That's where you'll find him."

"When is the bomb arriving?" Cara asked.

"In a couple of days. Serrano wants Roman to get it into the US and plant it for detonation."

"Where?"

"I don't know."

"Sit down," Kane ordered.

Cruz did as he was ordered.

Cara and Kane walked together until they were out of earshot. She said, "This changes everything. We can take Roman off the board but that will leave the weapon in play. We take the weapon, and we lose Roman."

"Then we have to take both at the same time."

"It's a big gamble, Reaper. We'll have to wait until they're both in the one place."

Kane turned and called over to Cruze. "Is the weapon going to the villa?"

"Yes."

"That settles that."

"I'll call Thurston," said Cara.

"What do you want to do with Rowe?"

"Fuck Rowe."

———

ROSANNA MORALES WAS ABOUT FINISHED with her examination. "You are just a multitude of bruises, Raymond."

He didn't correct her. She was about the only one he didn't. "Been busy, Doc."

"What's this bruise here?"

She touched it and he winced. "Got shot a few days back."

"This one?"

"Same thing."

"Do you have any bruises where you haven't been shot?"

Knocker shrugged. "Should have some new ones where I jumped off the balcony."

Rosanna shook her head. "One day you're going to really hurt yourself."

He gave her a big grin. "At least I'll have you to look after me."

She slapped the bare skin of his back. "Put your shirt on."

"Damn, Doc, that's a new bruise right there."

"Is the hyena giving the doctor trouble?" Kagiso asked as she approached them.

"You might want to check Kagiso out, Doc. She got shot the other day too. Same as Reaper."

"I already checked her over after she got hit."

Kagiso grinned. "You only want to see me with my shirt off, Hyena."

"Why Hyena?" Knocker growled, putting his shirt on. "Why not wolf or lion?"

"Because Hyena suits you better."

"Great."

"Are you done here?" Kane asked Morales.

"Yes, he is fine."

"Good. Knocker, on me."

The Brit followed Kane. "What's up?"

"The force at the estate was CIA black ops. They are under a man called Rowe."

Knocker scratched his head. "Wait, let me think. Rowe...Rowe...Congo?"

"That's him," Kane acknowledged. "I was leading the second Recon Marine force that day."

"Okay, what now?"

"There's going to be a meeting in the morning. I don't trust him."

"Roger that. Anything kicks off, I'll shoot him first."

Kane slapped him on the shoulder. "I knew I could count on you."

"There is something else."

"Uh-huh."

"There is a low-yield nuke coming into our AO."

"Bollocks. Why is it always shit like that?"

"We have a location of where it's going and where Roman is. Villa in the jungle. We have to wait until they're both together before we move."

"No, no, no. Snakes and spiders?"

Kane nodded with a grin. "Snakes and spiders."

"Damn it. You know I hate snakes after I got bit that time."

"I'm pretty sure the snake died after that," Kane said, his grin widening.

"Thanks. Up yours too."

"Get some rest."

"Rest? I'm so jacked up I doubt I'll come down before morning."

"Get Rosanna to give you something. I want you fresh in the morning."

Knocker nodded. "Whatever it takes?"

"Whatever it takes."

———

CARA KNEW it was early morning in Hereford, but Thurston needed to know the new developments.

"What's up?" Her voice was hoarse after being roused from sleep.

"Sorry, General, but we have a new development that you need to know about."

"I'm listening."

"We have a low-yield nuke incoming."

"Explain." All vestiges of sleep evaporated instantly.

Cara related the details they'd gained during the interrogation and about Rowe. When she was finished, Thurston said, "I'll reach out to MI6."

"What about the Americans?"

"Them too. I'll get back to you. What are you going to do about Cruz?"

"Sit on him until we're done then hand him over. Any news on Hunt?"

"Nothing. Keep me informed, Cara."

"Will do."

———

THE FOLLOWING MORNING, Kane had the whole team in kit. He wore his Synoprathetic suit beneath jeans, a shirt, and body armor. He also wore a baseball cap. Knocker was dressed in a similar fashion. There was much anticipation over the arrival of Rowe.

"You lot look like you're going out on an op," Cara said when she saw them.

"Can't be too careful," Kane replied. "Rani and

Teller have eyes in the sky, and Slick is dialed in to every camera for three blocks."

"We've got incoming," Slick said over their comms, almost as if he'd heard his name mentioned.

Kane nodded and said to Cara, "Shall we?"

"Do me one favor."

"What?"

"Don't kill him."

"I won't."

Cara turned away.

Kane glanced at Knocker.

The Brit nodded.

"How many vehicles, Slick?"

"Just one. Black SUV."

"Roger. Keep your eyes open. All right, let's see what they want."

Minutes later the black Range Rover SUV pulled up outside the hangar. Four people got out, three of which were black ops operators. The fourth was Rowe himself. Ten years older, a little grayer. He looked at Kane. "Well, well. We meet again, Mr. Kane."

"We met last night," Kane replied.

Rowe nodded. "So it would seem. My men certainly got their asses handed to them."

The CIA man didn't seem happy. Cara asked, "What is you want?"

"I want you to back off."

"Why would we do that?"

"Because the CIA want Roman," he replied.

"They had their chance when we were looking for someplace to take him," Cara pointed out. "Now, all of a sudden they want him? Makes no sense."

Rowe shrugged. "The cogs at the CIA move slowly."

"Then how about you take your slow-moving cogs and fuck off," Knocker growled.

Cara glared at him. Rowe said, "You must be the famous Jensen I've heard so much about. You know, I could use a man like you."

"So you can send me downrange and leave me there?"

Kane ran his gaze over the escort. They were poised to act if something happened. Cara said, "I'm afraid you've wasted your time. This jaunt that we're on has already cost too many lives. We're going to see it through."

"Are you sure you want to go down that path, Ms. Billings? If you let us have Estaban Cruz, we'll be on our way."

"You can be on your way now," Kane replied.

Rowe's gaze hardened. "The CIA mean to have Roman. We will get him one way or another."

Knocker said, "You heard the lady, fuck off."

"When the time comes, I'll remember you," said a big man with a black beard.

Knocker grinned. "What's your name, pal?"

"Buck Roberts. Why?"

"Just so I know what to have put on your headstone, you fucking pillock."

The man stepped forward. He grabbed Knocker by the shirt and shoved him back. Knocker being Knocker, pulled his sidearm and pointed it at the man's face. "Back off, motherfucker."

"Roberts," Rowe snapped and his man stood down.

The CIA man tried one last time. "If that is your final word?"

"It is."

"Then I shall bid you good morning."

They all climbed back into the Range Rover and sped away.

Cara turned on Knocker. "What was that horseshit?"

"Sorry, boss, but he pissed me off."

"Now you pissed me off."

"Something was off about him," Kane said.

"What do you mean?" asked Cara.

"The whole thing with wanting Roman now, the wheels at the CIA moving slow."

"I'll have Slick look into it."

———

IT WAS only moments later when Thurston called. "You have a knack of taking a big problem and making it bigger, Cara."

"I like the sound of it," she said sarcastically.

"It seems Rowe is acting alone. Whatever he's doing is unsanctioned. Apparently, he's made a habit of it over the past few years."

"So he's not here on CIA business?"

"No, and he's on the outer."

"Disavowed?"

"That's the thing, they won't give me a conclusive answer with regards to him."

"Deniable. But for who?"

Thurston said, "No idea, but I'm guessing that it relates to something in Roman's past."

"Well, he's done work for hire before. It could relate to something like that," Cara said.

"Maybe. But for who?"

"I'll have Slick keep digging with his already worn-down shovel."

"Watch your six, Cara."

"Before you go, Mary. Lofty?"

"His body has been retrieved and is on its way home."

"Thank you."

"Take care."

Cara found Kane who was talking to Knocker. "Are you prepping?"

He nodded. "The team will go just before sundown."

"Something you should know. Rowe isn't down here for the CIA. It's either deniable, or someone else is pulling the strings."

"He's not going to stop," Kane said.

"I know."

Cara's next stop was Slick. "How are you faring?"

"I've got six balls in the air, boss, and one arm. Other than that, I'm on top of it."

"Sorry, Slick," she said apologetically.

He saw the expression on her face. "Why do I feel like I'm about to get thrown a seventh ball?"

Cara told him about the conversation with Thurston. Slick sighed and said, "I'll add it to the list."

She stared at him. "I know you are busy, but you're looking troubled."

"Something is wrong," he replied. "I keep getting a signal and I can't work out what it is."

"Can't crack it?" she asked.

"No. It seems to be highly encrypted."

"Like something the CIA would use?"

Slick slapped his forehead. "Like something the CIA—how stupid of me."

"Easy, Slick, you've got a lot on."

He punched something into his computer and suddenly everything became clear. "...*extra ammo, Reaper, just in case we're on target...*"

"Shit," Cara growled. "It's a fucking bug."

They hurried to where Kane and Knocker were working. Cara grabbed the Brit and turned him around. "Hey, boss, what's up?"

"You're bugged."

"What?"

"I said there's a bug on you."

"Ah, bollocks. That prick who started the fight."

Cara nodded. "That would be my guess." When she found it, Cara held up triumphantly and said, "Fuck you, Rowe."

Dropping it to the concrete hangar floor, she brought down the heel of her boot and crushed it. Kane said, "They'll know about everything."

"They will."

"Which means we have to stop them before they screw it all up."

"There's only one thing for it," Knocker said. "We have to take them out or that nuke will be in the wind."

Cara pulled her cell. "Shit."

Thurston picked up. "What's wrong, Cara?"

"Rowe and his people know where Roman is. They had Knocker bugged."

"How the hell did they—you know what, never mind."

"They'll know about the nuke too. But that's not the problem. They will go after Roman and when they do it'll put the nuke in the wind."

"We can't have that then, can we? Damn it, why can't things be easy? Plan?"

"Only one I can think of," Cara replied.

"You're right. Take him out."

The call disconnected and Cara stared at Kane. "We've been green lit to take out Rowe."

"It's the only way," Kane replied, barely able to contain the smirk on his face.

The tablet in Slick's hands pinged. He looked down at it and said, "I know where he is."

CHAPTER 16

CIUDAD DEL ESTE

"Reaper Two in position," Knocker said over his comms.

"Hold, Reaper Two," Kane said.

This was a daylight assault. Something Kane didn't like. As a special operator, the dark was his friend. But upon their arrival, it looked as though Rowe and his people were about to move out.

The CIA man's base of operations was an old, dilapidated baseball stadium on the outskirts of the city.

Cara was with them, finding a suitable place to set up with a Haenel RS9 Sniper Rifle. It was a bolt-action weapon and was chambered for a .338 round. Beside her was Brick who was acting as her spotter. "Ares in position."

"Can you get a line on Rowe?" Kane asked.

"Negative."

"Roger that."

The plan was for Cara to take out Rowe with a

long-range shot. The team was there just in case things went to shit. They didn't want a close-in firefight, but they were prepared for it.

Cara's voice came back. "I see Reaper Two's friend. He's directing the gear load."

"Copy. Still no sign of Rowe."

"We have another vehicle incoming—no, make that two," Slick reported.

"Everybody hold what they're doing," Kane said. "Bravo Three, what are we thinking?"

"No idea."

As the two SUVs drove in and pulled up, four men alighted before one of them opened the rear passenger door on the second vehicle. A fifth man climbed out.

Cara said, "I want pictures, Bravo One."

"Roger that."

"Oh, shit," Slick gasped over his comms.

"Talk to me, Bravo Three."

"Can you see this guy's face?"

"Negative."

"Brace yourself. It's Jorgensen."

"You are shitting me," Knocker growled.

"That would explain how they found us," Kane said. "What do you want to do, Ares?"

"Slick, do we have a PID on the second male?"

"Affirmative."

"Talk to me, Ares," Kane said.

Cara settled in behind her scope, pulling the sniper rifle into her shoulder. "Brick, talk to me."

"Range 450 meters. Target near the front SUV."

"Ares, we have movement," Knocker said. "Looks like the rat is coming out of his hole."

"Copy. Brick?"

"Wind left to right, six mph."

Cara made her adjustments.

Rowe walked over to Jorgensen and they shook hands. Brick heard Cara whisper, "Come on, turn some more."

Brick killed his comms. "Boss, what are you doing?"

Cara then killed hers. "Two for the price of one."

"That's one hell of a shot."

"I can make it."

"Ares, sitrep?" Kane asked.

She opened the channel again. "Hold position, Reaper One. Brick?"

"Targets at two o'clock. Range, 777.24 meters. Wind same."

Rowe and Jorgensen moved. Suddenly the planets aligned. Brick said, "Targets in position. Send it."

The RS9 smashed back against Cara's shoulder as she stroked the trigger. The round exploded from the barrel and streaked across the gap between shooter and target. The .338 Lapua round smashed into the back of Rowe's head before exiting from his forehead and continuing with enough force to burn itself into Jorgensen's brain.

"Hit. Head shot," Brick said. "Both targets down."

Cara nodded. "Let's get out of here. All callsigns RTB."

———

"Well, Cara, you certainly kicked over a hornet's nest," Thurston said. "Pissing off the CIA and MI6 all in one go."

"Did you tell them why?"

"I did."

"And?"

"Six had no idea that Jorgensen was there or what he was doing. According to them he was meant to be on his way back to London for a debrief. The CIA were pissed we didn't consult them before we took out their guy."

"Bad luck," Cara said.

"They also want us to back off this nuke thing."

"What? Why would they want us to do that?"

"They want to watch and see where it goes."

"I hope you told *them* where to go," Cara growled.

Thurston went silent.

"Mary, no. What about Roman?"

"I'm sorry, Cara, stand down."

"We have eighteen hours until the bomb arrives."

"I know, now get your people ready to leave. Understood?"

Cara remained silent.

"Understood, Cara?"

"Yes, boss."

The call ended and Cara seethed quietly for several minutes before heading off to find Kane. She found him talking to Burner. "Reaper, a word."

"I'll leave you to it," said Burner who walked off to get something to eat.

"What's up?" Kane asked.

"We've been ordered to stand down."

"What do you mean?"

"Mary ordered us to stand down. The CIA want to take over and monitor the situation."

"Monitor?" Kane asked incredulously. "What if they lose it?"

"That's what I'm worried about."

"What did you tell her?"

"That I understood."

"Well, what are we going to do?"

Cara's face grew tight. "We're going after that bomb."

———

DECIDING to utilize the river with its proximity to gain access, Ferrero found a man willing to use his boat to insert them for a price. He was then to wait there until they were ready to leave. They moved slowly toward the target, traversing the dark jungle under a crescent moon, while overhead in the modified C-17, the rest of the team worked their magic.

Knocker was on point, followed by Kane, then Burner, Jones, Kagiso, with Brick on rear security. They walked a trail through the thick undergrowth toward the edge of the coca plantation.

Coming up on the perimeter, they circled around to a position they had selected, from which they could observe the villa. The going was easier than expected, and they reached their observation post with a couple of hours to spare. The sun was poking its head above the eastern horizon, the sky a crimson hue.

Kane said, "Knocker, Burner, you take first watch. The rest of us will get some sleep. Wake us if anything happens."

Two hours passed quickly, and Knocker was soon rousing Kane. "Time to change over, Reaper."

With a yawn and a stretch, Kane said, "Roger. Kagiso and I'll do it. Anything we should know?"

"They have a roving patrol which changed over an hour ago. Two walkers both armed with AKs. There is a machine gun post on the hill to the right. It covers the approaches. It'll have to be taken out."

"Serrano? Roman?"

"No sign."

"Okay, get some shuteye."

For the next hour, Kane and Kagiso watched the villa, observing armed men walking to and from different buildings. Kane said over his comms, "Bravo One, copy?"

"Morning, Reaper One. How's life in the land of green?"

Kane slapped at a bug. "Interesting. What's ISR telling you?"

"There are around twenty unidentified heat signatures on target. Nothing else to report."

"Copy. Out."

A short while later, the whole team came awake, stretching their bodies in preparation for what was to come. Now they had to wait for the weapon to arrive.

———

"Reaper One, we're going to have to go off station to refuel," Cara said.

It was now late in the afternoon, and the sun was starting to set. "Roger, Bravo. Time off target?"

Cara hesitated. "Four hours."

It was inconvenient, but they couldn't do much about it. Without fuel, the plane would fall from the sky. "Copy, off station for four hours. Reaper One out."

"Reaper One, this is Bravo Three."

"Go, Three."

"I'll still have feed while we're gone. I'll keep you updated."

"Copy."

It wasn't until the sun was almost down that the vehicle appeared. They were forewarned by Slick who detected it via his satellite feed when it was three miles out. "Reaper One, you have inbound traffic. A single SUV."

"Copy. Okay everyone, looks like the package is about to arrive."

A few minutes later the compact vehicle pulled up in the turnaround next to the villa. As doors opened, three men got out, the driver moving to the rear of the vehicle. He waited as the tailgate rose then leaned into the cargo space and pulled out what appeared to be a suitcase. Knocker said, "Packed for holidays."

"Yeah. I guess he plans on having a blast."

Moments later, Serrano appeared and at his side was a familiar face. Roman.

"Bravo, are you getting this?"

"Roger, Reaper One."

As the group disappeared into the villa, Kane turned to Knocker. "You take Kagiso and Jones. I'll take Burner and Brick. Assault from both sides like we discussed. But don't go loud unless you have to. Which means no grenades." Kane looked his friend in the eye to ensure he understood the order.

Knocker grinned.

"Don't," Kane growled. "Just fucking don't."

Splitting up into their teams they went to work.

Kane and his people used the coca field for their approach. Knocker circled and came in from the jungle side. When Kane reached the villa perimeter, he crouched low.

"Reaper One, Bravo One."

"Go ahead," Kane said, his voice was barely a whisper.

"I'll be your fairy godmother this evening. Right now, you need to hold position. You have two rovers coming toward you from the right. Fifty meters out."

"Copy."

The guards materialized out of the darkness. Kane and Brick were crouched side by side, their suppressed 433s up and ready. When the approaching men were within twenty meters of them, they both rose and fired. Two bodies dropped to the damp ground without emitting a sound.

Kane said, "We have two tangos down. Proceeding toward the house."

———

INSIDE THE VILLA, three men sat around the case which lay open on a coffee table in the center of the living room.

"Well?" asked Serrano.

"It's fine. It will do what you want it to," Roman replied. "Flatten everything for a few hundred meters, radiation another kilometer, then fallout you can add up to fifty kilometers more. Minimum of fifty thousand casualties."

Serrano nodded abruptly. "Good. That will show them I will not be messed with."

"Be aware, if you do this, the Americans will throw

everything at you. You will be lucky to live out the year."

"I do not care. My life will be worth the thousands I shall take from them."

"Just so you understand."

"You know how to arm it?"

Roman nodded. "Yes."

"Good, let me see you do it."

Roman shook his head. "No, I will not transport it armed."

"I want to see it done," Serrano said.

The cartel boss pulled a gold-plated handgun and pointed it at The Persian. Roman dismissed it. "You forget, Serrano. I am already a dead man. It is only a matter of time. But I am the only one who can get this into Washington for you."

Serrano didn't like it, but it was what it was. "How do I know you will go through with it?"

"I guess you will have to trust me."

Just then gunfire ripped through the grounds of the villa.

A man burst inside. "We have intruders."

Roman knew instantly who it was. "It is the mercenaries."

Serrano leaped to his feet. "Grab the case and follow me."

Leading Roman down to the basement, they stopped at the mouth of a narrow tunnel illuminated by a string of bare globes. "Follow it. There will be a vehicle waiting for you. The keys are on the visor. Go. Do what I have asked. We will buy you time."

Roman nodded and ran into the tunnel, his footsteps echoing loudly in the confined space. Serrano turned and ran toward the sounds of gunfire.

————

"Contact!" Knocker snarled. "That's bloody torn it."

They ran smack-dab into a patrol that had somehow been missed, and the shit hit the fan. Gunfire rattled throughout the night. "Push forward toward the house," Knocker barked. "We need to move now."

As they hurried forward, more cartel shooters appeared from every direction. Knocker shot one down, but three took his place. Jones swept them aside with the SAW. Kagiso hurried past Knocker, her 433 at her shoulder. As another cartel shooter appeared, she shot him twice, and he was dead before his body slumped to the ground.

"Keep moving," Knocker said to them.

As he started around the corner of the villa, he heard Cara in his earpiece say, "What's going on? Someone talk to me."

A swarthy man with a mustache was rounding the corner at the same time and was shocked to see Knocker in front of him. The Brit smashed the butt of his weapon into the man's face. The man staggered backward briefly before the Brit shot him. "Things have gone loud, boss."

"Damn it."

AK fire ripped through the darkness. The rounds seemed to pass harmlessly between Knocker and Kagiso. Kagiso saw the shooter before Knocker did and she opened fire, causing the shooter to stagger. She fired twice more, and the shooter died.

"Shit, that hurts," a strained voice said.

Knocker turned and saw Jones on his knees. "You okay, big fella?"

"No, I'm not. I got fucking shot."

"Where are you hit?" Knocker asked, crouching beside him.

"The chest."

Knocker started dragging him to his feet. "The suit would have taken it. Come on, there will be time to hurt later."

The three of them reached the side entrance near Serrano's pool. Like the pool house opposite, it had large glass windows from floor to ceiling. Knocker fired three rounds and glass rained down. "Knock, knock, asshole," he said and stepped inside.

———————

KANE SWORE when he heard the gunfire. "What's happening?" he demanded.

"Knocker walked into a patrol," Rani replied.

"How the hell does that happen? Never mind." He turned to the others. "On me. We need to get into that house."

The trio pressed forward. Unlike Knocker's team who had entered via the pool area, Kane and the others used the large undercover patio area. A motion sensor detected their presence and lights came on, suddenly illuminating them. Burner reacted instantly and fired at the lights.

As she did, a fusillade of gunfire ripped through the large sliding windows in front of them. Kane didn't hesitate. He opened fire in the midst of bullets ripping all around him. Hearing a cry of pain followed by a cessation of firing, Kane moved forward and found the shooter lying on terracotta tiles, blood pooling around him.

The three found themselves in the villa's kitchen. A shooter came running from a hallway and stopped suddenly as bullets from Brick's gun sat him on his ass. Another appeared and Burner punched his ticket.

Kane said into his comms, "Reaper Two, where are you?"

"Sweeping the front rooms," he replied.

"Anything?"

"Negative."

Realization dawned on Kane that the gunfire had stopped. However, there was no sign of Roman or Serrano. "Keep your eyes peeled."

The team was starting along a hallway when Serrano appeared. He screamed loudly and fired his gold-plated handgun. In his other hand was a round object. As Kane shot him, he realized what it was. "Grenade!"

As Kane and the others threw themselves flat, the grenade exploded violently. Razor-sharp shards ripped through Serrano, cutting his already dead corpse to pieces. The heat of the blast washed over Kane, and his head started to ring.

The walls were stripped and blackened from the blast and a fire had ignited, the hallway filling with dust and smoke.

Kane coughed, gasping for air. Behind him, Burner rolled onto her back and groaned, "Motherfucker."

"Brick, are you okay?" Kane asked.

"I'm still here, Reaper."

In Kane's ear he heard Knocker say, "Reaper, sitrep?"

"We're all good. Serrano is down. No sign of Roman. Sweep the whole villa."

"Reaper One, report?" This time it was Cara.

"Serrano is down, no sign of Roman or the nuke."

"Copy. Keep me updated."

Kagiso was the first to find the tunnel. As she entered the basement, the open mouth yawned obviously, not concealed by anything, and the lights were still blazing. Kane walked up and peered inside, observing the thick concrete walls leading away from him. "I have a bad feeling about this."

Before entering the tunnel, Kane called for Knocker's team to join them in the basement. When the second team arrived, it made sense to them why they had been unable to locate their target.

The subterranean escape extended at least 500 meters. When they emerged, it was in the jungle, and a rough track ran away from it. Knocker looked at his friend. "Reaper, this is not good."

Kane sighed. "Bravo, copy?"

"Read you, Lima Charlie, Reaper One."

"We've lost the package. I say again, we've lost the package."

———

"You HAVE GOT to be kidding me," Cara growled. "Everyone, I want to know where Roman and that nuke went. We need to reel him in as soon as possible."

A few minutes later, Slick said, "I've got him, boss. He's in a vehicle headed back toward the city."

"How do you know it's him?" Cara asked.

"I don't."

"Well, it's all we have. Reaper One, you need to find yourself some wheels and go after him."

"Roger that. Knocker and Kagiso with me. Brick, take the others back to the river and get to the rendezvous."

"Reaper, you can't let him get away."

"Roger that, boss. We'll get him."

Cara turned to Slick. "Slick, what is he doing?"

"Still headed toward the city."

"Copy. Regina, can you hear me?"

"Ma'am."

"I need us back in the air now."

"No can do, ma'am. There's been an issue with the refueling. Something to do with the pump. We don't even have enough to get back to the target."

"Shit. Slick, whatever you do, don't lose that son of a bitch."

————

HEREFORD, ENGLAND

The worst part about having ongoing operations in different time zones was the ungodly hours that her phone rang. "Thurston."

"I thought you were told to damn well stand down?" the voice on the other end demanded.

"Clemmons? What the fuck?"

Clemmons was the current director of the CIA. "Don't tell me you don't know, Mary. Shit, talk about a fuck-up."

"Whoa, just back up and go over it again," Thurston told him, completely awake now.

"Your people went into Sarrason's fucking villa."

"Don't you mean Serrano?"

"Whatever, I don't give a shit. What they did was screw up an operation. One that you were told to stand down from."

"Did you have people on the ground, Clemmons?" Thurston asked.

"No, we were using a satellite which we had re-tasked."

"Fuck, Clemmons. You know just as I do, an op like this requires boots on the ground."

"There wasn't time. We had a team—"

"What would have happened was you would have lost Roman and the nuke. If my people did attack, they did the right thing."

"Well, it's a damn mess, Mary. Sort your shit out."

The line went dead, and Thurston felt a surge of anger flow through her. Partly because of the call but mostly because Cara had disobeyed her. "Damn it, Cara, what are you doing?"

She made the call. Cara answered by saying, "I'm guessing you already know."

"I've just had the director of the CIA chew my ass for something I know nothing about. I thought I made myself clear that you were meant to stand down."

"You did."

"And so, you chose to ignore my orders."

"I did."

"Why?"

"Because we were here and the CIA wasn't."

"How do you know they weren't?" Thurston asked.

"Because they weren't. If they were we would have picked them up."

"I hope for your sake that everything worked out?"

"Not exactly," Cara replied.

Thurston closed her eyes. "What do you mean?"

"Roman escaped with the nuke."

"God damn it."

"Reaper, Knocker, and Kagiso are chasing him down. The rest of the team is making for the rendezvous. On the bright side, Serrano is no longer a problem."

"Keep me updated."

"Yes, boss."

"And, Cara, when this is over, you and I need to talk."

CHAPTER 17

CIUDAD DEL ESTE

"Reaper One, copy?"

"Got you, Bravo Three."

"Target has just entered a part of the city that is controlled by a prominent gang."

"Same as last time?" Kane asked.

"Negative, these are worse. They're affiliated with Serrano."

The three Team Reaper operators had found a Humvee in Serrano's garage. It was able to be remotely started, and they were soon on the road after Roman. When they reached the gang-controlled part of the city, it was almost as though someone had pulled back a curtain, the change was that dramatic. Now the streets and buildings were covered in graffiti and gang tags and burned-out wrecks. This was another place that local police refused to go.

"Bravo Three, this place looks bad," Kane said.

"The last time any type of enforcement went in

there, was when the government sent a battalion after one man."

"Sounds like fun," Knocker said as he suddenly stopped.

"What's wrong?" Kane asked.

"We should go on foot. This thing will stand out like dog's balls."

"Point taken. Bravo, we're proceeding on foot."

"Copy, Reaper One. You are two blocks from the target."

They climbed out of the Humvee and proceeded along the street, hugging the buildings on their left, avoiding the varied detritus littering the sidewalk. Up ahead at an intersection, they saw a small group of people. Three women and a man. As Kane drew close, the man stepped in front of him. "What do you think you are doing? This is Las Hienas territory, man." The man spoke in Spanish.

Kane hit him between the eyes with the butt of his weapon. As the man crumpled to the sidewalk, the three women stared at him, fear etched on their faces.

He said, "It's okay. I'm not here to hurt you. I'm looking for a man who doesn't belong."

They backed away from him, and he walked past. Knocker gave them a wink and said, "Ladies."

"Were they prostitutes?" Kagiso asked.

"Yes," Knocker replied.

"They are unlike the ones we have back home."

Not knowing how to respond, Knocker shrugged and kept walking.

They crossed the intersection. To their right the street was blocked by garbage and an old vehicle. The street on their left was clear, but there were more civilians along it, some standing around burning 44-gallon drums.

"Reaper One, target is stationary."

"Copy, Bravo. Bravo Three, what do you know about Las Hienas?"

"Nasty, cartel backed, often do a lot of the heavy lifting on the streets for Serrano. Advise to hit hard and run."

"Roger that. Zero, ROEs?"

"Advise to treat every fighting-aged male as a threat," Ferrero said. "Most of them will be armed. You're in a war zone."

Kane said, "Kagiso, you're on point."

"It is wise to send the lion to hunt the buffalo," she replied, bringing up her weapon.

"I bet you have a duffel full of those sayings," Knocker said.

"No, I just make them up as I go."

Knocker grinned. "You grow on me more and more every day."

Kagiso moved steadily out in front. She reached another intersection and paused. Around the corner to her right were three men, all armed, standing around a 44-gallon drum, the flames dancing merrily. It was likely they were sentries for the target building where Roman had gone. She pulled back.

"What's up?" Kane asked.

"Three men with weapons. My guess is they are guards."

"Then we'd better do something about them."

Kane lowered his weapon and took out his suppressed P320. Kagiso followed suit and they walked around the corner of the building, weapons held high.

By the time the gangsters realized what was happening, they were already shot and falling.

"You want to hide these guys, Reaper?" Knocker asked.

Kane looked around and pointed at an alley across the street. "There."

Dragging the dead men across to the street, they dumped them in the darkness. "Okay, let's keep moving. Bravo Three, sitrep?"

"You're on your own, Reaper One. I've lost satellite coverage. Last images show activity at the target building two hundred meters to your north."

"Copy."

"Bloody inconvenient losing satellite covers now," Knocker growled.

"Can't have it easy all your life, buddy," Kane said.

"Right. Bugger it. If we're going to walk into something, I'm going first."

Knocker took point while Kane brought up rear security. Stopping just short of the target building they took up position in a dark alley where they could observe it from the shadows. It was a single-floor building that looked like it had once been a bowling alley.

Knocker said, "Going in there blind isn't my idea of smart, Reaper."

"I agree."

After watching for a few minutes, they saw a single figure emerge. Whoever it was started coming their way. Kane said, "Here's our chance."

"I'll take care of it," Kagiso said and stripped her kit so that she was wearing only her jeans and a tight T-shirt. Tucking her combat knife down the back of her pants she walked out into the light. "Hey," she called out.

The figure stopped. It was a man. "Who are you?" he asked in heavily accented English.

"I am lost," Kagiso replied. "Who would have thought someone from Africa could get lost here. A different jungle I guess."

The man glanced around before approaching her. He stood back a few feet and tried to look cool. In the moonlight he had face tattoos in gang patterns. "You say you were lost, Mama?"

"Yes."

"I could help you. Come with me and I show you a good time."

"I do not think you could handle me," Kagiso replied.

Those words were enough to draw him in. He stepped closer, invading her personal space. Their faces almost touching, he said, "I can handle anything you want."

The gangster felt a prick under his chin and realized that the woman was holding a knife to his throat. Kagiso grinned, showing her white teeth. "How about if I cut your throat?"

"No, don't. I meant nothing."

Kane and Knocker came out of the darkness and secured him. They dragged him back and spun him around. Knocker gave him an icy grin as he took a handgun from the man's waistband. "Hello, chum. You're about to have a very bad night."

Kane clamped his hand over the man's mouth and Knocker buried his knife deep into his thigh. The man cried out and bucked against Kane's tight grip. He said,

"As you can see, we don't have time to fuck around. Now, tell me, there is a man inside with a case. Yes?"

The gangster nodded, tears of pain running down his cheeks.

"What is he doing?"

The hand came away. "He—he is looking to get out of the country."

"And go where?"

"America—Mexico."

"Why Mexico?"

"He says he knows someone who can get him into the country from there," the man gasped against the pain of the still-buried knife which he looked at anxiously.

"Do you know what's in the case?"

The gangster shook his head.

"It's a nuclear weapon."

"I—I didn't know," he said urgently.

"We're going to get it back."

The gangster nodded.

"How many people inside?"

"I don't know."

Kane clamped his hand over the man's mouth again just before Knocker twisted the knife. The gangster bucked again from the pain. Kane released his hand. "Try again."

"Ten—there are ten."

"Right, that's better. Are they armed?"

"Yes."

"How many ways in?"

"What?"

"Doors. How many doors?"

"Two," the man replied.

"At the rear?"

"Yes."

"Is there a guard?" Kane asked.

"Yes."

Knocker said, "Have you finished with this guy, Reaper? I want my knife back and he's bleeding all over it."

With one swift movement, Kane broke the gangster's neck and Knocker retrieved his knife, wiping it on the dead man's clothes. As he straightened up, Kane asked him, "You want the back?"

Knocker's posture changed and Kane knew he was grinning. "Ah shit."

―――――

KNOCKER HAD STRIPPED himself of his kit, keeping only his P320, knife, and lucky grenade. He had waited for Kane and Kagiso to circle around the back of the building before walking across the street. There was a guard outside who moved to block Knocker's progress.

The suppressed P320 came up and fired twice, making the gangster jerk wildly before collapsing onto the steps. Stepping over him, Knocker said, "Entering now, Reaper One."

"Copy. Waiting on your signal."

"You won't miss it."

The interior of the bowling alley hadn't changed much with the passage of time. It had, however, become more rundown and gained more artworks in the form of graffiti on the walls. There were six gangsters sitting talking among themselves while two were off to one side discussing something with Roman. Knocker pulled his grenade and removed the pin, holding the deadly egg at his side.

"Hello, gents. Nice evening?" His voice echoed around the cavernous space.

Everyone present turned their head to look in his direction. He heard Roman mutter something. "Hey, Roman. You're a hard man to catch up with."

"You need to kill him, Manuel," Roman growled.

"Who is he?"

"He is a mercenary. One of those I escaped from."

The man named Manuel signaled to the other group who were now on high alert that their territory had been invaded without their knowledge. They began moving toward Knocker who held up his grenade. "Any of you scousers seen a pin?"

They froze.

"Get him," Manuel snarled. "He wouldn't dare throw it. Not with what we have."

A big shit-eating grin spread across Knocker's face. "Do you want to tell him, Roman, or will I?"

Roman opened his mouth to speak but Knocker spoke instead. "Fuck it. I'll just show him."

With that, Knocker tossed the grenade at the group of gangsters.

———

KANE AND KAGISO were in position waiting for the signal. When they had arrived at the rear entry point, Kane had taken out the guard. Now they waited, listening to Knocker over the open comms line. Kagiso said, "Are you worried?"

"About Knocker? No. He can handle himself. About what he could do? That is a whole other story."

"You are good friends."

"We've been through a bit together. Hell, we all have."

"What do you think he will do?"

"It scares me to think about it."

"Hello, gents. Nice evening?"

"Hey, Roman. You're a hard man to catch up with."

"Any of you scousers seen a pin?"

Kane shook his head. "Oh, no. Knocker, don't do it."

"Do you want to tell him, Roman, or will I?"

Pause.

"Knocker, no."

"Fuck it. I'll just show him."

Suddenly the building was rocked by a massive explosion. Kane was up and moving. "Yeah, that's about it."

They went in hard, weapons raised. The passage from the rear door was narrow with openings on each side. Usual protocols would have had them clearing each as they went, but this wasn't that time.

When Kane and Kagiso reached the lanes, the air was filled with dust and smoke. A figure loomed out of the fog and Kane fired. The gangster, missing one arm, fell onto his face.

There were cries of pain filling the open room. Another figure charged out of the haze and Kagiso fired. He stopped as though he'd run into a brick wall.

The pair pushed further into the room which was eerily silent. Then they saw Knocker. He was standing with his weapon pointed at a figure on his knees. Beside that figure lay two bodies. The lone figure was Roman. "Hey, Reaper, what took you so long?"

"Everything secure?"

"Sure is."

Roman looked at Kane. "He is crazy."

Kane nodded. "Yes, he is. Kagiso, tie Roman's hands and let's get the fuck out of here. Bravo copy?"

"Copy, Reaper One."

"Both packages are secure. We're pulling out."

"Roger. Meet you at the RV."

———

RELIEF FLOODED Cara when she heard the news. To have both Roman and the nuke in hand was a tremendous outcome. She called Thurston.

"Good news?"

"Yes," replied Cara. "We have both Roman and the nuke in custody. Reaper and the others are moving to the RV."

"All's well that ends well, I guess."

"Yes, ma'am. Is there anything new on Borden Hunt?"

"Nothing this end. Has Slick found anything?"

"No."

"Okay, keep working on it. Have your plane land in Vélizy-Villacoublay Air Base. Roman will be transported from there."

"Then?" Cara asked.

"We still have two bishops to take off the chess board," Thurston said. "Only then will Chrysalis be dead."

Ferrero said, "He was being transported when the van was hit. There were five hijackers. Well drilled like they were military. They used motor bikes and explosive charges on the escort vehicles. According to one of the survivors, it was over in a heartbeat."

"Boss, why are we talking about this when we should be going after Hunt?" Knocker asked.

"Because Hunt is in Russia and Roman, as far as we know, is still in France. Don't worry, Mary has got people working on it. She'll let us know."

Knocker was unhappy about it like the rest of them. Then he realized something. There were two people missing from the briefing. "Where are Burner and Jones?"

"On their way to Hereford for training. Can we continue now?"

"Sure."

"Okay," Ferrero said. "We know bugger all about the hitters except for this. Slick."

Slick took over. "When I was scanning through traffic cams of the hit I came across this."

He passed around some photos. "What you are seeing is an arm with a tattoo on it. The sleeve pulled up and it was exposed."

"It looks like some kind of Arabic," Brick said.

Slick nodded. "This arm belongs to a Saudi Special Forces soldier."

"I thought they weren't allowed tattoos."

"They're frowned upon. But they still get them. This one says, *For the King.*"

"How do you know who he is?" Kane asked.

"I've come across it before. This guy used to be a king's bodyguard."

"Are you saying the King of Saudi Arabia is behind this?" Knocker asked.

"Not at all. Current bodyguards for the king are all present and accounted for. This guy was one in his past."

"So, is he a mercenary?" Brick asked.

"No," Kane replied, interrupting. "He's working for Khalid Al-Mansour."

"That would be my guess."

"Why didn't they just kill him?" Knocker asked.

"He's going to use him," Kane said.

"For what?" Cara asked.

"That's what we need to find out," Kane said. "But I'm guessing that it has something to do with money."

"I don't get it," Brick said. "They put a massive bounty on his head, now you say Khalid wants to use him. It makes no sense."

"Just remember, we've busted Chrysalis wide open." Kane looked at Cara. "Have their monies been seized?"

"What was found. They'll have backup."

"Then we have to find Roman before he gets out of France," Kane said.

Slick grinned. "I'm glad you said that. I've found someone who might know where he is."

———

PARIS, FRANCE

Kane and Cara stared across the street at the dry cleaning store. Cara asked, "Is it me or does this seem like a scene out of a B-grade flick?"

Kane nodded. "It does a bit."

The sign above was written in Chinese which made it even more like a movie scene. The owner was a woman named Li Yan who had connections to the Paris underworld and was suspected of people smuggling into Britain. Kane checked his weapon as did Cara. "Slick, copy?"

"Read you, Lima Charlie, boss."

Cara said, "We're going in."

"Copy."

Kane said, "Knocker, we're going in."

"Roger that."

They were in a white van, with Knocker, Brick, and Kagiso in the cargo bay. They were backup should it be required. Dressed in civvies, Kane and Cara climbed out of the van and walked casually across the street. They stepped up onto the sidewalk and Kane opened the door for Cara.

Inside there was a front counter with racks of plastic covered clothes behind the desk clerk. It also had a few rows of pigeonholes on the side wall which held other items of clothing.

The woman behind the counter looked up. "Can I help you?"

"Do you speak English?" Cara asked.

She nodded. "Yes."

"We'd like to see Li Yan."

A cautious expression came over the woman's face. "Is she expecting you?"

"No."

"Wait here."

It didn't take long before two big men appeared. Both looked to be pumped up on steroids. Kane stared at them and said, "They gave trees legs in this part of Paris."

Cara nodded. "They look like sequoias."

"You guys want to tell us what is happening?" Kane said.

A short Asian woman appeared. She said, "They are making sure that you don't start anything."

"What have you been feeding them?" Kane asked.

"Whatever they want."

"I'd believe that."

"The question here is, what do you want?"

"Are you Li Yan?" Cara asked.

"I am."

"Then we would like to talk to you."

She looked at them suspiciously. "Why? I don't know you."

"We hope you might be able to help us find someone. His name is Roman."

Li Yan turned abruptly. "No, go away. Get rid of them."

The two giants stepped forward. Kane moved swiftly and drew his P320. He used it on the first of Li Yan's bodyguards. Like an axe, it rose and fell. The big man's eyes rolled back into his head and he dropped at Kane's feet.

His friend closed the distance, but Kane pivoted and pointed the weapon at his face. "Don't. I'd hate to waste half a magazine putting you down."

"Who do you think you are?" Li Yan hissed.

Cara said, "We just want to talk. That's all. We don't care about what you do."

She stared at them and nodded. "Fine, follow me. But it doesn't mean that I will tell you anything."

They followed her past racks and machinery through the rear of the dry cleaners to her office. She sat behind a metal-framed desk in a normal office chair. The office itself was sparsely decorated and she saw Kane looking around. "Is something the matter?"

"I thought there would be more," he replied.

"It suits a purpose."

Kane nodded. He guessed it did. Why would you decorate it lavishly when it is only a dry cleaners. "Less attention that way," he said.

"Yes. Now, what are these questions?"

"Have you ever heard of The Persian?" Cara asked.

"Yes, I have. I know his name is Roman and I know he escaped custody from Interpol. Get to the point."

"We believe he was busted out by a team of Saudis," Cara explained. "They're going to need a way to get out of France."

"So, you came to me," Li Yan said.

"It is your specialty."

Li Yan nodded. "I heard your questions, now you can leave."

"You haven't answered them yet," Kane said, taking a step forward.

"Do not try to intimidate me," Li Yan cautioned him. "I come from China, remember. They have people better at it than you."

"We're not trying to intimidate you," Cara said. "We need your help. I'm going to say you know who we're talking about."

"I know."

"And?"

She stared at them. "None of this comes back on me."

"No, definitely not."

"Well, if I was going to get someone out of the country, they might do it in a container on the back of a truck. Not one of mine," she stated. "I'm not the only travel agent."

"Who else?" Cara asked.

"His name is Jules Moreau. He runs a shipping business on the outskirts of Paris. It is called Moreau Transport and he has lorries leaving all the time."

"So they could be already gone?"

"No. They will wait for things to die down. Maybe up to a week."

Kane said, "Makes sense. Where exactly is this depot?"

Li Yan told them. "But like I said, this does not blow back on me."

"It won't," Cara said. "But I'd advise you to get another line of work."

"Do you know how many people China executes each year? Thousands. Do you know how many shouldn't even be in jail? Thousands. So, if I can help just a small minority of them get to a better life, I'll keep doing that."

"Thank you for your help."

———

CARA CHECKED her suppressed Haenel RS9 Sniper Rifle and said, "Give me a few minutes to set up."

"You'll have to do without a spotter," Kane said.

"Close enough to do without," she replied then disappeared into the darkness.

"Bravo Three, how are we looking?"

"ISR looks fine."

"Bravo One?"

"The UAV is working fine," Rani said. "We can stay on station for the next four hours."

"You won't need that long."

A few minutes later, Cara said, "Ares in position."

"Copy. Reaper is moving."

Kane led out followed by Knocker, Kagiso, and finally, Brick. Approaching the perimeter fence on the south side of the property, when they reached it, Knocker set about cutting the wire. Once it was large enough, they slipped through.

The trucking yard was full of vehicles and trailers. Every eight minutes, three armed guards completed a perimeter cycle. At various intervals, floodlights lit those sections of the yard as bright as day.

The four operators crouched beneath a trailer and waited for a guard to pass. From there they used other parked trailers to close their proximity to the main warehouse. ISR detected eight heat signatures coming from the building. Kane guessed they were the five shooters from the hijack, two support personnel, plus Roman.

"Reaper One, hold position," Rani said.

In silence, they went prone under another trailer.

"I have a tango coming your way, Reaper One," Cara said. "Coming straight at you."

Kane saw the boots walking along the side of the trailer. Suddenly they stopped.

"Hold, Reaper One," Cara said quietly.

As they lay there, the silence was broken by the sound of running water. Then splashing, followed by the scent of hot urine. The bastard was pissing.

A minute or so later he was finished but instead of moving on, he remained there. Now this was inconvenient. Damn it.

"Reaper One, I have a shot," Cara said.

"Send it."

A heartbeat later the guard was down, a bullet in his brain. Kane grabbed him by the feet and dragged him under the trailer. "Ares, we're Charlie Mike."

"Roger."

Kane and the rest of the team broke cover once more. Keeping low they continued toward the warehouse. "Reaper One," Rani said, "the entry on the west side is clear."

"Copy."

Circling the warehouse the team began moving toward the west entrance. When they reached it, Kane tried the door but found it locked. He turned to Knocker. "Time to work your magic."

While the Brit picked the lock, Kane and the others kept guard just in case. Moments later they heard the lock snick and Kane turned back just as Knocker pushed the door open. He followed him inside.

The west side of the warehouse had been a good choice. There were lots of crates piled four and five high offering plenty of cover. Knocker took point and edged his way around them. The interior of the building was amply lit so visibility was good.

He was about to cross an exposed gap when he heard footsteps. Then Rani said, "Hold position. You have a rover coming your way."

Letting his 433 hang, Knocker took out his knife. He waited as the footsteps grew louder, then the rover was almost on top of him. The Brit sprang from cover and hit the man in the throat so he couldn't cry out. Then clamping a hand over his mouth to make sure, Knocker hit him three times with the knife: chest, inner thigh, throat.

Blood gushed.

Dragging him quietly into the shadows, Knocker wiped his blade on the man's shirt and put it away.

Using hand signals, Kane directed him to continue.

They moved silently, stopping when they saw a group of men sitting around. Counting only six, they knew it meant there was another somewhere else. Kane saw Roman. He was sitting further away from the other five. Kane slipped back behind the crates and took out a flash bang. He pointed at it and indicated for the others to do the same. Once they had them out, they pulled the pins. Kane nodded and then they threw them.

———

ROMAN TRIED to relax but found he couldn't. Ever since these men hit the Interpol convoy, he expected Kane and his people to come after him. It just wasn't in their DNA to give up. The five men who'd taken him were a small group made up from Khalid's security detail. They were all former Saudi Special Forces. The other two were the ones in command of the operation.

"Why are we waiting?" he asked Fahad Al-Mutairi.

Fahad looked over at him. "We have to wait for the right time to get you back to Khalid."

"The longer we wait, the more time Kane and his people have to find us."

"They will not find us."

"Then tell me," Roman said. "Why has Khalid gone

to all this trouble to get me out of custody? What does he want?"

"I guess that is for him to answer."

"He put a fifty-million-dollar price on my head. What's to say he won't kill me himself?"

"That was rescinded now that Chrysalis has been all but dismantled."

Roman was about to respond when the sound of metal bouncing across the floor got their attention. Immediately Roman could see what they were. He threw himself to the floor and shouted, *"Down!"*

———

As soon as the flashbangs detonated, the team broke cover. The HK433 in Kane's hands rattled to life spewing spent casings onto the concrete floor. A mercenary in front of him jerked and fell, blood blossoming on his chest. The man beside him lurched as his head snapped to the side, a bullet from Kagiso's weapon buried deep in his brain.

The team moved forward steadily as they fired, each taking out a target. By the time they stopped shooting, everyone except for Roman was down.

Almost everyone.

A figure appeared running from a nearby office. Knocker pivoted and put him down with two well placed shots. "Bad night, chum."

Kane said, "Ares, target secure. Take down the remaining rovers."

"Already done, Reaper One."

"Roger."

Brick picked Roman up from the floor. The

terrorist shook his head to rid himself of the cobwebs. He stared up at the team in front of him. Finally, his eyes came to rest on Kane. "I knew you would come, John."

"Was there any doubt?"

"Not one."

"What does Khalid want from you, Roman?"

"I do not know. Maybe he wants to shake my hand one last time." The German grinned.

"You have no idea?"

"No. I do know this, the bounty on my head has been rescinded."

"How do you know?" Knocker asked.

Roman nodded at one of the dead men. "Fahad told me."

Kane nodded. "Lucky you."

"You know this isn't over. More will come for me. The Israelis, the Americans, even the Germans and British. All have secrets they want to go away. And when they do, more people will die."

"Why would governments kill to get you when they can use diplomacy?" Knocker asked.

"Not governments. Individuals. Those whose secrets I harbor. They will send people after me and kill anyone who gets in their way. I can give you names."

"What price?" Kane asked him.

"I am a dead man," Roman explained. "I would rather someone kill me who I know."

Kane stared at him. Then he said, "Brick, Kagiso, secure the perimeter."

"You sure, Reaper?" Brick asked.

"Knocker and I can take it from here."

"Roger that."

Once they were left alone, Kane took out his cell and started to record. "Talk."

Five minutes later they had all Roman had to give. Names, and operations to go with them. Kane asked, "Do you have any proof?"

Roman shook his head. "Only names and jobs."

There was a long pause.

Roman said, "It is time to live up to your part of our agreement, John. It has been an eventful life I will—"

His words were cut off when Kane shot him in the head.

CHAPTER 19

SAINT PETERSBURG, RUSSIA

It was hard to get into Russia these days. The team couldn't just fly in, so they had to find another way. A fishing trawler in the middle of the night. Put ashore near Razliv, they were taken by truck to a staging point near Velikaya Zvezda Palace.

Inserted were Kane, Knocker, Brick, and Kagiso. Small team to get the job done. They were on a tight schedule. Once they breached the castle, they had two hours to get the extraction done and get to the airfield where their ride would touch down. They were using an Mi-24 Hind. It would pick them up and fly them to Finland where the others were waiting with the C-17.

The night air was cold, with a coverage of snow on the ground. Dressed appropriately for the conditions, the team's other kit was in duffels. They were trying to travel as light as possible. The man who picked them up in the truck worked for MI6. Yuri was an intelligence agent monitoring military movements. Thurston had called in a favor to make it happen. Even though there were some at the Security Service who were still pissed at Global.

"You must hurry," Yuri told them as they loaded the truck. "The darkness has eyes."

Once everything was aboard, he took them to their staging area: a large forest a short distance from the palace.

Here the team completed their preparations. Already dressed in black, they finished kitting up, including black masks and suppressed AK-12s. Nothing was taken in country that could identify them. Chatter was to be kept to a minimum. When required, it was to be done as a whisper over their comms.

Once they were ready to go, Yuri said, "Good luck. May God watch over you."

Knocker slapped him on the shoulder. "We've got something better, mate. We've got friends."

"You are so nice, Bravo Two," Rani said. "I think I love you."

"I always knew you would come around, Bravo One. I'll buy you dinner when we finish here."

"I'll check my twenty-thirty diary."

Knocker grinned behind his mask. "That a girl."

"Okay," Kane said. "Head in the game. Zero, we're ready to move."

"Copy, Reaper One," Ferrero replied. "I'm looking at our screens and everything is green across the board. Good hunting."

Yuri watched them disappear into the darkness before climbing back into his truck and driving away into the night.

Twenty minutes later as they reached the palace,

the rain began. It was a steady torrent which fell from unseen leaden clouds in the darkness above them. Not that the team was worried. The rain worked in their favor.

Velikaya Zvezda Palace was built like a medieval castle. It had large stone block walls with a parapet running around the perimeter. Inside the walls was the stone-built palace lit up by floodlights.

"Bravo One, I need a sitrep on the guards," Kane said.

"Looks like the rain is keeping them inside, Reaper One. Clear to move."

"Roger."

Kane waved Knocker forward with his grapnel launcher. He fired it sending the hook over the parapet. Once it was secure, Knocker hooked up his powered ascender and began rising up the wall.

Near the top he slowed and looked over. Everything was clear just as they'd been told. But he'd learned from experience, you couldn't be too careful.

Climbing over the parapet, he whispered, "All clear."

Next up was Kagiso. When she arrived, she took watch in the opposite direction. Brick followed her and Kane was last to arrive.

Moving as one along the parapet like a well-oiled machine, they reached the first guard house and found two sheltering from the weather inside. They shot them through the glass before moving on.

Descending into the yard, the team disregarded the immaculate grounds and well-trimmed lawns. There was a gravel turn around which they tromped across through the heavy curtain of rain.

Opening the door, Kane found a guard on the inside at the base of a large staircase. He fired twice and the man fell.

The foyer was huge as one might expect. Using hand signals, Kane indicated for Knocker to go one way with Kagiso while he went the other with Brick. They cleared the first room on the right. A substantial library with book-lined shelves covering each wall was devoid of life. The next was on the left at the base of the staircase. It appeared to be a formal living room, large and filled with overstuffed antique furniture. It too was empty.

Kane made a decision. "This is ridiculous. We can't clear a whole fucking castle."

"What do you propose?" Brick asked.

Kane took his sidearm, unscrewed the suppressor, and fired into the ceiling. "That should work. Bravo Three, copy?"

"Copy, Reaper One."

"Kill all outgoing communication."

"Roger that."

Kane turned to Brick and said, "Let the games begin."

Just then two shooters appeared.

———

KNOCKER AND KAGISO's mission was to get Hunt. The palace had been built with dungeons which was where it was figured Hunt would be held. As they walked cautiously down the stone steps into the darkness below, gunfire sounded.

Stopping with their backs to the wall, Knocker said, "Reaper One, sitrep?"

More gunfire sounded. Then through the comms channel he heard Kane say, "Just opening the ball, Reaper Two. Continue mission."

"Roger that."

Urgent footsteps. Running. They were coming toward them up the stairs. Two of them. As the armed men came into view, Knocker was ready. He opened fire and the two shooters stopped as though they'd run into a wall. Then they tumbled backward down the stairs.

When Knocker and Kagiso reached the bottom, the atmosphere changed dramatically. The air was cold, the walls were damp, and it felt as though they had stepped back in time. Knocker signaled to Kagiso to take the cells on the left while he went along the right, looking through small windows in the doors.

The first few cells they checked were empty. As Knocker reached the third one, he saw there was someone in it. He reached for the door. "Fuck."

"What is it?" Kagiso asked.

"I forgot to check those guys for keys."

Kagiso reached into her pocket. "It was a good thing that I did."

She threw them at him. "You're a good scout."

"I know."

Knocker unlocked the door and stepped inside the cell. It stank like human waste. "Bord? Is that you?"

The man looked up. His head wavered. Even with a straggly beard, Knocker could tell that it wasn't Hunt. "Bloody hell."

The Brit backed out of the cell, leaving the door wide open. He said to Kagiso, "That wasn't him."

"I have another over here," she replied.

Knocker tossed her the keys, and she opened the door. The room smelled the same as the one the Brit had opened. Kagiso said, "Borden Hunt?"

This one was a woman. She had short, matted hair and her face was covered in cuts and bruises. The woman said something that Kagiso couldn't understand. Most likely she was asking for help.

They checked four more cells; found prisoners in two. Kane's voice came over the comms, gunfire still sounding in the background. "Reaper Two, have you found the package yet?"

"Still working on it, Reaper One. This is a fucking human zoo down here."

"Copy."

As with laws of averages, the last place you look should have been the first. That was where they found Hunt. He was lying on the hard damp floor. His clothing was torn and his body battered and bruised. "Bord?" Knocker said.

Hunt looked up. "Hey, Knocker. Been a while."

"Can you stand?"

"Give me a hand up."

The Brit helped him to his feet. Hunt swayed and Knocker had to support him. "The bastards worked you over, huh?"

"Yeah. Petrov kept me alive as bait. They knew you would come."

"Where is he?"

"Here somewhere."

Knocker heard a small beeping sound. He frowned. "What the hell is that?"

Hunt gave a weak derisive laugh. "There's something you should know."

"What?"

Hunt adjusted his collar downward to show the origin of the sound. Around the former SEAL's throat was what looked like a dog collar with a small black box attached. In the center of it was a flashing red light. The box was the source of the sound.

Knocker's face screwed up when he realized what it was. "Ah, fucking bollocks. Reaper One, we have a problem."

"Copy, Two. Just get it sorted."

Knocker nodded. "Kagiso, time for you to go."

"What are you going to do, Raymond?"

He let the Raymond slide. "Whatever I can."

"All callsigns, all callsigns. You have incoming two miles out. Four vehicles traveling at speed."

"Well shit," Knocker growled. "Things just keep getting better. We have incoming."

"Get out of here, Knocker," Hunt said. "Nothing you can do."

"Like hell." He reached for his cell. After taking a photo, he said into his comms, "Bravo Three, I just sent you a picture. I need to know what to do and I need to know fucking yesterday."

———

IN THE FOYER, the bodies were starting to pile up. Intel hadn't revealed that there were this many shooters on site. It had said unspecified amount. Now there were more incoming, and Knocker was having problems of his own.

A shooter appeared along the hallway and died just as suddenly. The door to the library was opened and another shooter filled the void. The man must have come through the window. The shooter opened fire and bullets whipped around Kane's position.

Feeling a hammer blow to his left shoulder, he flopped back, left arm numb from the hit. Luckily the Synoprathetic suit stopping the round from tearing through flesh and bone.

"Reaper!" Brick exclaimed.

"Stay where you are," Kane grated through the pain. "I'm fine."

Although unable to hold the AK, he was still in the fight and grabbed his handgun. While his left arm was useless, he'd have to go with his right.

The MP-443 Grach came up and belched three rounds at the figure in the doorway. One found its mark as the man's leg buckled. Kane fired once more, and the shooter's head snapped back as he died where he'd fallen.

"Damn it, Reaper Two. What's taking so long?"

"We're having a bang up time down here, Reaper One."

"This is no time to fucking joke around."

"Oh, believe me, this is no joke."

———

THE CONVOY of incoming vehicles bounced along the road to the palace. Petrov was in the second vehicle, and the others were loaded with his men. The intruders had been detected in the forest around the palace by numerous motion sensors. He knew they'd be coming. Especially after he'd purposefully leaked Hunt's location so that MI6 would pick it up. Now he was springing his trap.

As they sped through the main archway into the palace proper, he could already hear the gunfire from within. Petrov climbed out, taking his assault rifle with him. His people split into four teams of four. His team would take the front door. The other three teams would make entry at different points around the palace.

Petrov followed his men to the solid wooden door. The sound of gunfire was loud from beyond. One of the assaulters grabbed a grenade and pulled the pin. He tossed it through the opening and waited for the devastating explosion.

———

"Grenade!" Kane shouted when he saw it bounce across the floor.

He threw himself flat, hugging the cold floor just as hard as he could. The explosion ripped through the foyer, tearing and shattering everything it touched. Kane's head rang and pain tore through his body. The blast had thrust him across the floor into a pedestal which had one been home to a bust of Lenin. That was gone, however. Torn apart in the firefight.

Kane dragged himself into cover as the shooters burst in, but he was rattled. Before he realized it, he was staring into the barrel of a weapon. He slowly raised his hands.

"Get up," the man barked in heavily accented English.

Kane climbed to his feet slowly. He was disarmed by a second man. Glancing to his left he saw Brick going through the same process.

Petrov came over to Kane. "So, you came."

"Seemed like the thing to do," Kane said.

"I was expecting you. When I gave the leaked information of your friend's presence, I knew you would be here."

"Surprise," Kane replied.

"What happens now?" Brick asked. "You shoot us and be done with it?"

"No, no, no. You have caused me much trouble. So, I have something special in store for you. A nice comfortable gulag." Petrov turned to one of his men. "Take them outside. The rest of you, find the others."

Three of Petrov's assault team went down into the dungeon. After a brief search, all they found in the cell where Hunt was supposed to be was the explosive collar.

Up above when Kane and Brick were outside, he heard Knocker say over his comms, "Just hang on, Reaper. We will come for you."

That was the last Kane heard from his friend for some time.

———

WHEN THE MEN reported back to Petrov that the others had escaped with the prisoner, he was livid. His plan had been sound. Perfect almost. Yet he'd lost a prisoner and gained two more. Not bad he supposed, but not perfect either. He was meant to have them all.

"How could they have escaped?" Petrov demanded. "We had all of the exits covered."

"The tunnels."

"What tunnels? I have lived here for years and have never known of such things."

"Well, there are, sir. I have seen them with my own eyes."

Petrov let out a yell of frustration before saying, "Get the others ready to travel to their new home."

———

THREE FIGURES MOVED through the snow-topped trees in the dark forest. Knocker wanted to go back for the others but to do so would be suicide. Through Kane's comms, he'd heard Petrov tell him that they weren't going to kill them, instead they had another plan for them. Then Petrov mentioned a gulag. This gave them more time. Kane and Brick just needed to hold on until they could come for them.

"Zero, we're moving to the extraction point. We are two bodies light."

"Say again, Reaper Two?"

"We are two bodies light, Zero. Reaper One and Reaper Three. Petrov has them in custody."

"Then get back in there and get them out," Cara cut in.

"No can do, boss. Not without getting killed."

"He would come for you, Reaper Two." Her words had a hard edge to them.

"We're just regrouping, boss. I'll explain when I see you next. Two out."

Knocker turned to Kagiso and Hunt. He picked the former SEAL up and put him on his back. "Come on, let's go."

They reached the extract point within the allotted time, and as the helicopter rose into the cold night air and flew across the snow-covered landscape to the sea, Knocker wondered if he'd done the right thing.

—————

GULAG 4127, KOLYMA, RUSSIA

They were forced off the helicopter in a blasting snowstorm. Officially Russia hadn't operated gulags in years. But that didn't mean they didn't have them. 4127 in Kolyma was used to mine gold. Here the weather was harsh and escape in the winter was impossible. To go out into the snow one was certain to die. The camp itself looked more like a concentration camp from World War Two. It was surrounded by barbed wire and had guard towers on each corner.

Kane stopped for a moment, looking through the curtain of falling snow. If he wasn't certain before, he was now. 4127 was hell on earth.

"This is going to be an interesting holiday, Reaper," Brick said.

"It is that."

Two guards shoved them forward. "Move!"

The cold wind bit at their exposed flesh. They staggered forward and were guided toward the commandant's office. Inside, it was warm and comfortable. Something Kane knew they wouldn't be getting anytime soon. Shown into his main office they found a middle-aged man seated behind a battered desk. He looked up at them and gave the pair a mirthless smile. "Welcome, gentlemen. I'm reliably informed that you are going to be trouble for me."

He paused waiting for a reaction. When one wasn't forthcoming, he slammed his palm down onto the desk and snarled, "Let me tell you now, that will not be the case. If there is any trouble from you it will be met with the harshest punishments you can imagine. Do you understand me?"

Kane and Brick said nothing.

"Do you understand me?" His voice became a shout.

"Yes," both men grunted.

"Yes, Commandant!"

"Yes, Commandant."

"Fucking Americans. Think you are better than everyone else." He glared at them. "My name is Commandant Nikolai Baranov. Remember it. Now, get them the fuck out of my sight. Enjoy your stay."

———

"You are American?" the big man asked. "I hate fucking Americans?"

"That didn't take long," Brick said.

Kane nodded. "By my calculation, five minutes and thirty-five seconds. Give or take."

"He's the biggest gorilla I ever saw, Reaper."

"He's the biggest anything I ever saw."

"My name is Boris," the big man growled. "This is my hut. And you do not belong here."

"You get the feeling we've been set up?" Brick asked.

"Yes."

"Do you want him, or should I take him?"

Prisoners began to gather around the three men. Kane stared at the big man. "He hates us both."

"Roger that."

Kane smiled and said, "Hey, Boris, where's Natasha?"

Then the two Reaper men charged.

Within the first minute both Kane and Brick had their bells rung and tasted blood in their mouths. It was like trying to move a mountain. But Boris didn't have it all his own way. He too bled. Both from his nose and a cut above his eye. He spat on the floor and waded back into the brawl.

Kane hit him in the face again and Boris shook his head. The Reaper commander wrung his fist. It was like hitting granite. Brick closed in and lay a few solid punches to the big man's gut. Boris flung a solid back-hand which caught the former SEAL in the face, sending him reeling. Then Boris turned back to Kane. "Come on, little man, your turn."

Now, Kane wasn't small by any means. It was just that Boris was bigger. Kane shrunk the gap between them and ripped two blows into the tree before him.

Another backhand and Kane was down spitting blood. Moving fast for a big man, Boris raised his right leg, preparing to bring his foot down on his adversary's head in a killing blow. Kane saw it coming and rolled away. The blow just missed eliciting a curse from the big attacker.

Meanwhile Brick had picked up a chair. He brought it crashing down across Boris's head and shoulders. Boris shook his head and turned to face the threat. Kane heard Brick say, "Ah fuck. Big man, you are not real."

Strong arms wrapped around Brick bringing pressure to snap his spine. Brick, in desperation, brought his head forward, catching Boris across the bridge of his already damaged nose. The huge Russian released him, and he staggered back.

Kane came in behind Boris and drove some solid punches into the man's kidneys. Boris buckled at the knees. It wasn't much, but it was there. He turned, pain on his face mixed with a vicious snarl. With outstretched hands, he lurched forward like a giant grizzly about to tear his prey apart.

"Fuck it," Kane growled. In desperation, he lashed out with his boot and caught Boris in the crotch.

The man mountain stopped cold, eyes bulging. His face changed color as he grabbed at his bruised balls. Kane watched as he slowly sank to his knees, a high-pitched keening sound escaping his lips.

Brick staggered over to Kane. He stared at Boris and winced. "Glass balls."

Kane nodded. "Thank God for that."

All throughout the hut everyone had gone quiet. From cheering to utter silence. Kane looked around half expecting the onlookers to rush them. Instead, a single, malnourished man stepped forward. He took Kane's hand. "Wonderful. Absolutely wonderful, Comrade."

"You wouldn't say that if you felt like we do," Kane replied.

"Boris has been our king for many years, and you come and finally his reign has ended. You are both heroes."

Kane nodded. "We'll see."

CHAPTER 20

HEREFORD, ENGLAND

ONE MONTH LATER

Team Reaper had been stood down for the duration. That was, until Kane and Brick could be found and rescued. Most of that time had been spent on training. Except for their initial return. They'd taken time to bury Lofty. The two new recruits, Knocker had worked hard, leading from the front. Since the absence of Kane, he'd stepped into the role of Reaper One.

Gone was the joker who'd kept them all amused. Instead, he'd been replaced by a no bullshit operator who expected the best and would take nothing less.

"Run the fucking exercise again," he growled after they had just finished a run through Global's Kill House.

The team was tired. He'd been working them hard all day and to be honest, they had responded to his criticisms each time. Except their time wasn't low enough. He wanted better.

Kagiso said, "Can we take five minutes?"

"No, you can't. You can have five minutes when we're done and that time comes down to a respectable number."

"Raymond, a moment. Now."

Knocker whirled in anger but bit his tongue when he saw Thurston. "Ma'am."

They moved off to one side. Thurston asked, "What are you doing?"

"Boss?"

"Look, I know you want to find Reaper and feel hopeless just sitting here. But don't take it out on your team."

"We're stood down. What the fuck else am I meant to do, General?"

"Just take it easy, Ray. You'll have them worn out and they'll be useless when they go into battle."

"When?" Knocker queried. "Do you have something, boss?"

"I'm not sure yet, but there might be something in the wind. You're officially on standby to leave for Alaska."

"Why Alaska?"

"You'll be told when the time comes."

"Boss."

"One more thing, you'll need to confer with Ketterson and Julian Cross for planning once you're green lit."

Knocker knew both men. Ketterson was a good operator. Strike Team Badger's commander, Julian

Cross was former SAS. All his team were except for Silas Quinn. He was SBS.

"Panther and Badger?"

"That's right."

"Consider it done, boss."

"Right. Now give your team a rest."

"Before I go, how are the new people faring?"

"They'll do."

"Before you fly out, I want you to pick a new member. Not Burner or Jones. I'll give you a list."

Knocker was confused. "What the fuck, General?"

"I'm forming a new strike team. Mongoose. Thorne Maddox will command it. He'll be training them up for African operations. I'll give you a list of who's available."

"Did you tell Cara, General?"

"I did. She said you could choose because you know most of the people on the list. She's going to be on the ground with you when you go in. Luis will command Bravo while she is on the ground."

"Sure."

"Another thing, I want all of you trained to fly our toys. Don't rely on one person."

"Roger that."

Thurston reached into her pocket. She took out a piece of paper. "Before I forget. The list."

Knocker opened it and started to read.

As Thurston walked away, he called after her. "Jett Conway."

Thurston turned. "The Australian?"

"Yes."

She nodded. "All right, you tell him and the others."

"Roger that."

After Thurston was gone, he went over to join the others. "All right, this is what is happening."

"Why do I get the feeling that this is bad news?"

"Depends on how you look at it. You and Jonesy's time with us has come to an end."

"What?" Burner exclaimed. "We're being RTU?"

Knocker shook his head. "No. You're going to be part of a new strike team. It'll be called Mongoose."

"Shit," Jones growled.

"It is what it is, I'm afraid. Your commander is Thorne Maddox. He's a good soldier. Listen to him and you'll learn a lot. After you're trained up, you're all being sent to Africa."

"Great," said Burner. "I'll be eaten by a fucking lion."

"I doubt it, Rosie. Leo will take one look at you and decide there's not enough of you to be bothering with."

She grinned. "Fuck you. I'll say this, it's been interesting with you guys. A change of pace will be welcome."

"Oh, it'll be a change of pace all right. Africa is a whole different kettle of fish. Anyway, it's been a pleasure to have been down range with you. Now, piss off."

———

JETT CONWAY WAS A LEPER. When it came to teams he'd been through three and now no one wanted him. Which was why he was working in the armament stores and contemplating leaving Global for good. He just hadn't gotten around to it yet. When Knocker found him, he was at the inside shooting range blowing off rounds through his handgun. He'd just finished his second magazine when the Brit approached him.

"Conway, stand down."

Conway lay down the handgun and took out his earplugs as he turned. "Knocker Jensen, how're they hanging, mate?"

Knocker ignored the question. "You still working stores?"

"Not for much longer. I'm getting out. Can't get on a team."

"I wonder why," Knocker stated.

Conway bristled. "What's that supposed to mean?"

"You're a loose cannon, Jett. Disobey orders, turn up to work drunk, leaving your teammate in a firefight. Do I need to go on? The list is bloody endless. Shit, you're lucky you're getting the chance to walk instead of getting tossed."

"What the hell is this, Jensen?" Conway snarled. "You come down here just to give me shit?"

"I came here to give you a chance, Jett. Possibly your last one."

"What do you mean?"

"I need a shooter for Reaper. For the life of me I don't know why, but I chose you."

"Me?"

"Yes."

"On Reaper?"

"Are you fucking nuts?"

"I think so. Do you want the position or not?" Knocker asked. "Make the choice."

"Of course, I bloody do."

"Fine, you're in. But you stuff it up, and I'll bury

you downrange myself. You won't get the chance to be kicked or to walk. Understood?"

"Roger that."

"Right, in the kill house in the morning. Be there."

———

From Conway, Knocker went to see Cara. She was in her office going over some notes. He knocked and entered. Cara looked up and said, "Speak of the devil."

"Pardon?"

"I was just talking to Mary. She said she'd been talking to you about the changes."

"Oh, that. All done and dusted," he told her.

Cara nodded. "Just one question, Ray."

"Why Conway?"

"Yes."

"For all his fuckups, he's a good operator. The last time we needed someone for the team he was in the mix. Reaper and I talked about him. But instead, we chose Lofty."

"I hope you know what you're doing," Cara said.

"Don't worry, I already told him this was his last chance. I'll leave him dead down range if he screws up."

Suddenly Slick appeared. "Boss, I have them. I know where they are."

———

"They're in Gulag 4127, Kolyma, Russia," Slick told them.

Gathered around were Thurston, Knocker, Ferrero, Ketterson, and Julian Cross. It was Ketterson who said, "I thought the gulag system was shut down."

"That's the official line," Slick replied. "But they still operate under a different name."

"Is this why we were told to get ready to fly to Alaska?" Knocker asked.

"Yes," Thurston replied. "We had a feeling that was where they were, but we had to be sure."

"Are we sure?" Cross asked.

Slick brought up a picture on the big screen. "We are now."

Knocker frowned, then squinted and asked, "Are we looking at snow?"

"Yes, but more to the point, it's what's in the snow."

Knocker moved closer and then saw it. JRK. "He's sent a message. But how the hell did he know?"

Cara said, "He knew we'd be looking. It was only a matter of time."

Knocker turned to Thurston. "But you knew before this. How?"

"MI6 have a person on the inside. A security officer codename Arctic Fox. We got a cryptic message telling us to look there."

"When do we go?" Knocker asked.

"Wheels up in two hours. That will give you enough time to have all your equipment ready."

Knocker looked at Cara. "Are you commanding?"

She shook her head. "No, you're Reaper One. I'll be Two like before. Luis will be in command of the airborne platform."

The Brit nodded. It was Ketterson who voiced what they were thinking. "It's easy enough to get in," he said. "But how the hell do we get out?"

"We're going to fly in a C-130, land it on the strip near the gulag, and get you the hell out of there," Thurston replied. "Weather permitting."

"We're going to need sat pictures," Knocker said. "And every scrap of intel we can get our hands on."

"You'll get it," Thurston said. "Also, you'll jump clean. Nothing to identify yourselves whatsoever. Masks as well."

"Twelves?" Cross asked.

"No, normal weapons."

"What if it all goes to shit and you can't get us out?" Ketterson asked.

"You make your way toward the coast. We'll get you."

"Roger that."

"Anything else?" Thurston asked.

No one spoke. The Global commander nodded. "Okay, let's get to work."

CHAPTER 21

OUTSIDE GULAG 4127, KOLYMA, RUSSIA

The teams got lucky with the weather and dropped three kilometers from the gulag. From there they split up to take up their positions. The plan was simple. Panther and Badger would secure the compound while Reaper would go after the packages. For them the mission was to move hard and fast to secure them before anything could happen to either Brick or Kane.

Opposite to Antarctica, Kolyma had around fifteen hours of darkness this time of the year. Good for the teams on their approach. All were equipped for the cold weather and wore NVGs. Most had had Arctic Warfare training which put them in good stead. That experience they passed on to those that hadn't.

Knocker and his team reached the fence. They had limited time to cut their way through before the search-lights swept back. This was a one-man job, and Knocker took the responsibility upon himself to get it done.

As the light swept back, he dropped to the snow, his

white suit helping him blend in with his surroundings. Even their assault rifles were camouflaged for the conditions.

Once the light had passed once more, Knocker finished the cut. Then took cover as the light swept back. He whispered into his comms, "Reaper Team ready to breach."

"Panther ready."

"Badger ready."

"On my mark, take out the lights. Three...two... one...execute."

Suddenly all the lights in the guard towers exploded as they were hit by gunfire. The perimeter went dark, and Knocker said, "All teams go."

Moments later, shouts were met with suppressed gunfire. Knocker got through the fence and waited for the others. A sentry came out of the gloom, and Knocker fired at him. The man cried out and fell to the snow.

Behind Knocker the others came through the opening in the fence. Once they reached him, they all pressed forward. There was no time to stick to the shadows or move from cover to cover. Their time sensitive mission wouldn't allow it.

Two more figures appeared to their front. Knocker took one while Cara took the other.

An explosion off to their right rocked the gulag. It was followed by another. Someone was throwing grenades. If Knocker had to guess, he would have said that it was Cross's boys.

"Contact Left," Kagiso snapped as she opened fire at a handful of Russians storming from a hut.

Conway joined her, his weapon rattling with

deadly efficiency. The Russians didn't know what hit them.

"Keep moving," Knocker ordered them.

He was moving toward the target building by memory. He'd studied it enough. In his head he remembered Thurston saying, "Stick to the schedule. Once they realize what is happening, they'll call for help."

"Can't you just jam it?" Knocker had asked.

It was Slick who'd said, "Most likely not. This place is old and probably has old landline systems in place. Can't jam those."

The only backup they could possibly call was air power. And they didn't want to be there if they arrived.

"Target building ahead," Knocker said.

All around the gulag now gunfire split the night with multiple explosions. From what he could gather, Panther and Badger were getting the upper hand.

Three more Russians appeared to their left. "Contact left," Knocker barked.

He fired his 433 and a man died. Cara joined him and soon the Russians were down before they could react.

When they reached the hut, Knocker said, "Cara, Kagiso, stay here. Conway, on me."

Knocker opened the door and flicked on the flashlight attached to his weapon and started to shine its beam around the hut. The prisoners were awake and standing around the small room. "Kane, Peters, up online."

No one moved for a moment then a big, mountain of a man pushed through the crowd. "Are you looking for the Americans?"

"Yes."

"They are not here."

"Shit. Where are they?"

"In hole."

Knocker was stunned. "They killed them?"

"Nyet. In solitary."

"Show me where."

The big man walked toward the door.

"What's happening?" Cara asked.

"They've been moved," Knocker explained. "Lurch here is going to show us the way."

Once outside, he ambled along between two other huts. The gunfire from around the gulag had died down but was still there. The big prisoner stopped outside a concrete block house. "In there."

He turned to leave when the rattle of an AK sounded. The burst caught the big man full in the chest and he buckled then straightened. Swearing in Russian, he staggered forward. In the meantime, Conway had turned and unleashed a torrent of fire at the shooter.

The shooter threw up his arms then fell to the earth dead. The big prisoner cursed once more then fell like a tree into the snow. Knocker glanced at him and said, "Thanks, pal."

Opening the door into the solitary block they were faced with a dark hallway lined by steel doors along the left side. "Kane and Peters."

A voice sounded from one of the cells. "Reaper, does that sound like a Raymond to you?"

"Sounds like a Raymond," Kane replied. "But it can't be him. The Raymond I know would have been here fucking weeks ago."

"Ought to leave both you pillocks here," Knocker growled. "And don't call me fucking Raymond."

"Definitely him," Kane said.

"All we have to do now is get them out. Luckily, I came prepared," Knocker said.

He reached into his pack and took out two small blocks of explosive compound. Attaching them to the locks he added the detonators. Knocker stepped back and said, "Fire in the hole."

The explosives blew and the doors jumped open. Knocker grinned. "I always wanted to say that."

Kane and Brick lurched out of their cells, clothes torn, beards and hair matted, and evidence of beatings front and center. "You two look like shit," Cara said.

"I don't know," Kane replied. "Five-star resort. Swimming pool, meals every day."

"Whatever."

Knocker said, "Bravo, Jackpot, I say again, Jackpot. We're coming home."

"Copy, Reaper One. Well done," Ferrero said. "Extract inbound."

"Conway, help them get some better clothes on," Knocker ordered.

Kane frowned. "Where's Burner and Jones?"

"Long story. I'll tell you over a beer."

Just then news broke over the net, and it wasn't good. "Bravo One to all callsigns. You've got fast movers inbound. Get the hell out now."

The team broke out into the night. The gunfire had finally subsided. Over the comms Ketterson said, "Compound secure."

Knocker replied with, "Panther One, Badger One, fall back to the rally point. Do it now."

Although they were banged up, Kane and Brick moved quickly, their bodies crying out with pain.

Ignoring it, they were hot on the heels when the first Su-34 fighter bomber screamed overhead.

Moments later explosions rocked the gulag. "What are they doing?" Conway shouted.

"They can't get troops here. The easiest way is to destroy it all," Knocker said.

The second Su-34 came in and dropped some of its payload. More explosions shattered the night. Glancing over his shoulder, Kane saw burning figures running across the snow. Prisoners.

Meanwhile the first Su-34 came back around and hit again. An explosion hit close to the team, and they were all thrown forward. Bells ringing. Knocker dragged himself to his feet. "Sound off."

One by one they called out. Everyone was good. "Right, now fucking move."

The second Su-34 made its run as the team reached the fence. Explosions. Then the comms channel lit up. "Man down! Man down!"

"Who?" Knocker asked urgently.

"Ketterson," came the reply. "He's taken shrapnel."

"Is he mobile?"

"Negative, we'll have to stabilize here."

"Shit. Cara, keep going to the RV. Panther, I'm on my way."

"I'll come with you," Brick said.

"Piss off," Knocker replied. Then he disappeared into the burning horror that was the gulag while the thunder of jet engines roared overhead.

———

KETTERSON'S TEAM was gathered around working on him when Knocker arrived. Blood stained the snow, and the screams of pain told the Brit all he needed to know. Knocker looked down at the Panther commander. Even though he'd been wearing a Synoprathetic suit, they weren't designed to stop the razor-sharp shrapnel from an exploding missile.

"How is he?" Knocker asked.

The operator known as Fossil looked up. "We're trying to stop the bleeding from his leg and arm."

Ketterson lurched upward from a sudden infusion of pain. "Give him some more morphine."

"He's had too much already," Fossil said.

"Give him more, he's going to need it. Wrap those wounds as tight as you can then we're moving."

"Roger that."

"Ket, this is going to hurt you more than me, mate," Knocker said.

"Just fucking get me on that bird. I'm not dying here."

"We're ready," Gregson said.

"All right, get him over a shoulder and let's go."

The group set off for the fence forming a guard around their leader. Behind them more explosions sounded as the two jets made another pass. Ketterson screamed with pain, but Gregson ignored his pleas to put him down. At some point the Panther team leader passed out.

When they reached the fence, they climbed through, then after checking Ketterson again, disappeared into the dark.

CHAPTER 22

HEREFORD, ENGLAND

TWO WEEKS LATER

Ketterson made the trip and was shipped to a military hospital in the US where the doctors patched him up. He'd lost his leg and would be in hospital for some time. Apart from him, there were no other casualties for such a high-risk mission.

Kane and Brick were given a week to recuperate and were back at work. Hunt was also back at work. This time, Thurston gave him a team. Strike Team Scimitar. It was another new team to add to the growing list. Global was now becoming one of the world's fastest expanding private security/terror fighting organizations.

In the meeting room the team sat around drinking beer. It had been a hectic couple of months, and they enjoyed their downtime.

Cara entered and looked around the room. "It's good to see you all relaxing."

Knocker shook his head. "The sword of doom is about to fall."

"What makes you say that?" Kagiso asked.

"Because it's true," Cara said. "A quick in and out job. Nothing is too dangerous. I need two volunteers."

They all looked at one another.

Cara nodded. "Thank you, Reaper. Thank you, Raymond."

"Ah, be fucked," Knocker growled. "I hate volunteering."

"Me too," said Kane. "When do we leave?"

"Now."

———

SHAYBAH–OMAN HIGHWAY, SAUDI ARABIA

It was commonly called Empty Quarter Road. A dual-lane highway surrounded by a sea of sand and huge dunes. At that moment the weather was baking hot and the two men watching the highway from their layup position had been feeling it for the better part of six hours.

"He's late," Knocker said.

"You've said that about ten times already," Kane replied. "You're sounding like a cracked record."

"Bravo Three, is there any sight of the target yet?"

"Negative, Reaper Two. We got word he's on his way. We just don't know when."

Both men were dressed like locals and carried HK G36s which were common military weapons for the

Saudis. Their main issue was being discovered. Mercenaries on Saudi soil, especially there to assassinate one of their most prominent citizens, would be met with instant death.

Another hour slipped by before Slick said, "Heads up, One and Two, your target is five mikes out."

"About bloody time," Knocker growled and reached for the detonation trigger beside him.

Down on the highway, they had set up a line of claymores on both sides of the blacktop. Once the vehicles entered the kill zone, Knocker would set them off and their target would be no more.

Kane used his binoculars and looked back along the highway for any sign of the small convoy. Eventually they appeared.

"Get ready."

The convoy came on. Their target, they were reliably informed, was in the middle vehicle. Today would be Khalid's last day on earth. After that he was going wherever he believed he would end up in death. And the remnants of Chrysalis would be down to one.

The convoy was traveling fast. They were headed for Oman where Khalid was going to invest in a new oil field that had been discovered recently. However, he wasn't going to make it. Not today.

The first vehicle, a black SUV just like the others, entered the kill zone. Then the second...then the third.

Knocker clacked off the claymores.

Two lines of orange laced with black appeared on either side of the highway. The three vehicles were caught in the hellstorm of violence unleashed by the explosives.

All three of the SUVs were torn apart including all

those inside them. Orange flames engulfed the vehicles, and a column of black smoke rose into the clear sky leaving a dark smudge.

Kane and Knocker climbed to their feet and stared at the carnage below. Kane said, "Bravo, are you seeing this?"

"Copy, Reaper One," Cara replied.

"Mission successful. Moving to extract."

"Roger that. Helicopter inbound."

"That just leaves our Russian friend," Kane said.

"It does, but he'll keep for another day. Come home, Reaper One. Good mission."

———

HEREFORD, ENGLAND

"So that's it?" Ferrero asked. "Petrov keeps for a rainy day?"

Cara nodded. "I'm not sending a team back into Russia just yet. We've got people on him, so we'll know when he leaves the country. That's our best bet."

Ferrero nodded. "You're right."

One of the ops room staff came over to them and passed Cara a piece of paper. She unfolded it and scanned its contents. Looking up at Ferrero, she said, "Strike Team Mongoose has disappeared in the Congo Basin. They were chasing poachers. We're wheels up in eight hours."

Ferrero sighed. "No rest for the wicked."

"Let's hope we can find them alive."

A LOOK AT:
KANE: TOOTH & NAIL

FROM THE AUTHOR OF THE TEAM REAPER SERIES COMES KANE.

When John 'Reaper' Kane is forced to gun down a fourteen-year-old boy in self-defense, the combat-weary warrior becomes disillusioned with the endless cycle of blood and violence his life has become.

Going off-grid in the remote mountain town of Vesper Lake for a week of soul-searching, he steps in to help a young woman, and his two-fisted interference finds him running afoul of the local sheriff. In the violent aftermath, he discovers that the town suffers under the crushing stranglehold of Nazareno 'The Nazarene Dragon' Pedregon, a ruthless drug lord commanding his criminal empire from inside Black Bog Federal Prison, a cesspool of death and corruption.

Framed for murder, Kane is dragged into the prison and forced to fight for his life when Nazareno finds out who he really is. Alone, exhausted, and outgunned, with enemies closing in on all sides, the odds are stacked against him. But when the hunt turns primal, Kane knows that the only way to survive is by tooth and nail.

AVAILABLE NOW

ABOUT THE AUTHOR

A relative newcomer to the world of writing, Brent Towns self-published his first book in 2015. *Last Stand in Sanctuary* took him two years to write. His first hardcover book, a Black Horse Western, was published the following year.

Since then, he has written twenty-six western stories, including some in collaboration with British western author, Ben Bridges; several action adventure novels, such as his bestselling *Team Reaper* series; the novelization to the 2019 movie, *Bill Tilghman and the Outlaws*; as well as scripted a handful of Commando Comics. Not bad for an Australian author, he thinks.

Often up until the small hours of the night, bashing away at his tortured keyboard in Queensland, Australia, Brent loves to lose himself in the world of fiction. If you're interested in sharing your thoughts in more detail, scan the QR code below! Your feedback is invaluable to him—and often helps shape his future writing endeavors.

ABOUT THE AUTHOR